WAR HERO

Novel by

M K Devidasan

Coopyright@2020   M K Devidasan

ISBN-13: 979-8665381787

All rights reserved.

No part of this book may be reproduced in any form or by electronic or mechanical means including information storage and retrieval system without permission in writing from the publisher, except by interviewers who may quote the brief passage in a review.

Some characters and events in this book are fictitious and any similarity to a real person, living or dead is coincidental and not intended by the author.

Dedication

I dedicate this novel to all defense officers and men of the Army, Navy, and Air Force who participated in the 1971 Indo-Pak war.

M K Devidasan

Preface

I was on the posted strength of one of the air force units near the border before the commencement of the 1971 Indo-Pak war. For three months, I was away on temporary duty to an army unit in Jammu and Kashmir area from the first week of September and came back on 3 December and I reached my unit at 5-30 evening. While opening my temporary house, located near the runway, I heard the sound of ack-ack gun firing and saw the enemy planes flying over the airfield showering bombs. The Indo-Pak war of 1971 had started. I was with my wife and two-year-old daughter. We moved out to town and stayed with a friend.

On 4 December few fighter aircraft took off on various missions in enemy territory, but four did not return. The news of missing aircraft did not deter the courage of our pilots and they were ready to cross the border to accomplish their assigned mission. The spirit of those pilots, who participated in the mission, was heard in the officer's mess bar after the day's hectic activities. The narrations of a narrow escape from missile attack and ack-ack guns fire, by experienced pilots, were horripilation. Their morale was very high with never-dying enthusiasm. Everyone's desire was unique; cause maximum damage to the enemy to paralyze their fighting potential.

A highly spirited close friend of mine did not return after his sortie on 4th December. It was customary to declare such cases as missing in action.

After retirement, I developed a passion to write and bring into the notice of public various experiences I gathered from the officers who had participated in that war. This novel is partially based on a true story and the struggles of an officer after bailing out in the enemy territory. Firm determination and high morale gave him enough courage to cross over the border with the help of a Pakistani. But in Indian soil, he had to face a series of troubles before meeting his newly wedded wife.

Prologue.

Flight Lieutenant Prabhakar, an ace pilot with years of experience of flying was detailed to undertake a certain mission on the third day of Indo-Pak war, 1971. He wanted to accomplish the mission with satisfaction and for accuracy of destruction, he flew very low. When his Hunter aircraft came within the range of anti-aircraft guns, the enemies did their job well. He was hit and while the tail was on fire, he continued with his mission and completed the assigned tasks. When he was sure that further flying would entail in an explosion, he bailed out and landed up in a jungle. From then on, his struggle to escape from the enemy territory commenced. He got helps from few Pakistanis and he finally crossed the border.

M K Devidasan

-1-

The atmosphere was calm and quiet. The sky was very clear without any patches of clouds. The Gulmohar flowers from the trees on either side of the road leading to the briefing room kept falling in the morning cool breeze. The lullabies of small birds that circled the flowers to suck honey were very prominently heard in the silence prevailed. For attending the daily briefing, all aircrew of the station and other small units started trickling down to the briefing room one by one. Most of them were either wearing the 'G' suit or flying overall. After a while, exactly at seven o'clock unit commander Wing Commander Mukerji and Officer in Charge Flying entered the briefing room. With respect, everyone got up and wished them 'good morning'. After that, other unit commanders also came and took their seats.

Flight Lieutenant Gupta, the officer in charge Meteorological Department, came in front of everyone and took permission from Officer in Charge Flying and other Unit Commanders and started the day's briefing. He explained about the weather condition all over India with specific detailed importance to local. He clarified everyone's queries and withdrew after satisfying one and all in that room. Once the senior officers left the room, the Flight Commander Squadron Leader K N Singh asked four officers to remain there as he had to brief them separately on the day's flying activity. He explained to them all about the formation flying that was planned to be conducted by all of them. The formation was planned to be led by him. The names of officers who were to form on either side behind him were readout. They were briefed in detail with the height and the distance to be maintained from one another with precision. The activities to be performed at various stages of their formation by each one of them were also explained. Though everyone was conversant with the emergencies, he was particular to repeat each such situation and reminded them of the actions to be performed by them to come out safely. He even reminded them of the aerodromes to be contacted for landing in case of an extreme emergency. When the briefing was over, few officers shot out their doubts and he patiently cleared them all.

Flight Lieutenant Prabhakar adjusted the 'G' suit and picked up the helmet and walked to the tarmac with all other officers. From a distance, he saw all fighter planes on the tarmac shining in the morning sun. He moved close to the allotted plane and carried out the mandatory routine checks. Fully satisfied, he moved to the ladder and climbed up and took his seat inside the cockpit. After carrying out all essential checks, when he was fully satisfied with the performance of the plane, he looked at the technician standing on the side, at a distance. That technician went running to the plane and closed the hood and removed the ladder. He removed the choke from the front side of the wheels and raised his thumb indicating that everything was in order. The plane was ready to move out. As directed by the leader, he moved his plane slowly forward. The technician gave smart salute wishing him to come back safely.

Each plane entered the runway as directed by the leader and took off. The last one to take off was that of Prabhakar. As briefed, after flying for a while, each one of them started coming closer to get into the formation. Keeping the leader in the front, each one of them got into the formation maintaining the height and distance from one another. When all were in proper formation, the observers in the flying control expressed their happiness over their efforts and capability. After flying in the formation for a while, they started peeling off one by one and carried out eye-catching performances such as rolling, pitching, and diving. That was a wonderful performance and the observers all around the flying control and on the technical area appreciated them vehemently.

When pre-planned tasks were over, one by one sought permission from the flying control to land. The leader was the first one to land and others followed. Prabhakar was the last one to get permission to land as he was the last to take off. He pressed the landing gear switch. But, the usual green light when the wheels were down was absent. The red light kept glowing indicating that the wheels were still not down. The indication made his two or three heartbeats to miss, but without showing any panic, he informed the flying control of the particular situation he was facing. He followed the drill to be carried out in such situations to bring down the undercarriage. But, all attempts went futile. There was no total failure of electrical or hydraulic systems. All other systems in the plane were functional. That made him more confident and he thought of ways to bring down the aircraft safely. The very thought of the huge loss to the exchequer if the aircraft crash-landed made him feel uncomfortable and he thought of ways to save the aircraft somehow. When all his efforts failed, he informed the ground of his inability to bring down the aircraft safely. Air Commodore Sinha who was informed of the emergency, came to the flying control and instructed Prabhakar to fly around till the fuel tank was emptied and then carry out belly landing on the grass, by the side of the runway.

Prabhakar kept flying over the airfield. During this time, all arrangements to meet the emergency were being made on the ground on a war footing. Crash tenders and an ambulance with a doctor and all essential medicines for first aid were ready near the flying control, ready to move to the site at short notice. All emergency arrangements as per the air force procedure were taken with precision and all were ready to meet any eventuality. Officer in Charge Flying supervised every preparation and expressed satisfaction. When the fuel in the tank was about to be over, Prabhakar informed the flying control of his descent for a belly landing. Suddenly, the countenance of one and all in the flying control changed and the anxiety-stricken eyes got glued to the horizon with the mounting heartbeats. They started praying to close their eyes waiting for the ear breaking sound of the approaching plane. The plane was sighted by their naked eyes. Everyone's eyes were glued to the incoming aircraft at low speed. That touched the grass on the outer side parallel to the runway and kept moving forward. All crash tenders and ambulance moved fast towards the runway. The plane kept moving. That was to stop only by friction as the wheels were not out to apply break. Suddenly, a minor fire was observed on the rear side of the plane due to friction. The aircraft was moving forward. Due to everyone's prayers, the plane came to a halt. Immediately the fire tenders got into action and started spraying the form over the entire tail portion of the aircraft. The form covered the plane thus stopping oxygen and within seconds, the fire was extinguished. Simultaneously, water jets sprayed over the plane helped to cool the surface. Meanwhile, another vehicle moved towards the aircraft with a ladder and one technician climbed up to open the hood of the plane. When Prabhakar was seen coming out, more people started gushing forward in anxiety, but Officer in Charge Flying stopped them for fear of possible explosion. He wanted to avoid any casualty, in case of an explosion that could not be ruled out after belly landing. Not heeding to the warning, Prabhakar's friend Flight Lieutenant Sudhir moved fast to the aircraft and helped him come down the ladder. Sudhir continuously kept inquiring about his health and kept touching his different body parts to ascertain everything was in order. Prabhakar kept trying to recover from the great shock he suffered from the belly landing, but he felt his tongue was not taking his commands. He hugged Sudhir and sobbed. His eyes got filled, but he immediately regained courage and looked at everyone around with a smile. The doctor and medical assistants helped him to lie down on the stretcher and immediately carried him to the ambulance. Though Prabhakar kept repeating to his Commanding Officer and Officer in Charge Flying that he was perfectly alright and there was no necessity to take him to the hospital, the medical officer insisted that he was to be kept under observation and took him to the army hospital immediately. Sudhir accompanied him in the ambulance.

The whole station was happy that nothing untoward had happened to Prabhakar. In the majority of belly landings, the damage to the aircraft and the pilot used to be of a higher order. The fire due to friction and burn injuries to the pilot was of routine affairs, but due to good luck, nothing had happened and everyone thanked God for that.

Prabhakar tried to get up from the stretcher. 'For what you people are taking me to the hospital? I am perfectly normal.' He begged.

The doctor smiled. 'I know that. But we have to carry out a complete check-up to ensure you are perfectly normal... It is a usual check-up after the belly landings.' He chuckled.

'No doctor. Please.' He looked at Sudhir and said. 'Why don't you try to make him understand? I am perfectly fit.'

The doctor looked at Sudhir. 'For that, we all thank the almighty. But, certain procedures are to be followed. That is mandatory. We can't avoid that.'

XXX

In the hospital, the doctor who examined Prabhakar could not find anything unusual. Still, he was admitted there for the sake of observation, for one day. After some time, the unit doctor and his assistants left the room. Sudhir also did not stick around there for long and left saying he would be back after lunch.

While Prabhakar was dozing off, he heard someone knocking on the door. He opened the eyes and saw Sneha, the daughter of Air Officer Commanding of the air force station, Air Commodore Sinha, entering the room with mild smile and anxiety.

'What happened?' She stood by his side and inquired with anxiety.

Prabhakar smiled. 'I was experimenting with land aircraft without wheels.'

Sneha shook her head and smiled. 'Then, was the experiment successful?'

'That's why I am lying alive.' He grunted.

'Good. That means all future aircraft can be manufactured without undercarriages.' She looked at him with a forced smile. 'Due to someone's good luck, nothing happened to you. Otherwise...'

'Otherwise?'

'Don't make me say otherwise.' She pretended anger and said. 'Nobody even thought of informing me of this. I came to know of this as my father informed the hospital superintendent. My father informed him in the morning, but that person informed me only now. Sooner, I came to know of this, though many patients were waiting for me, I left the hospital without telling anybody and rushed to see you.'

'You did not take the permission from your hospital superintendent?' He chuckled.

She looked a little perplexed. 'No.'

Prabhakar smiled. 'Sometimes when you go back, your name would have been struck out from the register.'

Thinking for a while she said. 'If so, I don't care. If not there, I am sure to get a job in any other hospital. There is a great shortage of doctors everywhere.' She moved close to him and lifted his legs and hands and examined him. 'The moment I came to know of the belly landing, under my imaginations I saw a different Prabhakar. Half burned face and broken limbs.' Suddenly she corrected. 'Oh, no. I was just joking. I was very confident that nothing would happen and you would come out scratch-free.' She moved her hand over his head and smiled.

'Oh, good. Did you start joking also? But, before cutting a joke, please be kind enough to inform.'

'For what?'

'Then, I will be prepared to laugh.' He chuckled.

She showed mock anger and murmured. 'There is a limit for teasing me.' She expressed her displeasure.

After some time the doctor entered the room followed by the nurse. Prabhakar turned his head and eyes to that doctor and introduced Sneha to him. 'Doctor, this is doctor Sneha. She is working in Batra hospital.'

That doctor wished Sneha. Is she your wife? When she is with you, our visits are not required.' He smiled.

Those words brought a broad smile on her face. Her face shined as if a thousand watts bulb was lit. She looked at Prabhakar expecting him to react with his comment that 'very soon that would get materialized'. But, she had to turn her face with disappointments.

The doctor gave some specific directions to Sneha and left the room.

Sneha continued to sit in that room reading a novel. Frequently she got up and recorded the blood pressure, pulse, and temperature. Towards the evening, Prabhakar said looking at her.

'Why don't you go back home? It is getting late. Your father may not like it when he comes to know that you had been spending the whole day with me.' He showed uneasiness.

'That's ok. Today I am supposed to be on duty for twenty-four hours. In the morning, before leaving for hospital I had mentioned that to both daddy and mummy.'

Prabhakar looked at her with mock anger. 'That means, you tell lies.'

She smiled. 'Otherwise, survival is difficult. One can tell at times minor lies, provided that doesn't harm anyone.' She looked into his face. 'Don't you tell lies?'

He hesitated for a moment. 'If you ask me...... Yes. Sneha, is there anyone who doesn't tell lies? If anyone claims otherwise, either he is telling another lie or he is insane.'

Both of them laughed.

The entire night she spent in that room lying on the divan with the sincere intention of looking after him. In the morning, the doctor came and examined him in detail, and finding everything alright permitted to go back to the unit. After receiving the discharge order, she held his hand and walked along with him to the portico. Asking him to wait, she ran to bring her car to the portico. She opened the car and made him sit in the front. He was against the way she was caring for him like a child, and many times he resisted her personnel assistance on his every movement. Often, he tried to keep her hands away from his body, but she kept insisting complete rest without violent movements at least for a day or two more. She drove the car slowly and left him in his room. Before leaving that room, she said.

'Don't think of going to the unit for a day or two. You need to complete the rest. I will come back in the evening. If you do not observe what I said, I will behave like a doctor and scold you.'

Both of them laughed.

-2-

In the evening, Sudhir knocked on the door of Prabhakar's room and entered. Throwing his glance towards the incoming friend, Prabhakar closed the book he was reading and tried to get up.

'Don't strain yourself. Keep lying down.' Sudhir moved quickly towards him and compelled to lie down.

'Not required. I am perfectly alright.' Prabhakar slowly dragged himself towards the wall and leaned on to that.

Thinking for a while, looking at his friend Sudhir asked very casually. 'Which is your favorite God?'

With a broad smile, Prabhakar said. 'Lord Ayyappa.'

'You developed that devotion on your own or under guidance from parents?'

'Why do you ask?' Again, he smiled. 'On my own.'

'What was the reason for that? I am sure there would have been some incidence or reason due to which you developed a special feeling towards that.' Thinking for a while he said.

'If you are interested to narrate, I will be happy to listen. Because I am also a god-fearing person.'

Prabhakar smiled. 'Before that let's have tea.' He yelled for the bearer.

Knitting the brows, Sudhir said. 'What nonsense? Don't talk rubbish. Who will have tea at this time of the evening? After six in the evening, a soldier will never take tea or coffee. Should not offer also. He will enter the bar.' He chuckled.

Prabhakar looked at him. 'If so I will have to respect your feelings. The bottle is here. I hope, you are not very particular about going to the bar and drinking.'

Sudhir liked his friend's attitude. 'No problems.' He looked around the room as if searching to find the bottle.

With slight hesitation Prabhakar said. 'I have no soda here. I hope, you have no allergy for liquor with water. If particular, I will get a soda.'

'Seventy percent of our weight is of water. We should not disregard that.' He smiled. 'Water will do.'

Responding to the call, when the bearer came, Prabhakar directed him to go to the mess and bring a plate of groundnut fried with plenty of onion and lime juice sprinkled over. Before the bearer left, he was also instructed to fix two drinks for them taking the liquor bottle from the cupboard. The bearer poured whiskey and water in two glasses and gave them.

Taking one sip, Sudhir looked at Prabhakar and said. 'Now, let me hear why you became an ardent devotee of Lord Ayyappa.'

Prabhakar wondered why his friend was so keen to know of his likings. He sipped the liquor and started. 'I was born and bought up in Kerala. I am a Punjabi. Years back my parents came to Kochi and got settled down there. Father is a businessman. For years, he had been visiting Sabarimala every year to have a darshan of Lord Ayyappa. Even now, he continues with that, without break. During my childhood, I was made to accompany him during his trips to Sabari Mala. The experiences I got during those trips made me an ardent believer of that deity, Lord Ayyappa. Those who never moved on their legs received the blessings of that Lord and started walking in front of that temple. The dump could yell out the name of that powerful God in front of that deity. Likewise, many miracles I could observe there, which have no scientific explanations. Every year the number of devotees visiting that shrine is on the increase, as you probably know. Without sufficient cause and belief, I don't think so many will take so much of pain of forty-one days religious fast without non-vegetarian food and take the trekking to the mountain to see and pray that powerful god. No.' Taking a sip of whiskey, he continued. 'Now I will narrate my own experience. 'Four years back, while on annual leave, I was driving my father's car from Trivandrum to Kochi. Before Alappuzha, one lorry came losing the control of the driver and hit the car head-on. The car was smashed completely. Luckily, I was all alone in the car and nothing had happened to me. Those who assembled there immediately after the accident never believed that the driver survived.' He sat mute and continued.'Likewise, many minor incidents. My experience of yesterday itself is an incident to narrate. Have you ever heard of any plane not catching fire after belly landing? Without even a scratch, the pilot escaped yesterday. When I realized the problem of the undercarriage, I repeatedly prayed Lord Ayyappa and he came for my rescue.' He took another sip. 'Though many argue otherwise, there is something for which, one can't give explanations. The one who talks against such beliefs is ignorant and fools.' He looked at Sudhir for reactions and drank. 'I haven't told these things to anyone so far. Since you tried to probe, I just opened up my heart. I do not expect anyone to believe what all I narrated. It is purely my belief'

    The bearer brought a plate full of lime juice sprinkled ground nut fried with onion garnishes and kept on the table.

Sudhir took few ground nuts in the spoon and put in his left palm and ate. 'Your intimacy with Sneha also is with the blessings of this Lord?'

Prabhakar laughed. 'She is an innocent girl. She likes me very much. She is a very good friend.'

'Nothing beyond that?' He grunted.

Prabhakar put a few nuts in the mouth. 'No. I haven't thought of anything beyond just friendship. I don't think she also has anything beyond that. Just friendship between two adults.'

Both of them remained silent.

Sudhir broke the silence. 'You have the habit of reading a lot. Shall I ask one question? What are the essential factors in life for a person to remain happy?'

Prabhakar laughed. After thinking for a while, he said. 'I don't think there is any yardstick for measuring personal happiness. Happiness is a condition that is to be developed by each individual. If a person can derive happiness from any situations that confront him, that is the greatest quality of that person. Some people will never find an element of happiness from any situation. Having a broad mind to take things lightly, can find himself always cheerful with a smiling face. I don't mean that even in sad situations, one should try to smile. But, if a person is capable of overlooking the factors that enter in his life to destroy happiness, he could try to remain cheerful.' He drank whiskey. 'I don't know what all I said.' He leaned towards Sudhir. 'Why? Do you have any unhappiness?'

With slight, hesitation, Sudheer opened out his mind. 'I have a lot of problems in my personal life.'

With anxiety, Prabhakar looked into his eyes. 'What is that? It is news to me. If you think that the causes of your unhappiness should not be let out to anyone, don't tell. Otherwise, you may share it with me. We can jointly try to find out possible solutions.'

'I got married four years back. To date, I am not lucky to have a child.' Those words were melancholy filled.

Prabhakar laughed. 'That is not a problem friend. Many couples get a child only after years of married life?'

Sudhir suddenly turned sad. 'Here, it is not like that. She has a medical problem. She will never get conceived. This is the conclusion of the doctor after a detailed examination.' He turned his head down and remained silent. 'I haven't told her this. Her firm belief is that I have some medical problems. After such feelings crept into her mind, there is a sudden change in her behavior towards me. She gets annoyed fast. She tends to oppose whatever I say.' He looked around and lowered his voice. 'To be frank enough, I hesitate to go home.' His melancholy filled voice chocked. 'I don't think, happiness would ever come back to my life.' His eyes were filled. 'God has given me everything; enough income, a respectable job. But life is purely mechanical without happiness. In front of everyone, she is very respectable and loving. But, her behavior towards me is unacceptable. Her behavior towards the servants at home is also very cordial. Not towards me. Educationally and financially, I am much superior to her. Still, in all possible ways, she tries to undermine me.'

Prabhakar felt sorry for his friend's plight. At the same time, felt like laughing but controlled. From the love and respect, the couple exhibited made for each other There was never any indication of discord. Prabhakar had been visiting their house frequently, but at no point of time, he felt any indication of disharmony in their marital life. He used to frequently comment on their happiness for which he had even felt envious of. During mess dinner dance parties, the couple used to hit the floor and dance together for hours which was considered to be the sign of an ideal couple. They did not have offspring. That was a fact. But everyone was of the impression that was part of their planned program. He was certain that the cause of the present talk was either the momentary outcome of some misunderstanding with his wife before coming there or due to intoxication. Anyway, Prabhakar was not interested to prolong such meaningless talk. When he looked at the bottle, he could confirm that a good portion of the liquor was already consumed by his friend.

'Why don't you make her understand her deficiency showing the medical report?' Prabhakar said very casually. 'Then, you will see the difference in her behavior towards you. Probably she might start adoring you for still loving her knowing fully well of her shortcomings.'

He laughed with sarcasm. 'I tried even that. Then, her reaction was that I was lying.'

Flight Lieutenant Ahluwalia entered the room, knocking on the door. Neither Sudhir nor Prabhakar talked about that subject further.

Looking at Ahluwalia in white trouser and tee shirt with white canvas shoes, Sudhir asked. 'Coming after games?'

Without responding to him Ahluwalia lifted the bottle and said casually. 'Both of you have consumed the whole?'

Sudhir said with mock anger. 'You did not answer me.'

Looking at Sudhir he said with a smile. 'This is not a court for me to answer every question you put across.' He turned his head and eyes towards Prabhakar. 'I just went to play.'

'That's was what I asked.'

Sudhir smiled.

Without looking at anyone Ahluwalia said very casually. 'I don't answer everyone's questions.'

Sudhir did not like that. He decided to finger him. 'I heard your name was there in yesterday's formation flying.'

'There is nothing unusual. Sometimes they put my name, but I used to get that taken out.' Ahluwalia smiled.

Prabhakar indicated Sudhir not to unnecessarily annoy him.

'What I would do? Have I done anything wrong in deciding not to spoil the costly aircraft unnecessarily?'

'How?'

'When I have loose motion, is it correct to fly the airplane? Especially, when I do aerobatics, can I order my stomach please do not give me problems as I am doing aerobatics?' He laughed. 'Stomach will not wait for my instructions.'

Prabhakar agreed with a burst of wild laughter. 'You are right. During aerobatics, what you said could happen.'

Getting support from Prabhakar made him happy. 'That's right. These things can't be appreciated by Sudhir, who is an accounts officer.' He lifted the bottle again and tilted and said. 'You both have completely emptied this.'

'You are right. Sudhir may not be having that much knowledge about flying to appreciate the pilot's problems. But, these frequent stomach problems surfacing while detailed for flying duties is not a good habit.' Prabhakar said with mock anger.

Ahluwalia smiled. 'Because of that, you could show the whole world that even without bringing down the wheels the aircraft could be brought down safely.'

Everyone laughed aloud.

"To be frank enough, I don't like to fly fighter planes," Ahluwalia said.

'Then, why did you become a fighter pilot?'

'What can be done? They made me a fighter pilot. I was interested to become a transport pilot. One thing is there. You can see my logbook. I have done enough of hours of flying.' He leaned towards Prabhakar. 'To be frank, somehow, I want to get medically unfit for flying and get converted to administration or logistic branch. There the life will be more enchanting with no risk factor'

Sudhir shot out a naughty question. 'Why don't you resign from the air force itself?'

'Oh, no.' He looked at Prabhakar. 'Where else will I find such a wonderfully secured career? Nowhere else. Good salary and respectable job. I can't even dream of that in any other organization.'

Sudhir laughed. 'Good. You want to work in this organization without doing any job.'

'I have no problems. That's what I am trying to.' Ahluwalia squeezed his forehead.

Sudhir looked at Prabhakar and laughed.'

Ahluwalia suddenly became serious. 'Jokes apart.' He slowly moved towards Prabhakar. 'How do you feel? Anybody pain or other uneasiness?'

Prabhakar replied with a smile. 'Oh, I am fine. By the grace of God, I have absolutely no problems.'

'That was what had helped me also.' Ahluwalia smiled and said.

'How?'

'Otherwise, I should have taken that aircraft. If so, surely you would have attended one funeral. I don't think I could have belly-landed as he had done without even a scratch. I would have caused a lot of damage to me and the plane.' He looked up. 'Surely, you are great. You have saved me and I would admire your presence of mind.'

Everyone looked at each other and sat mute thinking of the whole episode of emergency belly landing.

-3-

When he got the information from the commanding officer's PA, on phone, that he was wanted by him immediately in his office, Prabhakar had many questions in his mind. Immediately, he proceeded to the Unit Head Quarters on his scooter and asked the PA to inform the Commanding Officer of his arrival. When he got permission to enter the office, knocking on the door, he entered the office and stood in front of the commanding officer Wing Commander Mukerji.

Mukerji kept the file he was looking at aside and asked politely Prabhakar to take a seat. From the cordial behavior, Prabhakar could understand that he was called for some friendly chat. Sitting on the chair opposite to Mukerji, he said respectfully.

'Yes sir.'

Mukerji looked at him.' I called you to talk about a party in the mess on this Saturday. I am giving you the responsibility as you are the food member of the mess. We should serve Chinese food.'

Prabhakar felt more relaxed. 'Yes sir.'

'We have a cook in our mess. What is his name?'

'I think you are mentioning the cook who prepares Chinese food. His name is Sundaram.'

'Yes, yes. He should be asked to prepare good food. I am inviting our Air Officer Commanding. Also, there will be two of my civilian friends. They are local business magnets. That's why I am giving these specific instructions.'

'Ok, sir. I will prepare a menu and show you.'

'It is not required. If you want, you may take the help of Sneha, the daughter of Air Officer Commanding. She has a fair knowledge of Chinese food preparation. I understand she has done a course.'

'Yes sir.'

'Another thing. You will function as the Master of Ceremony. The assembly will be at eight in the evening. From then on till nine, you may have a few party games. Not difficult ones. Very simple to spend time with fun and laughter. Drinks will start coming from the time of assembly. Should serve tasty snacks. From nine to ten-thirty dances on the floor. Immediately after that, dinner should be announced. The guests have expressed their desire to leave by eleven. Once they leave, you people may continue. Ok? Any doubt?'

'No sir.'

Prabhakar directly went to the mess. While talking to cook Sundaram, Sneha came there.

'You both might be talking about Chinese food items, isn't it?' Sneha looked at Prabhakar and said with a smile.

That was quite unexpected from her and expressing surprise Prabhakar inquired. 'How do you know?'

She was casual. 'Mukerji uncle had called me. He told me that you have gone to the mess and wanted me to meet you with a menu prepared by me.'

'Then?'

'I have prepared and brought one menu.' Sneha opened her handbag and took out a piece of paper and handed over to him.

Opening that paper, he looked at her with a meaningful smile conveying that she was much clever than expected and read the contents aloud.

After hearing the menu Sundaram said. 'I can't prepare many of these items.'

Sneha said looking at him. 'Don't worry. I know.'

Looking skeptical, Prabhakar asked. 'Will all these items be liked by everyone coming for the party? Chinese food started appearing on our dining tables since recently only. You should not forget that. It is doubtful that these items will be liked by the civilian guests.'

'I don't think so. They will like.' She sounded positive. 'What you are trying to convey?'

'Just expressed my opinion; that's all.'

Thinking for a while she asked. 'Which item do you think will not be liked by all? We will avoid those items. Before coming here, I had read out this to Mukerji uncle.'

'Then there is nothing to think about.' Prabhakar looked at Sundaram. 'Isn't it?'

Sundaram did not utter anything, but his smile had conveyed that there was nothing to disagree with.

On the day of the party, most of the unit officers had started assembling much before seven fifty with their lady wives and started occupying the chairs placed on the sprawling lawn with hedges decorated with color bulbs to give a festive look. Officers were in their pants and full sleeves shirt of pastel colors with a tie. And the lady wives were in sarees. Other modern attires were usually not permitted in formal mess functions. There never used to be a necessity of mentioning that to anyone as that was customary.

Western music was being played in low volume.

At about two minutes to eight, Wing Commander Mukerji came in his car with his wife and special guests. To receive them, the Flight Commanders and their lady wives were waiting on the road. Prabhakar also had joined them. They were received and escorted to the specially arranged sofas. Looking around, they appreciated the elaborate decoration and other arrangements and took their seats. Within a few minutes, the Air Officer Commanding, Air Commodore Sinha with his wife and daughter Sneha arrived. Seeing his car from a distance, Wing Commander Mukerji and wife went and received them and led them to the sofa reserved for them.

Prabhakar took permission from Mukerji and went to the dais and stood in front of the mike and drew everyone's kind attention. 'Ladies and gentlemen, I request every one of you to make this evening most memorable in your life. On my right, the bar counter is open. If you are not having enough patience to wait for the bearer's arrival to your seat with the glasses, you are most welcome to come down to the counter and pick up the drinks of your choice.'

Observing a surge to the bar counter, Prabhakar again announced. 'Please do not get stuck to the bar counter. With your glasses, please get back to your seat. A lot many interesting games are planned and I request everyone's participation.'

When Wing Commander Mukerji got up and walked to the stage, everyone's eyes followed him. He said, Prabhakar. 'Let me have a few words. Games can be played after that.'

Looking at him, Prabhakar moved aside.

Standing in front of the mike Mukerji said after looking around. 'I do not intend to waste your time or bore you out.' All eyes and ears got sharpened as they expected something important to be uttered by him. They knew Mukerji would not have taken the mike unless something special was to be announced and their anxious faces were visible to him in the dim light. 'Ladies and gentlemen, this is my private party.' Again, he looked around. 'You must be anxious to know of the occasion for that. I will tell you. Today is my fifteenth wedding anniversary. There is another special reason also. I am being promoted to the rank of Group Captain. With effect from the first of next month. I stand transferred to Western Air Command, New Delhi.'

From the lawn, he could hear countless congratulatory words. He looked on either side and thanked, one and all, with a broad smile. 'Today's party is purely by me and no bill will be paid by anyone. Keep enjoying and make this evening a memorable one as just now Flight Lieutenant Prabhakar said.'

The exodus of 'thank you sir' started pouring in and Mukerji could not control his broad smile and waved his hand expressing satisfaction. When he left the platform, Prabhakar again took the mike. 'Moments of happiness and melancholy. The news of our beloved Commanding Officer leaving us makes us quite unhappy, but that he is going on promotion overpowers that feeling.' He looked around and continued. 'I think we should not waste our time. First, we will play a few simple party games. The first game is finding your partner.' He gesticulated to the officers who were arranged before, to distribute the papers. They handed over everyone folded papers.

'Please do not open those papers. Only after everyone gets that, that will be opened. Ok?'

Prabhakar also got one.

Once Prabhakar got the confirmation that all have got the paper, he announced.' Now you may open those papers.' He looked at the people and found them busy with opening and seeing what was written on that. 'Now we will take one number from this pot.' He lifted the pot. 'The number written on that slip will be called. Then, the person with that number should raise his hand. After that, he should find out the partner who has the paper with the same number. Both of them should come here and perform something. Either song or dance or mimicry. Whatever you feel like. Ok?'

'Ok.' Everyone agreed.

He called one person from the crowd and requested to pick one number from the pot. That person picked one and handed over to Prabhakar. He opened that and called out 'Eight.' He looked around and asked. 'Who has, with eight written on the paper, in your hand?'

Squadron Leader K N Singh raised his hand.

'Ok, sir. Now you must find the lady partner who has this number.'

K N Singh moved among the ladies trying to find out who has the paper with eight written on that and succeeded. Air Commodore Sinha's wife. She got up and walked towards the platform with K N Singh. After discussing, they performed bangda dance singing themselves.

Everyone applauded.

When they went back to their seats, Prabhakar got another paper picked by the same person. Prabhakar opened and called out 'Number one. Who has got?'

No one raised hand. Then, one person said loudly. 'That could be with you Prabhakar.'

He opened the paper with him and said with a coy. 'It is with me.' He moved down to find the partner.

Seeing him trying to find the partner, Sneha opened the paper of the lady sitting by her side and quickly swapped that. When Prabhakar came near her she opened and showed him the paper and moved with him to the floor.

'What will we do?' She inquired in a very low voice.

He thought for a while and said.' You are a dog and I am a cat. We will make sounds as if they are fighting.'

That did not appease her. 'No fighting' she said with unhappiness. 'I have an idea. Why not we make a love scene?'

'No. I do not know.'

'You just say; I love you.'

'No.'

'Then let us sing a love song.'

He expressed his consent.

She, holding him tight, sang an old Hindi song and he sang with her. A duet!

Everyone gave a big hand to them.

That game was felt very interesting for all. When it was played for long, Prabhakar decided to commence the next game. The next game they played was passing the parcel. Many ladies and gents sat around and the parcel was passed with the music on. When the music was stopped the person holding the parcel was to open that and read and perform what was written in the paper inside. That was also liked by all. Towards the end, the person who had opened the parcel got a gift.

At nine, the games were stopped and everyone was called to the dance floor. Fast music was played. Many joined on the dancing floor and they danced picking their partners. Sneha danced with Prabhakar keeping their bodies very close which was noticed by most of the people.

Before ten, the arrangements for dinner was made in the lawn itself. The bearers brought all food items from the kitchen and arranged them on the tables. At ten, Prabhakar got the signal from the chief waiter that everything was ready.

'Ladies and gentlemen, the dinner is ready.' He moved to the mike and announced.

First, all ladies moved towards the table. When it was confirmed that all ladies have filled their plates, others moved one by one.

Everyone liked the food. The guests did not forget to mention the worth of Chinese food served there. Mukerji called Prabhakar and praised him in front of others.' I did not make a mistake in giving you the whole responsibility. I was confident that you would take any responsibility given in the right spirit and get executed to the utmost satisfaction of everyone. Thank you for everything.'

'Sir, the whole credit goes to Sneha.' When Prabhakar said those words, everyone could notice the great happiness that bloomed on her face equivalent to a thousand watts bulb. He raised his hand towards her and waved.

-4-

While coming out from the briefing room, Squadron Leader K N Nair, of Packet aircraft squadron, asked Prabhakar. 'Tomorrow one aircraft is planned to go to Kochi. Are you interested to come?'
'Packet plane?'
'Yes. I will be piloting that.'
'When will you be back?'
'Day after. It can be delayed by one more day. Not more than that'
Thinking for a while Prabhakar said. 'I will take a few days to leave and come.'
'Welcome.' He tapped on Prabhakar's back. 'I will be happy to be accompanied by you.' He smiled. 'You are getting a free lift, courtesy Air Force.'

Prabhakar thought very seriously of availing the lift and talked of this in the crew room. All suggested he avail a few day's leaves and relax at home. For quite some time he had not paid a visit to Kochi and met parents and was badly in need of a few days' rest. Few thoughts of naughty things he did along with friend Jayaram in home town came to his mind and made him smile unknowingly. He knew, unexpectedly without prior intimation, while seeing him, all in the home town would show surprise and happiness. Usually, he went on leave without informing anyone and used to derive pleasure out of others' surprise and complaint about not giving advance information. He decided to avail of a few day's leaves and go home and enjoy.

With the filled leave application in hand, Prabhakar walked into the office of Flight Commander and apprised him of his intention of availing a few day's leaves. As he had not availed any leave during that current year, the Flight Commander did not have words to refuse. With his recommendation for twenty days leave Prabhakar handed over the leave application to the unit adjutant. After a few minutes, he was informed of the approval for the applied leave of twenty days by the Commanding Officer.

On the following morning, at six-thirty the packet aircraft took off to Kochi. There were few airmen also as passengers. They were all proceeding on their annual leave and all were in the uniform. After some time, Prabhakar opened the cockpit door and sat on the seat between the pilot and copilot. Looking at different indicators and meters inside the cockpit, Prabhakar sat silently. Nair, who was piloting the plane took out the headgear and looked at Prabhakar.

'All meters and indicators of the transport planes will be entirely different from that of your fighter planes.'

With a pleasing smile, Prabhakar said. 'I know.'

'When are you planning to return?'

'I am on twenty days of annual leave.'

'That means you will not be returning with us.'

'I am coming to Kochi after a few months.'

'If you want, I will stay for one more day.'

'No sir.' Prabhakar said showing courtesy.

'Today I will go home.' Nair said. 'Tonight, I will spend time with my father and mother. Sometimes, I will stick around for one more day. Co-pilot is a Malayali, from Tiruvalla. He is also planning of going home.' After a pause he said.'If you are interested to come with us, you are welcome.'

Prabhakar smiled. No sir. I have some work at home. Within two days, I do not think I can finish all those.'

Nair shook his head and smiled. 'These works cropped up as this plane came now?'

Prabhakar smiled without answering.

'You are from which place?'

'Kochi itself.'

'I came to know that you are not a Malayali. How did you get settled in Kochi?'

Prabhakar smiled. 'Sir, that is a long story.'

'Oh, my lord! If you can complete it before we land at Kochi, it is ok. Otherwise no.'

Both of them laughed.

Prabhakar started. 'My grandfather came to Kochi with a few gold ornaments to sell. Later he opened a shop. Then, it seems, he did not like to leave Kochi. Later, that shop became a big one with a lot of gold ornaments.' His face suddenly turned gloomy. 'He died. Now the business is being looked after my father.'

'How is business there?'

Prabhakar smiled thinking. 'It is going on.'

'Gold business is full of competitions, isn't it?'

'It is. But, we have good business. People have a general belief that gold in our shop is pure. Hence our business is going on well. Sir, if you have money, the gold business is always profitable. While buying old gold ornaments or selling new, the shop is sure to make a huge profit. That's why these shops give huge discounts and gifts.'

Nair showed interest to know more about his family. 'All your relatives will be in Punjab, isn't it? Do you all go there to meet them often?'

'All our relatives are in Punjab. You rightly said. Frequently we all go there and spend a few days with my uncles. My father's brother is also in the same business. There is Punjab.'

'Father married from Punjab or from Kerala itself?'

He smiled. 'From Punjab. My father frequently mentions going back to our homeland. But, at the same time, he is reluctant to leave this beautiful place. I am sure, he will not do that. Also, we hear frequently from him that after two more generations we all will be pure locals here. We will stick around here itself. To be frank, I and sister do not like to leave this place. We will continue to live here only. The culture and peace of Kochi will never permit us to leave.'

'It is very difficult to uproot from the present location to another; isn't it?'

'Definitely. I don't like it.'

After landing at Agra the aircraft was refueled and the further journey continued. As per Prabhakar's request, Nair had contacted on wireless, Flight Lieutenant Unnikrishnan of air force unit at Kochi, and informed him of his arrival. The request to his friend was to arrange a taxi at the airport for his onward journey.

XXX

The aircraft landed at Kochi. In the technical area, after switching off the engine, when the door was opened, Prabhakar saw Unnikrishnan at a distance with his old standard 10 car waiting for him. As he stepped out of the aircraft, the waiting car came to his side. Thanking Nair, Prabhakar got into the car after the exchange of pleasantries with his friend Unnikrishnan.

After setting the car into motion Unnikrishnan asked Prabhakar. 'Where you want to go?'

'I want to go to my home. You do one thing. Just drop me outside the gate. I will take a taxi and go.'

Unnikrishnan looked at him very seriously. 'No, no. Nothing doing. If I can come to tarmac and pick you up, I can leave you in your home also. For that, I have enough petrol in this car. Though she is old, she can be trusted.' He hammered on the steering wheel and laughed. Looking at the packet aircraft, he inquired. 'Where that pilot is going?' He looked at him curiously. 'Did I show any indecency towards him? I did not talk to him anything.' He switched off the car. 'I will just go and ask him. Otherwise, what will he think of us Malayalees?'

Prabhakar looked at him. 'You start the car. He is also a Malayalee. The vehicle will come for him.'

'Are you sure?' When Prabhakar shook his head in affirmation, he started the car. 'I will leave you at your house.'

'During the working hours, if someone asks for you?'

Unnikrishnan laughed. 'If I am not available for some time in my unit, no emergency will arise. Everything will function normally. When you took leave and came, has anything happened in your unit? Nothing, isn't it? Similarly, here also nothing will happen. Not that alone, I have informed the concerned people of my absence for two hours.'

Prabhakar was astonished to hear the way his friend talked. During the training period, he was too timid and shy. He looked at him and smiled wondering how such changes took place in him.

After crossing Venduruthy Bridge, when the car reached Thoppumpadi he stopped in front of a fruit shop. He got out of the car in a hurry and walked fast to the fruit shop saying he would be back soon. Leaving the briefcase in the back seat, Prabhakar also followed his friend.

'What for you are buying these fruits?'

'It is not proper to come to your house empty-handed.' Unnikrishnan looked at him and smiled.

After buying the fruits, before entering the car, Prabhakar passed his gaze to the back seat and was shocked to realize that the briefcase was missing. The bubbling enthusiasm and happiness suddenly got extinguished and Prabhakar's face turned bloodless. 'Someone has stolen my briefcase.'

Unnikrishnan felt sorry for the loss and inquired. 'Was there anything valuable?' Unnikrishnan's throat was choked. He suddenly became gloomy with the feeling of guilt, as that had happened due to his stopping the car in the crowded place.

'No, nothing valuable.' Prabhakar said. 'My few dresses and the bank checkbook. Otherwise nothing useful to the thief.'

Unnikrishnan was still feeling sad. 'We will go to the police station and complain.

Knowing fully well of the notorious thieves masquerading in Kochi and the efficiency of the police, Prabhakar asked. 'For what?'

Under compulsion from Unnikrishnan, they went to the police station. Entering the police station, Prabhakar saw his classmate Vishnu as the Sub Inspector there. Though meeting after a long time, they recognized each other and hugged. When he was informed of the theft of the briefcase, Vishnu did not give an iota of hope of getting that back from the thieves. Realizing his mistake of leaving that in the car unattended, Prabhakar had by then had reconciled to the loss and did not show any hope of recovery. He expressed his happiness of meeting his good old friend Vishnu, many times.

'Kochi is very famous for the notorious activities of thieves and goons. Every effort is being taken by all our police force to get that eradicated. But, that is impossible and beyond imagination. Once few are caught and put behind the bars, others emerge.' Vishnu looked at Prabhakar and said.

'Not required. Your explanation is out of context and we are not interested to hear.' Prabhakar looked at Unnikrishnan and said. 'I forgot to introduce you to him. 'He turned towards Vishnu. 'This is my coursemate Flight Lieutenant Unnikrishnan. He is stationed here in Kochi. He is also a pilot.'

Vishnu shook hands with him. 'Glad to meet you.' With a smile he said. 'In case you need any help, you may contact me.'

Unnikrishnan did not like to give importance to that offer. 'Oh, it is not required. We have our police and we have a very smart policemen.'

Vishnu took that as an insult and looked at him with raised brows.

'Then, we are moving.' Prabhakar looked at Vishnu and said. Before leaving, Prabhakar gave his house phone number to the Sub-Inspector.

"If I get any information, I will ring you up and inform.' Vishnu said walking behind him.

Unnikrishnan wanted to cast sarcastic comment but controlled for fear of insulting him further.'Ok.'

XXX

The car reached Prabhakar's house. When the mother heard the sound of the car, she came out and was surprised to see her son Prabhakar coming out. She moved fast to the car and holding the hand of her son, inquired. 'Why in uniform?'

'One aircraft was coming to Kochi. I took a few days to leave and came in that.' He looked towards the house. 'Father will be in the shop, isn't it?'

'From Punjab, your uncle and aunty have come.' She smiled.

'When?' Showing extreme happiness, he asked.

'Yesterday.'

'Deepthi has also come?'

Her face suddenly turned happier with a broad smile. 'Why? Are you very anxious to see her?'

He presented as if he did not understand what she meant by that. 'I know, when uncle and aunty come, they will not leave her alone in Punjab.' He smiled. 'Still for the sake of asking I just happened to raise that query. Nothing else. Please do not take in any other meaning.' Looking toward the house, he asked. 'Where are they?'

'They all have gone to M G road for buying something.'

'Then, my younger one Sunanda? Has she also gone with them?'

She is there in her room. I think she is yet to know of your arrival. Otherwise, she would have come running.' She smiled.

When Prabhakar introduced Unnikrishnan to her, she said. 'I know him. He had come here earlier also. He often cuts jokes; I remember.'

Unnikrishnan felt happy. He said looking at her. 'These days I avoid telling jokes. That has made me get into trouble many times. Hence, I am very careful these days.' He walked along with Prabhakar towards the house. Entering the house, he kept the fruits cover on the central table and sat on the sofa.

'Hello, who is this?' Sunanda entered the sitting room and asked aloud. Looking at Prabhakar curiously from top to bottom, she said. 'You look very smart in uniform.' She held his hand and asked looking at Unnikrishnan. 'Who is this?'

Showing surprise, he asked. 'Haven't you have seen him earlier?'

Thinking for a while she said confidently. 'No'

'My friend and coursemate Unnikrishnan. He has stationed here itself.'

After an hour a phone call came from the police station informing that someone has handed over the lost briefcase to them saying, that was found lying on the road. The news made Prabhakar happy and he said looking at Unnikrishnan. 'Poor thief could not have found anything valuable inside except a few shirts and pants. From the cards inside he would have identified the owner to be a poor air force officer and out of pity handed over that to the police station. Anyway, the thief has some sense of respect for the defense person. His good-hearted behavior has helped me to avoid unnecessary expenditure on buying those items.' He sounded happy.

Mother and sister looked at each other not able to understand what he was talking about.

'Mother, we will just come. Some work is there to visit the local police station.'

Mother could not understand and she looked perplexed. She kept looking at his children with anxiety.

Unnikrishnan could read her face and said. 'No sooner landed here your son was created by someone.'

'What?' She became more curious.

'Someone stole his briefcase from the car.'

Keeping her finger over the nose, she asked. 'Thieves are so clever to flick from the running car? Has Kochi improved so much?'

Hearing her Unnikrishnan said. 'Mother is very humorous.'

Prabhakar said. 'The car was stopped in front of the fruit shop.' He smiled. 'Thieves of Kochi are capable even to pick from the running car.'

-5-

Both Prabhakar and Unnikrishnan came back from the police station after collecting the briefcase. Leaving Prabhakar at the gate, Unnikrishnan said bye and left to his unit. When Prabhakar entered the house, he saw uncle and aunty sitting in the sitting room and talking. He looked around as if searching for someone. Observing that, aunty yelled for Deepthi. Hearing the call for her, Deepthi who was busy talking to Sunanda in her room came in a hurry to the sitting room. Seeing Prabhakar, her speed got reduced considerably and she bit her kerchief showing shyness.

Observing her unusual behavior, the aunty said in a teasing tone. 'Look at her. So far, she had been inquiring why Prabhakar Bhavya has not come, repeatedly. Now she is wriggling with coy.' She taunted.

Prabhakar's mother Bharati who was sitting by her side decided to protect Deepthi. 'She is no more a small baby. She is grown up. It is natural to have little shy.'

'What is a necessity? After a few months, they have to live together.' The aunty knitted her brows.

'That is later.'

The conversation there gave Prabhakar a sudden shock. 'What am I hearing? Whose decision is this?' He thought and looked at his mother and aunt. He saw Deepthi smiling with coy biting the kerchief.

'Let me change the uniform. I got into this in the early morning.' Saying so he withdrew to his room.

When Prabhakar suddenly withdrew from that room without any indication of reaction to what she said, the aunt was unhappy. She moved close to Bharati and asked. 'Bharati, why he did not even have a word about their marriage? He did not say anything when I hinted that. Haven't you told him about their marriage so far?'

Bharati brought a forced smile on her face. 'Deepthi is studying now. Let her education be completed.' She looked at Deepthi.

Aunt's face suddenly changed. She made faces to show her dissatisfaction. 'Oh, her education is complete. What else she has to study?' Sarcastically she said and turned her face away.

The uncle who was listening to their talk so far silently decided to open his mouth. 'Degree completed. She has gained sufficient education required for a girl. She has expressed her desire not to go for any further studies.' His words contained the meaning that only the next step left was her marriage.

Bharathi suddenly became serious. Without looking anywhere, she said. 'Prabhakar is still very young to think of marriage. When the time comes, we will tell him about that.' She was assertive.

Suddenly the aunt changed her attitude. She talked very mildly. 'Actually, we had decided to fix everything during this trip. She has completed her degree. Not interested in further studies. In that case, we think it is better to get her married.' She looked at Bharati and pleaded.

Bharati was confused. She did not know what to tell her. She could not find proper words to console her and kept looking at her without opening her mouth. She wished her husband should have been there during such conversations. She had half a mind to tell them to open the topic only during his presence but somehow controlled her tongue scared of her brother and wife shouting at her. She could bring on her face her helplessness on the issue which others could read easily.

Brooding over the issue, the aunt said with slight discomfort. 'Years back it was decided.' She turned her face towards Bharati. 'Deepthi is very fond of Prabhakar. Many proposals keep coming, but she refuses all. IAS officer's and IPS officer's proposals had come. Many engineers and doctors' cases also came. All these boys came and liked Deepthi. But, she refused to accept any proposal. She wants only Prabhakar.' She paused thinking. 'My desire also is the same. I kept encouraging her on this. Since their childhood, you too have been telling that Deepthi is for Prabhakar.'

After hearing her, the uncle shook his head and supported. 'You are right.'

Sunanda came there to hear their conversation and took her seat on the sofa. Deepthi who was standing behind the sofa joined her.

Looking at Sunanda the aunt asked. 'Have you not completed your engineering degree?'

Sunanda shook her head. 'Yes.'

Aunt looked at Bharati and said. 'Her marriage also should be conducted without much delay.'

Bharati did not say anything. Instead, she decided to remain quiet.

Aunt suddenly turned happy and said. 'Then, both marriages could be conducted on the same day.'

When Bharati did not react, the aunt said. 'Since you people came to live in Kerala, these children's marriages are getting delayed. Would that have happened had you been in our place? When children grow up, every parent must get them married at the earliest. Otherwise, the bad stigma will get attached. Even if you take bath in Ganga, that stigma will never get washed away.'

Deepthi did not like her mother's unnecessary talk. She expressed that, by saying; 'Ma, please keep quiet. When the father is sitting with you, let him talk.'

She expressed unhappiness. 'It doesn't matter whether he is there or not. Both are the same.' She looked at her husband. 'Since long he has been sitting here. Has he ever opened his mouth to say anything on this?'

Uncle did not like that insult. He raised his voice. 'Would you mind keeping quiet?' He turned his head towards her. 'Prabhakar is the son of my sister. That means I am his uncle. I am confident that he will do whatever I say. Have we ever spoken to him about this or has he ever said no to this proposal? No. Then, these conversations are meaningless and futile.'

The aunt's face suddenly turned gloomy. She expressed her displeasure by making faces and decided to keep mum.

When Prabhakar entered the room after changing the dress, he observed everyone in the sitting room maintaining silence. 'What is the cause of this silence?' He looked at Deepthi. 'Why your face is swollen?'

Looking at Prabhakar, Sunanda said. 'Here, a serious matter was being discussed. The topic is your marriage.'

'Why to remain gloomy for that?' He casually asked with a smile.

'Uncle got annoyed and shouted at aunty.'

'Husband getting annoyed and shouting at his wife is very common.' He moved close to the aunt and held her chin showing affection. The aunt's face suddenly changed and she smiled and caught hold of his hand.

'We desire to get the marriage of you and Deepthi conducted as early as possible. That was the topic here.

You both grew up together and, in your mind, also there would be a desire to live together. We must realize that and do what is required to make you both live together. Now we have come prepared for that.' Throughout she had been holding his hand and talking very happily looking into his eyes.

Prabhakar laughed. 'For that, I have not attained the age for marriage aunty.'

Thinking for a while she asked. 'Now you are twenty-seven. When will you be of marriageable age?'

He smiled. 'Thirty.'

'At the age of thirty, children should start going to school.'

'That is the practice there in Punjab. Here, youngsters think of marriage only after thirty.' With the intension of not continuing that topic, he said very firmly. 'I like to follow the system of this place.'

Accepting defeat, she looked at her husband and shook her head indicating him to talk to Prabhakar. He however decided to keep mum and sat looking downwards.

After some time Prabhakar's father Kishanlal came from the shop.

Afterward, no one dared to open that topic.

At night, after dinner, everyone went to their rooms.

Mother Bharati stepped into the room of Prabhakar. Sitting by his side on the cot, she said. 'They have come here to make certain decisions. That is what my brother told me.'

Prabhakar looked into her eyes. 'I could guess something from their conversation.' He moved close to her.

'What is your decision?' She asked very firmly.

'Ma, I like Deepthi. But, I cannot see her as my wife. It is correct that both grew up playing together. We know each other for years. She knows me well and I know her too. But…'

'That 'but' has some specific meaning, I know. What is that?' Mother asked.

'You know me well.' He smiled.

'Are you still keeping that Menon girl firmly in your mind?'

With a head shake, he smiled.

'But, will they agree for that, son?'

Holding her hand to his chest he said. 'Even if they do not give consent, she is willing to come with me leaving everything behind. As good parents, if they do come on our way that will be good for everyone. They should permit us to live together.'

'They too should realize that. Will they?' Her words were full of uncertainties.

'That's right.' He looked at her face.

Seeing the sadness on her face he continued. 'Ma, I and Sujatha grew up together from class one. The relation we developed on those days continues. I like her very much and similarly, she likes me sincerely.'

'Has she ever told you that?' She asked to clarify.

'It is not necessary to mention. That could be felt. Our relationship is such.'

'That is not sufficient son. She should express that and her parents should agree to the relationship.' She opined.

'Ma, her parents shall do anything only as per her decisions and likings'

'Has she ever mentioned that to you?'

Thinking for a while, looking at the wall, he said. 'She hasn't told so specifically. But has hinted at. Ma, her father is a politician who has some extra sense.'

'You can't believe all these politicians. Some of them are even goons.'

'Ma, are you scared of him? Not required ma. I am a defense person who enjoys various types of protection.'

When the mother went away from that room, Prabhakar lifted the phone and called Sujatha. He was confident that as the phone was in her room no one else would attend his call. But against his expectations, the phone was lifted by her mother. When he identified himself, her voice was full of affection that he could feel over the phone. Before handing over the phone to Sujatha, she did not forget to tell him good night. Her affectionate talk during the short conversation on the phone generated some confidence in him. He felt happy.

'I came to know that you have come.' Sujatha said politely.

Prabhakar talked very mildly to give a feeling of him talking from far away place. 'Who said that? I am talking from north India.'

Laughing aloud she said. 'It would be correct if you say that you are speaking from the north house.'

'I see. That means you people have come to know of my arrival.'

'Why not? Coming in a vintage car in uniform with peak cap and walking in front of the house up and down many times - you mean that wouldn't be noticed by your neighbor?'

'Oh, I see. That means you did not go to the hospital today?'

'I went. Mother saw you coming in the car with another officer in uniform.'

He laughed. 'That means, your mother's job is to keep watching the neighbor's activities?'

Hearing the terrific sound of that vintage car she was attracted to look at thinking what the tractor was doing in that house.'

Prabhakar could not control his laughter.

'When can I meet you tomorrow? Can you take a day's leave?' His voice was full of love.

Thinking for a split second she said. 'After going to the hospital, I will take, not one day, but for two days leave.'

'Good. That means you love me.'

She did not like those words. With mock anger she said. 'Oh, that is a new invention!'

'Please don't get annoyed. I was trying to make you laugh. Instead, I found you getting annoyed. You could not understand my humor?'

She laughed. 'Mine was also humor.'

'Ok. Good night. Then we will meet tomorrow.' He disconnected the call.

After some time he again picked up the phone and called her.

'Why, you are not getting sleep?' She asked.

'No. I feel some sort of uneasiness.' His words were erratic.

'What is the reason?' She tried to cajole him. 'Sleep well. You must be tired of a long journey.'

'I wish I had some supernatural powers'

'For what?'

'To come to your place and meet you.'

She laughed. 'That you can do on the phone also.'

'To embrace you?' Very reluctantly he said.

'I see. Keep that desire for later days. For the time being keep that in your mind alone. If still unable to control, take the help of a pillow. And sleep now.'

'Ok madam.'

She laughed.

'I just called to know when we will meet tomorrow.'

Thinking she said. 'As soon as I reach the hospital, I will ask for leave and wait outside. You can come and pick me up. Ok?'

'Ok. Then once a more good night.'

-6-

The next morning at about eight, Prabhakar got ready to go out. After breakfast, he came out and took the father's Benz car out of the garage with his permission. Before starting the car, he passed his gaze to the adjacent compound. No one was seen outside Sujatha's house.

Aunt came outside and inquired. 'Where are you going early in the morning?'

'I have some work aunty.' He said very respectfully. He turned his head and looked at her. 'Shall I go aunty?'

Without waiting for her reply, he started the car and put it into motion. He drove the car directly to his friend Jayaram's house. Stopping the car on the compound, he went and pressed the calling bell. Jayaram's mother opened the door.

'When did you come' She raised her brows and asked showing surprise.

'Yesterday.'

'On one-month leave?'

No, aunty. Only twenty days.'

Jayaram came out to verandah putting the shirt's buttons and saw his friend standing out in front of the mother. He asked with an anxiety-filled voice. 'Hai. When did you come? Why are you standing outside? Come inside. When you came to Kochi?'

'Yesterday.'

'Without informing anyone.'

'The thrill lies there. I always used to come like that.'

Jayaram laughed looking at him. 'I know, I know.'

Looking at Jayaram his mother asked. 'What is that?'

'Nothing. I just laughed.' Jayaram said looking at his mother.

She knew, Jayaram sometimes would go out with his childhood friend without taking breakfast. To avoid such immediate outing, she said looking at her son. 'You go out only after breakfast.' She turned to Prabhakar and inquired. 'Did you have your breakfast?'

'Um.' He said running his hand over his stomach. 'Generally, I do not go out in an empty stomach.' He entered the room and asked curiously. 'What is breakfast here?'

'Dosa and coconut chutney.'

'If so, I will just have one.'

They went to the dining hall.

After serving them she asked Jayaram. 'Wouldn't you be going to school today?' She doubted whether her son would
 skip the school, as used to generally happen when Prabhakar comes on short leave.

Prabhakar felt that it was his responsibility to remove her suspicion. 'He will go to school. After leaving him in front of the school, I will go.'

While both were on their way to school, Prabhakar said. 'Recently I had met with an accident.' He explained everything in detail about undercarriage malfunctioning and belly landing and the hospitalization. 'After that only I received the letter from Sujatha.'

Jayaram turned his head expressing curiosity. 'What was in that?'

'She had spoken to her parents about our affair and they have given a green signal.'

Jayaram showed happiness. 'Very good.' He hit on his thigh and said. 'This is the most pleasant news' He looked at his friend. 'You have to give proper treatment for this.'

'I have not mentioned this to anyone else; even to my mother. Because she can't be taken all for granted.'

'That's ok. You tell me about the treat.'

'No problems. Today itself we will have. You tell me where I should take you. Hotel or bar? You are at liberty to choose.'

Jayaram tried to be a bit naughty. 'How about little local toddy?'

Expressing slight hesitation Prabhakar asked. 'Should we?'

'What is there in that? You just can't get the taste of local toddy in any bar or hotel.' He asked. 'Do you remember the toddy shop we visited some time back?'

'I remember. Being a senior air force officer, is it worth visiting such a shop?' He scratched his head.

'Then also you were an air force officer.'

'Correct. But....'

'If you have such reservations, just forget. We will not go.'

Prabhakar thought that he should not have talked of his position and felt sorry for talking downgrading his friend's status. Without showing the signs of regret, he expressed his desire to visit the toddy shop. 'Yes, we will visit the same shop. Forget about our position and status as officers and teachers. We both are having some respectable positions in society. But, the people coming there will not know that.'

'Ok. Agreed.' Jayaram shook his head in agreement showing happiness.

War Hero

'But not in this car. Going to the toddy shop with this Benz car will attract everyone's attention. We should avoid that.' He turned his head.

Jayaram could read on his face the embarrassment he was scared of. 'Ok. We will go to my ambrette scooter.'

'That is a good idea.' In agreement, Prabhakar shook his head.

Sitting among the locals on the common bench of toddy shop and having toddy with the open bottle in the front and hearing the cheap jokes of people would be very interesting. The very thought of the whole situation caused little embarrassment. However, he was sure that the atmosphere there would be giving utmost happiness forgetting yourself which one cannot even dream of in a five-star bar or officer's mess bar. Different frames in the toddy shop leaped into his imagination and derived some unknown pleasure and he smiled unknowingly.

With a tinge of jealousy, Jayaram said after maintaining silence for some time. 'How many girls are there to love you? I am jealous. There in your air force station, Sneha, in Punjab Deepthi and here your favorite Sujatha.'

Prabhakar laughed. 'To your surprise, Deepthi has come here. Uncle and aunt are also here. They want me to marry Deepthi as early as possible. The main purpose of their visit is that.' He laughed again. 'I do not know how to wriggle out of all this mess. My main worry is all about this.'

'You are really lucky to have so many girlfriends. You are the reincarnation of lord Sreekrishna. Everywhere you have a girlfriend. Even Lord Sreekrishna, who had sixteen thousand and one girlfriends, will say hats off to you. Very lucky man.'

'To be frank enough, I am not aware of the reason for this. I know that I am not very handsome to get attracted by the opposite sex.' He turned his head towards Jayaram. 'What could be the reason for this peculiar phenomenon? Do I have some magnetic power?'

Hearing his funny question Jayaram felt like laughing aloud. 'Handsomeness is not the main cause of this. Any girl for that matter gives maximum marks for social security. They need a man with a good job. Some girls who know the value, prefer defense officers comparing to civil service officers; I mean IAS and IPS. Same salary, most secured job. Even one wants to quit, the organization would not allow it. At the same time, no much of responsibilities as others have. These are the factors the girls give maximum marks. Handsomeness and beauty take back seat as the time passes. Your Air Commodore's daughter Sneha, uncle's daughter Deepthi and even Sujatha give maximum importance to these factors. These girls are capable of thinking far ahead of their future, comparing to men. We men give importance to the beauty of face and body shape. But their important line of thought is social security. They prefer to have only a person capable of leading a life with respect to society. Without money and position a person, however handsome he might be, will get the only back seat in any society. Haven't you heard that a person without money gets the respect given to the grass only? That is quite correct.'

His speech without any break was interesting and Prabhakar kept listening to him without interrupting.

When the car reached in front of the school, Jayaram asked. 'Aren't you getting down to meet our headmaster? He is fond of meeting his old students. You just meet him and then go.'

War Hero

Prabhakar got down from the car and walked down to head master's office. With respect, he opened the half-door of office and entered after taking permission. The master could not recognize
the old student immediately on entry. He raised the spectacle once or twice up and down and recognized him. Showing respect and love he suddenly got up from his chair and moved forwards, as if to receive him.

Quickly Prabhakar moved forward and showed utmost respect by touching his feet.

The headmaster held his shoulders and he got up. Looking at Prabhakar he said. 'This is the specialty of north Indians. Touching the feet to show respect. This practice is unknown to our culture.' He kept his right hand on Prabhakar's head and wished. 'Only good things will happen in your life.' He looked at Jayaram who entered the room after Prabhakar. 'He is one of my students who has attained a very high position. When I meet such people, the extra strength and good feeling that get germinated in me are countless and unexplainable. And that is the great treasure a teacher can expect. And their good feelings are our assets. He ran his hands over his body and asked. 'Nothing happened to you on that day's accident? No fracture or major bruises?'

The mention of the accident by the headmaster raised a few questions in his mind. Which accident he was mentioning about? He wondered. He knitted his brows and asked innocently. 'Which accident?'

'Don't try to hide anything from me. I came to know everything. It appeared in one English newspaper. In Indian Express. When the airplane wheels did not come down, the pilot cleverly brought down the plane without much damage to the plane and the pilot was safe. Your name was also there.'

Prabhakar was taken aback. He stood stunned. 'Then, why father and mother never inquired or talked about that when I came?' He murmured with suspicion. That was not with any expected answer from either headmaster or Jayaram; just murmured.

The headmaster looked at him with sympathy. 'They know. Probably would have decided not to remind you of that nightmarish event. Here a lot of people know of this accident.'

'That would have been the reason of Jayaram's expression of innocence and lack of anxiety when I mentioned and explained all about the accident to him.' Prabhakar thought.

Again, the headmaster ran his hand over his body and asked. 'Surely nothing had happened to you, isn't it?'

Casting a glance with affection he said. 'No sir.' With a smile, he continued. 'With the affection and prayers of all of you, any major accident will pass off very lightly.'

Those words made his eyes to get wet. Looking upward he said with respect. 'Everything is decided there.'

After spending a few more minutes in his office, Prabhakar came out seeking permission.

From there he went directly to the hospital where Sujatha worked. While he was getting out of the car, he saw Sujatha waiting outside for him. Standing outside holding the door, he gestured her to come to the car. Lifting the front of the sari, she looked on either side and came down the stairs in a hurry.

'Since long I had been waiting here. Why you got so late?' Her words were full of anger.

'I had to get down at school. The headmaster was too excited and happy to see me.'

They got inside the car.

'First, we will have a coffee from Indian Coffee House'. She suggested.

'Only coffee. Nothing else.' He was firm. 'My two breakfasts are already over.'

Showing surprise, she asked. 'Two breakfasts?'

'Before coming out of the house once from there. Another from Jayaram's house.'

'Then, as you said only coffee.'

They entered the coffee house and found a vacant table in one corner and occupied that. While having coffee Prabhakar asked her. 'How did you present our case to your parents?'

She smiled with little coy. 'One of his father's friends brought a proposal for his relative's son. When this was brought to me I took the usual method of avoidance saying I want to continue my further studies and hence I do not want marriage now etc. When I found that the grounds advanced by me were weak, I opened out the facts. Luckily, I got the support of my mother. On the next day, after considerable thinking of various parameters, I received the consent of the father. Probably he might have thought that these two had grown up playing together and permit them spent rest of their life also together.' She smiled. 'After that, he spoke to your father also. There also, I think, everything moved smoothly. After that our horoscopes were checked and they were found to be matching. I think these things are not known to anyone except for both fathers. Even mothers are not informed. Unless you give ok, it was decided to keep that within them.'

'When our minds have good resonance, do you think our horoscopes will not match? That will be matching perfectly.' He laughed.

'Yes. I told you that.' She kept the coffee cup down and said.

'That means this is going to be an arranged marriage.'

'Yes, yes.' She looked more jubilant. 'Then only my father can get maximum mileage. The daughter is getting married to a person from another state and caste. This will be the headlines in the newspapers. That will be a good addition to the father's political image.' She smiled.

With mock anger he said. 'I don't like your comments about my father.'

She smiled. 'I had taken your horoscope to the astrologer.'

He became curious. 'Then, what did he say?'

'Long life. Many quick promotions. You will also become the topmost officer in the air force.'

Hearing her words, he could not control his laughter.

'That was the reason that accident went off very lightly. The astrologer also said that you will always have god's blessing and will come out of any dangerous situations without much hardship.' The glow on her face while she said those words was unexplainable.

When they realized that others were observing them sitting and talking since long with the excuse of two coffees, they decided to quit.

After getting inside the car, they did not have a clear idea as to where to go next. Without any aim, they kept driving and came near the Venduruthi Bridge. Parking the car before the bridge, they walked towards the center. There they stood, watching the anchored ships, not caring for the scorching sun. They started perspiring and Sujatha started showing uneasiness. She kept wiping the forehead and said. 'I think we both are really mad to stand in this scorching sun.'

'At times we should stand directly under the sun. Let our bodies receive sufficient vitamin D. You being a doctor, I don't need to remind you of this.'

Looking to the farthest she asked. 'It will be very nice to travel on those ships, isn't it?'

'What nice? You can just sit inside looking at each other. What else? Are you interested to travel in a ship?'

After thinking she said. 'You are right. After a certain distance, you will see only water all around. It will be boring without the sight of land. The same will be the case while you travel in a plane also. Isn't it? Instead of water, you will see the sky throughout.'

'But that will be only for a short duration. Not for days together. In huge passenger ships, different facilities will be available. Playgrounds and theatres. I believe, the future passenger ships will have many comforts.'

When the heat was unbearable Sujatha requested. 'Now let us go from here.'

Straight they went to Ernakulam boat jetty. Sitting in the park, they kept looking at the passengers going and coming and passed comments without anyone hearing. When lunchtime approached, they moved to a nearby hotel.

When the waiter came to their table Prabhakar asked her.

'Veg or Non?'

'For me the only veg.'

'Why? Have you not started with non-veg yet?'

'I will eat whatever is prepared at home. Not from outside. I just can't be sure of the cleanliness while cleaning the raw and also while cooking.' She squeezed her forehead. 'I don't like. Just can't take for granted.' She grunted.

'Don't take. Just eat' He smiled.

She did not like that humor and she stamped mildly on his foot by her foot. As that conveyed the message, he nodded and smiled.

After taking order for two vegs. Food, when the waiter left the table, she asked. 'When we talk in front of waiters we should be slightly careful.'

Showing surprise, he asked. 'What did I say?'

'We should maintain our status.'

'What? What did I say for that?'

'What will they think of us when we talk about such cheap things?'

'What status? As a class one officer or as a doctor?'

'Both.'

'I keep my status and ego at my unit. When I come home on leave, I am an ordinary person who likes to move along the crowd enjoying all around us. We are grown up in these surroundings and we should try to adjust and merge with this style of living. Afterward, we will not be able to live such life barred by our position and maturity. Now we are young and this is the time we should enjoy all living styles. After a few years, we will be seniors with three or four kids and then we just can't think of having such freedom of expression.'

'What? Three or four kids?' She raised her brows.

'I see. You are not happy with four. Ok. Maximum five. Not more than. We will not be able to afford more than that.' He chuckled.

She was not amused by that humor and again stamped on his foot.

The food was brought. Rice, sambar, and curds were liked by Sujatha and she ate well. Prabhakar could not enjoy in the absence of any non-veg dish. After ice cream, they paid the bill and came out. Both of them thought of various ways of spending time.

When Prabhakar suggested roaming around in the car, she showed reluctance. The suggestion to sit in the marine drive was also shot down by her as it was too hot. Then the unanimous decision was to take shelter of any cinema theatre. They found out that one cinema titled 'CID Naseer' was being played in a theatre on M G road. They proceeded to that theatre. That was the latest movie of the year and the actors were familiar with them. Premnaseer, Jayabharathi, AdoorBhasi, and Jose Prakash. The movie was very interesting with a few songs, comedy and a good story. Both of them liked the selection of movies to spend time together.

Coming out of the theatre, Prabhakar looked at the watch and said. 'Oh god! In the evening I have a program. Ok, let us go back.'

Showing surprise over the discomfort suddenly shown by him, she tried to probe. 'What is the sudden development? Where you need to go?'

'I and Jayaram have plans to go to one place.'

'Where?'

With a smile he replied. 'Toddy shop.'

She raised her brows. 'What? What did you say?'

He laughed. 'Since long I haven't visited a toddy shop. It is fun to have such an ambiance and drink a bottle.'

'There are so many other methods to derive pleasure. Will you do?' She expressed her displeasure.

'It is not as you think. The shop is very far away from here. Five-star type. Only standard people go there. If interested, you may also come.'

Those words gave her a consoling effect. Her anger got extinguished. 'This is what you meant by saying you will do all things as a local, while on leave here?'

'Sujatha, these are the moments one should be able to keep with himself to remember during our old days.' He smiled. "Even we can amuse our grandchildren saying all about the toddy shop and the evenings there.'

She remained silent. 'If somehow father comes to know?' She was apprehensive.

He tried to pacify her. 'Don't tell that your father will have informers planted in all toddy shops around here.' He smiled. 'Nothing of that sort will ever happen.'

While they were driving home, she asked. 'All those coming there would be very poor people, isn't it?'

'Where?'

'Toddy shop.' She grunted.

'I told you that it is a five-star toddy shop. Only rich and business people come there. Some government employees also come.'

She felt consoled. 'Jayaram also will be there?'

'Yes. In the morning we planned this trip.'

With a smile, she said in requesting tone. 'Should not drink more.'

'No. Never. At the most one bottle.'

'Oh my god! One bottle. Wouldn't it make you drunk?'

He looked at her with a smile. 'No. It is just like one glass of beer. You will not feel that you are consuming liquor. It is a good health tonic. Every day, having a bottle of toddy purifies the blood. You wouldn't have read in your medical books all these things. For knowing these, you should have general knowledge. I have a good impression that you have that enough. Don't make it to me to change that.' He held her chin and fondled.

She threw her glances with love towards him.

After dropping her in front of her house he drove to the garage and ran home. Straight went to the room and changed the pants and wrapped a dhoti and went out in a hurry.

Aunt and Deepthi who were observing his urgent movements kept quiet wondering what he was up to. When he moved out of the house, aunt inquired. 'Where are you going in such a hurry?'

He looked at her. 'Aunty, I will just go to the nearby riverside and see if I could some fresh river fish.' He said casually. 'Sometimes I may get delayed. If I do not get, I will use a fishing rod to catch a few.' He laughed within himself.

-7-

Sitting on the pillion of the ambrette scooter, Prabhakar proceeded to the earlier visited toddy shop, with Jayaram. Riding on the narrow road with paddy fields on either side was a good experience. The evening light breeze carried the aroma of bloomed flowers from the field and it was cool and pleasant. Often, they tried to keep the hair from flying hither thither by pressing down, especially when the breeze was slightly strong. Jayaram was riding at a good speed. Both were without a helmet. In the air force, riding two-wheelers without a helmet was considered as a punishable offense. High speed was forbidden for two-wheelers. Such messages and instructions used to be frequently published in all daily routine orders, as many officers had lost their lives in two-wheeler accidents than that in flying accidents. The very thought of that caused a chill to pass through his spine and he requested his friend to reduce the speed. But, Jayaram did not pay attention to him. Saying, the pilot who flies aircraft with more than the speed of sound should not be scared of this tiny scooter, he refused to decrease the speed. He often looked back and teased him.

From a distance itself, they could make out that the toddy shop, which they had visited earlier, was not functional. The coconut tree leaves with which that was made was almost found eaten by white ants. No one was seen in the vicinity. They parked the scooter near the shop and looked around wondering what the next course of action could be.

'This is permanently closed down. Very sad.' Jayaram said showing concern.

'Very bad.'

'Here we had good privacy.' Jayaram said. 'The small cubicles made of coconut tree leaves were a good hiding place for gentlemen to have two bottles without anyone noticing. All gone.' He looked sad.

'Sometimes that would have been shifted to some other place. That could be.'

'I don't know.'

'Then we will go back.'

'Then, it is ok.' Jayaram turned the scooter.

'Too bad. Our dream of enjoying with toddy had taken a premature death.'

Jayaram felt bad. 'You had desired so much?'

'Yea. Even I had taken Sujatha's permission to have one bottle.'

Jayaram cast a sarcastic gaze and said firmly. 'Then, let us find another suitable place for us.' Stopping a person on the road they inquired. 'The toddy shop which was here earlier has been shifted to some other place?'

'No. That shop was made to be closed down by the excise authorities. That shop owner was giving some harmful chemicals mixed in water with some other ingredients. There was a liquor tragedy a few months back. Few people lost their eyesight. That owner is in jail now.'

The news gave a jolt to both of them. They too had come and enjoyed the toddy and curries many times. They thanked God for saving their eyesight.

'Is there a decent shop anywhere nearby?' Jayaram was firm on his mission.

That person looked at Jayaram. 'You mean with privacy? Such shops are not available anywhere nearby. But there is a place you get good country toddy. Pure toddy.'

'Where?' Both asked in chorus with anxiety.

Pointing to the distant location he said.' If you go on this road for two kilometers, you will find one. You will get the best there.'

Sooner he heard him, Jayaram started the scooter and asked his friend to take the pillion.

Holding the scooter handle, Prabhakar took out the key and looked at Jayaram seriously. 'Should we?'

'If I can't get your desire fulfilled, what is the use of me claiming to be your friend?'

Prabhakar looked more jubilant. 'If so, yes, we will proceed.'

The scooter moved to the place suggested by the other person. It was getting slightly darker. They could see the toddy shop board from a distance. A hurricane lamp was found hanging. Parking the scooter at a distance, they walked slowly with slight hesitation towards the toddy shop. In the dim light of the hurricane lamps, they could not see the people sitting in the shop. Few benches were seen with people sitting and the desk in front of them was decorated with toddy bottles and glasses. The whole ambiance was not felt conducive for them to spend the evening and Prabhakar held his friend's hand and moved back towards the scooter. They heard someone calling them from the shop; 'Sir.' As it was the customary practice of every shop owner to address the customers as sir, they did not pay attention to that. When he felt someone approaching them from the back by running, Prabhakar looked back.

'Sir, why are you going back after coming up to this place?'

Looking at the approaching person Prabhakar searched for words to reply. 'Oh, nothing.'

'Sir, it is not correct for you to go away after coming up to this place.' That person stood in front of him and said with the utmost respect.

Cursing that person in mind Prabhakar said. 'We came in search of one person. He is not found in this shop.'

That person smiled. 'Sir, that can't be believed. Sir, I am also from the the Air Force. Medical assistant. My name is Francis. On that day of the accident, I was there to accompany you to the hospital in the ambulance.'

Jayaram drew the attention of Prabhakar by tapping at his back and shook his head asking what was the next.

Francis looked at both. 'Sir you will get pure coconut toddy here. Very good item. Another thing, the chicken curry and fish fry of this shop are very famous. Having come over here, I request you to come and at least taste these items and I can assure you that it will be a great experience for both of you to cherish the hospitality of these people around here.' Francis was found adamant to escort them to the shop.

Unable to take a decision both friends exchanged glances asking what was to be done next.

'Sir, I am sure you both have come to this place in search of a toddy shop. May not have the expected standard, but I can assure you both that the items served in this shop are pure and clean.' Francis did not have the intension to leave them free.

They changed their mind and decided to enter the shop.

They walked behind Francis and entered the shop and looked around to see the people sitting by the table with glasses and bottles in the front. One person was found drinking directly from the bottle itself.

Francis drew the attention of everyone there and said pointing to Prabhakar. 'This person is a big officer in Indian Air Force. A very senior officer who flies fighter planes. It is the rarest opportunity this shop can get to treat such a great person. I just happened to see them passing by and I compelled to enjoy our hospitality.' He looked at Jayaram and inquired. 'Sir, I could not recognize this person. Who is this sir?'

Jayaram said. 'I am working in the Gulf.' He said a lie so as not to get a bad name for the teacher community by visiting the toddy shop.

One person drew quick breaths and said. 'That is the reason for this nice fragrance since they entered this shop.'

'Sir, the crab curry of this shop is a specialty.' Another person said looking towards the cash counter. 'Give them one plate each. Let them enjoy.'

Francis said looking at everyone. 'This sir is the only Malayali officer in our station. The peculiarity of this officer is that he will speak only in Malayalam to all airmen from Kerala. I have seen some other Malayali officers. They will never speak a word in Malayalam. They feel it is against their status to speak in their mother tongue. But, this officer is not like that.' He turned to all there and asked. 'Do you know the power of this officer? He can charge sheet anyone and can even put anyone behind the bars. If someone commits a crime.'

One person did not like that. 'How can anybody put someone in jail? Unbelievable.'

Francis looked at that person and said. 'I said if someone commits a crime. Probably you did not hear that.'

They both were made to sit comfortably and the shop owner placed two bottles and glasses in front of them. Francis sat at a distance and drank from the glass. 'You know, this sir will take the plane very high and come down like a top, spinning at high speed. The plane goes like an arrow. It spins dives and does all sorts of aerobatics. Once you happen to see his aircraft exercises, you will not feel like pulling out your eyes from that.' He drank again. 'There is an officer from my neighborhood. He will not even look at me. Leave alone talking to me in Malayalam. He feels that even while on leave he should not talk in mother tongue to anyone.'

'That means, even to his parents he will not talk in Malayalam?' One person raised his doubt.

After finishing one bottle each, both Prabhakar and Jayaram decided to leave. When they asked for the bill, Francis intervened. 'No sir. That is not correct. I will pay your bill. After coming to my place, if you pay the bill for a bottle of toddy, it is a shameful affair for me. What these people will think of me?' He looked around and asked.

'You are right.' Few supported him.

Prabhakar looked at the board hanging inside with the price of each item in the shop. He calculated the amount for what they consumed and opened the purse and took out notes and kept on the table. Francis expressed his objection and took those notes and placed them back in his pocket. 'Sir, I will pay for this. Otherwise, these people will shout at me when you leave.'

Everybody there supported him and showed their teeth with a broad smile.

Prabhakar looked around and showed his happiness over their love. 'How loving and simple these people are?' He murmured.

They both waved their hands looking at everyone in the shop and came out.

Francis followed them to their scooter. Before Jayaram started the scooter, Prabhakar inquired. 'Francis, will I be able to get river fish from anywhere?'

Straight he asked. 'Sir, what sort of river fish you want?'

'Any river fish will do.'

Requesting them to follow him, Francis walked quickly towards the shop. Looking at him Prabhakar said. 'We are not interested to have anymore. We are going.'

Francis turned back. 'Aren't you interested to have river fish. It is here sir. Live fish of your choice.'

Looking at each other they showed surprise and followed him wondering what he was up to. They saw Francis talking something in low voice to the shop owner.

'Come with me, sir.' Francis took them behind the shop. 'Here they grow all fish required for the shop. As per the requirement they catch and prepare. Fresh fish. That is the specialty of this shop. Similarly, they have chicken also. They do not buy these things from outside. They prepare curry using these chickens only. These chickens are healthy and well-fed. In other toddy shops, you can't be sure of the health of the birds they use for curry and fry. They use sick birds and even dead ones. But, not here.' For that reason, the customers come from different places in the district. This shop owner is my relative. Usually, he will never sell the fish he grows. As I spoke to him, he has agreed.'

Prabhakar expressed happiness. 'Thank you very much.' They saw in the feeble light of descending sun, the chicken in a cage, and fish in a small pond.

'Sir, do you need crabs?'

'No.'

'How about chicken?'

'No.'

When a bag with live fish was handed over to him, Prabhakar asked the prize.

'Sir, this is my gift to you. No money will be charged. As I said this is my relative's shop.' He was very firm.

Not knowing what to do, both friends looked at each other. Finally, under compulsion, without satisfaction, the bag was accepted and Jayaram hung that on the hook at the bottom of the seat.

Francis was seen running towards the shop saying one minute. He was seen running back towards them holding a card. He handed that card to Prabhakar saying, 'this Sunday is my marriage. If both of you could come, that will be considered as my luck and I will be very happy and I will never forget that in my life.' He smiled very pleasingly.

Accepting that Prabhakar opened the cover and tried to read the card. Francis helped him read in his torchlight. Putting the card back into the cover he said.

'Let's see. If possible, we will come.'

Jayaram started the scooter and moved forward. 'Are you the king of your station? The respect and affection showed by him identify you as one like that.'

Prabhakar laughed. 'My friend, if a human being considers others also to be human-like you, respect will come automatically from others without being demanded. If you try to show your position and power to others, you can't expect that.'

Jayaram turned his head back. 'You are perfectly correct. Those people will find only good moments in life.'

'That I do not know. But one thing, I am very confident. Those people will have many friends. I can't say they will not have enemies. That can happen anytime.'

Jayaram suddenly stopped the scooter. When asked for the reason, he said. 'Just see on the road ahead.'

A huge snake was found lying across the road. In the headlight of the scooter, it was not fully visible. As the road width was less, it was not possible to take the scooter forward avoiding it.

'Why is not giving us the way?' Jayaram asked.

'Either it is badly injured by some vehicle running over that or lying immobile after eating huge prey.'

'How can we go forward? Shall I take scooter over that?'

'No. That might die sometimes, if not already dead.'

'I think it is lying dead.'

'Poor thing.' Prabhakar showed sympathy.

Observing Prabhakar's concern for the snake, Jayaram wondered how he is so simple-minded being a soldier.

Prabhakar got down from the scooter and pulled out a piece of branch from the nearby plant and tried to move its tail out of the road. The snake slowly moved out of the road. Observing that Prabhakar said with a smile. 'It is not dead. It was lying after eating prey.'

They again started their journey.

After a certain distance, Jayaram asked. 'Should we go for marriage?'

'What is your opinion?'

'Since we are obliged, I don't know what to say.'

'If so, is it not correct to attend that with a small present?'

Jayaram laughed. 'I think.'

XXX

When reached home, it was later than expected.

With the bag containing fish, Prabhakar entered the house singing an old Hindi song. When no one inquired what was in the bag or talked to him, he felt something had gone wrong. But without trying to find out the cause for the silence, he directly went to the kitchen and handed over the bag to the servant and went to his room. He could not imagine the causes of the total silence there. After a bath, he changed the dress and went to the sitting room and found uncle and aunty sitting on the sofa looking at each other and conversing something seriously. Though they saw him, hardly paid any attention by any of them, from which he could guess that the subject of discussion could be very serious.

He tried to intervene. 'What is the subject of such serious discussion?'

'No. Nothing.' Aunty said. 'We are discussing our return.'

He could feel the tinge of unhappiness in her words. He moved close to her and asked. 'Why all of a sudden you are thinking of going back?'

'We have stayed here for four days now.' Uncle said with a smile. 'We have a lot of jobs after going there.'

The unhappy face of both indicated some discord. He preferred to refrain from the further probe and went to Sunanda's room and sat on the bed by her side. She was found reading a book and seeing him by her side, she closed that and kept away.

'Where is the mother?' He asked. 'I couldn't find her in the kitchen.'

'Uncle was heard talking to her with a raised voice. She must be sitting upset in her room brooding over that.'

'What had happened?' He showed anxiety.

'Matter was your marriage. In the evening, when father came back from his shop, he informed the mother about the telephone call received from you would-be father, asking to proceed with the matter. Though the mother very tactfully introduced the subject to uncle, he suddenly became furious and made a commotion. He blamed both mother and father for not maintaining the words given to them from years and shouted by saying it all happened, as we are living here in Kerala. Finally, when they saw the mother's tears, they cooled down. Now they are planning to go back by the earliest means.'

      Prabhakar felt sad after hearing the whole. He had a feeling that the relationship was getting eroded due to him. Expressing unhappiness overstraining of good relations he went out of the room without uttering anything.

-8-

Observing father Kishanlal sitting on the chair outside on the verandah and reading the newspaper and sipping tea from the cup kept on the table, Prabhakar stood leaning over the door frame for a while. He moved close to him and sat on the chair adjacent. Sensing the presence of the son, he folded the newspaper and kept aside and observed him from bottom to top.

'What is today's program?' He asked

'Nothing particular to mention.'

'Today we are going to Rajesh's house. You too should accompany.'

That was unexpected welcome news. With happiness, his mind started jumping up and down. Without showing any signs of anxiety, he asked very casually. 'Who are all will be going?'

Kishanlal could read the mind and face of his son. Casting a smile, he said. 'Me and mother.'

'How about uncle and aunty?'

Kishanlal smiled. 'They are planning to go back to Punjab today itself.' He looked at his son and continued. 'They are disturbed.' He emptied the teacup and placed it on the table. 'Yesterday Sujatha's father Rajesh had phoned me up. He said he and his wife are coming here today to talk about the marriage proposal. I blocked their plan. You know, here your uncle and aunt are sure to create problems with unwanted talks. I wanted to avoid such scenes. I suggested that we will visit their house for a discussion.'

Prabhakar felt sorry for Deepthi and sat without showing any sign of unhappiness.

'We can't blame them totally.' Kishanlal said. 'From your childhood, very often, this uncle and aunt kept saying that their daughter Deepthi is your girl. But, at any time mother never said any word against. I too have heard them saying so. But did not say against, suggesting such decisions could only be taken after knowing their minds, once both are grown up. Every parent desires to send their daughter to a financially and socially sound family. That is what they also desired. Had we instilled our thoughts in them, this situation wouldn't have come across. They sincerely hoped all will be in their favor'

'None ever asked me for my opinion.' His voice was hardly audible. 'Not only that, but I have also seen Deepthi as my younger sister only.'

Looking towards the horizon Kishanlal said. 'Marriage can't be forced on anyone. The whole life of a person is decided in marriage. Once you commit a mistake in selecting your life partner, the whole life is ruined. It is not correct on the part of even parents to compel children to marry someone of their choice and liking.'

At ten o'clock, Kishanlal, Bharathi, and Prabhakar walked down to the adjacent house of Sujatha. To receive them Sujatha's father Rajesh and mother Ramani were waiting outside on their verandah. They were ushered into the drawing-room and showed sofa to sit. Ramani called Sujatha who was inside her room. She responded to her call and came to that room. Ramani hurried to the kitchen and brought a tray with water-filled glasses. Sujatha took that tray from her and placed it on the central table.

Kishanlal turned his head toward Sujatha and inquired. 'You didn't go to the hospital today?'

That question raised laughter in Rajesh. 'Had she gone, you wouldn't have seen her here.'

'For the sake of asking something I just did so.' Kishanlal looked at Rajesh and said trying to hide his folly.

Looking at Prabhakar, Rajesh said. 'You both can go inside and talk anything freely.'

Kishanlal was amused. 'It is not required. They always keep chatting.' He said humorously.

'Then, not required. We all can sit together and discuss future plans.' Turning to Kishanlal he said. 'You are at liberty to ask or tell anything being the groom's father. Let us hear from you.' Rajesh smiled.

'I have nothing to say specifically.' Looking at Prabhakar he said. 'You know, he can't get leave whenever he likes. All of you know that perhaps. Hence, my demand is that this should be conducted as early as possible'. When he said so, the extra glow with happiness on the face of both Prabhakar and Sujatha was observable. He looked at Bharati for taking her clearance with a nod.

'I also want the same.' Ramani said with a smile. 'I got both horoscopes checked with the famous astrologer here. Both match perfectly. I got even checked off the muhurta. One good muhurta is on this twentieth.'

Kishanlal raised his brows. 'For that only a few days are left.'

Rajesh was mused. 'Why do you worry? For the groom's side, the work involved is hardly any. Just come to the hall and tie the thali and take the girl home after taking part in the feast. What else? All works involved are on the bride's side. We are ready for that. Then what is the problem?' He looked at Prabhakar and asked. 'Any problem?'

Thinking for a while, Kishanlal held Rajesh's hand and said. 'Alright. We are ready.'

Prabhakar expressed slight uneasiness on his face. 'My leave is up to twenty-fifth of this month. I have to return on the twenty-second.'

Rajesh looked at both Kishanlal and Prabhakar without showing any uneasiness. 'What is there in that? Nobody is going to hold you back. After the marriage ceremony, there will be two days. Our both families are known to each other. Then what is the problem?' He looked around at everybody. 'No difficulty.' He smiled. 'See I am a politician. I like everything to be conducted quickly. I have no patience to wait. From now on, we have ten days to inform all our relatives and friends. Wouldn't that be sufficient?' He shook his head with raised brows as if to take everyone's concurrence.

Kishanlal leaned towards his wife and whispered something. Then he looked at Prabhakar. 'Can't you ask for a few more days?'

'I will send a request. I will extend my leave for another ten days more. But, can this date of marriage be extended?'

Rajesh grinned. 'Can't. We will not get another good muhurta soon. And this muhurta is very good as per the astrologer. Looking at Kishanlal he asked. 'Wouldn't it be possible for you to complete the arrangements within these ten days?'

Kishanlal said promptly. 'No problems. Agreed.'

Rajesh suddenly turned jubilant. 'In front of both these houses, huge pandals will come up. After marriage, a feast will be here in our pandal and the evening party to treat the people coming from here to bring back the groom and bride to this house will be in your pandal.' Rajesh imagined the whole event and smiled expressing utmost happiness. He looked at Kishanlal. 'We will come to buy gold in your shop. You must give us a reasonable discount. Otherwise, we will go to some other jewelry shop.' He laughed aloud. Others also joined him.

When the serious conversation among the elders continued, Prabhakar signaled Sujatha to go inside. Coolly she looked around as if to take their permission for going from there. She got up and walked towards the room. She kept looking behind to confirm that Prabhakar was following behind. They both entered the room and sat on the cot.

With bit surprise he said. 'Your father is more anxious to get this conducted as fast as possible as we both are. Usually, the people from the girl's side ask for more time for preparation. Here it is just the opposite.'

She did not know what to say. She smiled and said. 'After all, he is a politician.'

'I never expected such a hurry from your father. As if otherwise I may run for some other girl.' He laughed.

She also laughed. 'You know what the reason could be?' She hesitated slightly. 'You know, now he is an MLA. The next election is on the cards. Expected to be announced at any moment. I think he may not get a ticket for the coming election.' She looked into his eyes. 'Every politician would like to get the marriage of their daughter conducted while in power. Understood?'

Shaking the head Prabhakar said with a smile. 'Now understood.'

They remained silent for some time.

'When I introduced our subject to father, first he vehemently opposed. Later he realized that mother also is in favor of my desire and then he reluctantly agreed. There is some problem in my horoscope. I don't know what that is. Many proposals came and father got checked their horoscopes with mine. But nothing was found matching. But our horoscopes were showing a perfect match. And he agreed.'

'So far, everything is in favor of us.' He held her hand and said very mildly. 'After this leave, you must permit me to go back to unit alone.'

She laughed.' Why? Can't you take me along? I think you do not want to forget your bachelor days so fast. Once I am with you, the freedom for living recklessly might be a hindrance. Isn't it?

'Oh, shut up. Even if you are with me, my life will continue to be the same; without any change. Not that. Number one; reservation by train for our journey. Number two; a living house.'

'We will stay in your room until one house is arranged.'

He knitted his brows. 'Best.'

Expressing dissatisfaction, she said. 'After the marriage, no question of me living alone.'

'Sure?' He held her chin and asked.

'Yes.' She held his hand with coy. 'Reservation will be arranged by the father. He will get that in emergency quota'.

'Really, you are your father's daughter.' He whispered.

When Prabhakar heard his father Kishanlal saying aloud that they were about to start back home, he along with Sujatha moved to join them. Though Rajesh compelled Kishanlal to have lunch and go, he excused himself saying that many occasions were ahead for that and he had to go as some urgent jobs were to be attended to. When Kishanlal moved out, others followed him.

XXX

That evening, Prabhakar went to friend Jayaram's house in his car. Jayaram had just come from the school and was having tea sitting outside on the verandah. Seeing

Prabhakar, Jayaram called the mother and asked to bring tea for him.

While taking tea, Prabhakar explained all developments of that morning to his friend.

Jayaram could not believe, how much serious decisions could be taken so fast. 'Within ten days, a marriage? Usually, this urgency was seen in the case of gulf employees who come on leave for a few days. For that, there would be a specific reason. Towards the end of the leave, a suitable match they find, and if not married immediately the girl will not wait for another two years; the slated waiting period of most of the gulf employee for next leave. In your case, I don't find anything of that sort. You can take leave and come at any time. Then, why are you in such a hurry?'

When Prabhakar explained what Sujatha had mentioned to him, the friend got convinced. 'Then, we can expect in your marriage a lot many politicians including few ministers as guests.'

'Who is interested in that?' Prabhakar did not believe in the pomp and show usually seen in marriages. 'I like a very simple marriage with few immediate relatives and friends. A humble one. Really.'

'That is your way of thinking. But not of others. The majority of people want to make the marriage in their home an event to attract other's appreciations.' Jayaram suddenly slipped into deep thoughts.

Looking at his friend, Prabhakar asked. 'What are you thinking about?'

'The decorated pandals in front of both adjacent houses with color papers and color bulbs would be a subject to talk. Beautiful'. He kept smiling.

-9-

In the morning when Prabhakar entered the sitting room, he saw uncle and aunty sitting on the sofa and talking. Sooner, she saw him, the aunty got up and inquired 'Did you have your tea?' Her voice was sweet with lots of affection and love.

Observing the unexpected concern from her, Prabhakar wondered what the reason for such a sudden change could be. He had expected different behavior from her as the development of the last day was not in her favor. The usual angry face and taunt he expected from her was found absent and he teased his brain thinking of the probable cause for such diametrically opposite behavior. 'Yes aunty, I had. How about you both?'

'Yes, yes.' Uncle turned his head towards him. 'You sit down here.' He indicated to sit by his side.

Like an obedient child, Prabhakar went and sat by his side.

Uncle adjusted himself and moved close to Prabhakar. 'See, we were not aware of your liking towards that girl on the next door. When we came to know that you were very close from your early childhood and at this juncture both families accepted to approve your affair, we are happy and have nothing else to offer other than our blessings. From the childhood of Deepthi, we had been nurturing the desire of marrying her to you, but we never thought it necessary to find out what was in your mind. We never thought it necessary to ask you or mention that.

Apart from that, neither your father nor mother had ever talked of in favor of your living together with her. All were our desires.' In those words, a tinge of guilt was predominant.

Those words of uncle tickled his senses and felt sorry. Without uttering a word, Prabhakar moved some more close to him and kept looking outside through the open front door. He felt sympathy towards uncle, aunt, and Deepthi. He suddenly thought about how he could face Deepthi who craved to marry him for years. Probably she would have been dreaming often of leading a life with him with utmost happiness and the very thought of him being the cause to get that extinguished suddenly made him gloomy. He found no way to rescue from the depth of despair she was subjected to. He looked at an aunt who was sitting aside with swollen eyes without uttering a word. Probably she would have thought of not causing additional embarrassment by expressing her feelings of unhappiness.

When all were sitting embracing silence, Deepthi came there. Prabhakar observed her swollen eyes and doubted her listening to her uncle's talk, hiding behind the door. He saw her wiping her eyes before she came in front of them. He could imagine her mental condition as everything had gone out of her reach and control. 'She had come to Kochi with lots of hopes of certain positive major decisions of her life, but everything had gone shattered like a pack of cards. Her mental condition, he could imagine.

Sitting by the side of Prabhakar, Deepthi looked into his eyes and asked. 'Why are you sitting as if you have lost something? It is not good for a soldier to keep mum like this; brooding over unnecessary things.' She sounded firm.

He tried to smile but failed.

She rolled up the kameez sleeve and exposed the left forearm and showed what was tattooed.

Looking at his name tattooed on her forearm he could not control his emotions. His eyes suddenly got filled and silently sobbed. With the kerchief, he cleaned his eyes and nose and turned his head away from those tattooed letters. He looked at an aunt who was sitting silently without caring for what was going on by her side. On the day of his arrival on leave, an aunt was very voracious with taunts and laughs, but she had gone completely silent with despair. When he looked at her he could see her struggling to control her emotions with wet eyes. He could not watch her emotions and pulled out the gaze suddenly from her with guilt.

He fondly held Deepthi's hand and asked. 'Are you angry or annoyed with me?'
She looked at him and tried to smile. 'No.' She cleaned her nose. 'Why should I? My innocence made me develop certain desires. I will be alright soon. I am already back to normalcy.' Her throat was choked.
Prabhakar felt very sad and left for his room. He kept brooding over various things. He felt as if the peace of mind was getting lost. When he thought of unhappiness of different people due to him, he felt his head was on the verge of exploding. After changing the dress, even without having breakfast he took the car and proceeded to Jayaram's house.
Observing the swollen eyes, Jayaram asked him. 'Did you shed tears?'
'If I say no, that may not be correct.'
'You mean?'
He repeated what his uncle had said. 'When I saw the tattoo on her forearm, I lost my balance.'
Jayaram moved close to him and tried to pacify. 'You are not responsible for what others do without even

knowing about your likes and dislikes.' He patted on his back. 'There is no reason why you should spoil your peace of mind.'

Prabhakar turned his head towards him. 'I just came here to get little peace of mind. Not to hear your philosophy.'

Sitting by his side Jayaram kept smiling mused over his condition. 'What should I say? In which way I can console you. You are one who has learned the decision-making techniques. In situations like this, which way you will take decisions. Keep attributing marks for each parameter and see which one has more importance. In the case of Deepthi, you are not interested but she is. In that case, the mark is one. Similarly, in Sujatha's case, both of you are interested to live together. Hence there, the mark is two. As per that simple theory, just forget this. Today's talk and expression of sentiments would have probably hurt your mind. But, you have no way other than just forget that.'

'I fully agree with you. I am capable to realize that. But, my worry is how to take these people out of the present mental condition?'

'Your question is genuine.' After thinking he asked. 'Shall I tell?'

Prabhakar turned his face anxiously.

'I don't know.' Showing mock anger, he said. 'What is the use of crying now after creating all unnecessary humbugs?'

Prabhakar did not like what he said. 'What humbug I created?'

'You should have thought of all these consequences while you were on a spree of falling in love with so many girls.' Jayaram sounded angry with little jealousy.

'But, I have never given words to anyone. I can't discourage anyone who shows love towards me. It is meaningless to tell all those who show affection to you, not to show that with the intention of marrying. If I say so, they will underestimate me as lunatic. Someone might be showing affection as a brother. It is foolish to think of marrying all those who show affection to you.'

'In case of Deepthi, they would have mentioned that to your parents, isn't it?'

'Would have. But, that was not mentioned to me at any point in time, by anyone. Without anyone mentioning what was in their mind, how can I even think of expressing my like or dislike?'

'That's is correct. I fully agree with what you said now. Then, have you told this to Sujatha?'

'No.'

Looking outside through the window Jayaram said. 'Your case is typical. Envious of you. So, two families are proposing their daughters for you. One your uncle's daughter Deepthi and the other your neighbor's daughter Sujatha. You are the reincarnation of Lord Krishna. There is no doubt at all.' Looking at him with the care he asked. 'Is this, just you are being an air force officer or being handsome with good complexion?'

Prabhakar looked at him with anger. 'I am not good looking. You are more handsome than me.'

There appeared shyness on Jayaram's face. 'Till now none has come to love me. So far, by the grace of God, no girl has ever expressed little affection towards me.' He looked upwards. 'For that, one has to be lucky.' He smiled and looked at him.

Prabhakar laughed. 'I think, you are lucky if what you are telling is correct. No tension like this.' With a naughty smile, he said. 'But, I fully can't believe you.' He winked his eyes.

Jayaram sat brooding over. 'You like Sujatha more. And you like to spend the remaining part of life with her. Hence, you are just thinking of that only. All other minor or major issues will be resolved over some time. Marrying a girl without fully satisfied will make you sick throughout life. The time can not cure such sicknesses. Any patchwork will have little projection and that will keep troubling you. Do you know, with family discord, how many families play drama in front of others and pass the days throughout their life? Any marriage with compulsion or by mistake will always be a failure.

Without passing any comment, Prabhakar sat with a smile.

Suddenly Jayaram remembered and asked. 'Today is your air force chap's marriage. Francis. Are you planning to go? Or forgotten?'

'No. I haven't forgotten. I have brought and kept one ring as a present. In case we plan to go, should not be empty-handed.'

XXX

On their way to attend the marriage of Francis in the Benz car, they saw the toddy shop they had visited earlier. They looked at each other and smiled.

'Do you feel like entering?' Jayaram's naughty question.

Without answering, Prabhakar laughed.

'To get rid of worries, on the way back one bottle can be gulped in, isn't it?'

'Good idea. In Benz's car and this dress? You are really mad.' Jayaram quipped.

Directly they went to the house of Francis. The marriage party was ready to proceed to the church. From a distance, Francis saw the approaching guests and he hurried to receive them. Everybody there wondered seeing the excitement of Francis and looked at the new faces wondering who they were. Francis held the hand of Prabhakar and told loudly. 'This is an officer of the Air Force. He flies fighter aircraft. A very senior pilot.' He introduced Prabhakar to everyone near him expressing great happiness.

When Prabhakar presented the gift to Francis, he opened and showed the ring to all in the pandal with a broad smile. 'This is a valuable gift from my officer.' He wore that ring on his finger and said. 'For me, more than your gift, the most valuable thing is your presence. I am very happy sir. I feel privileged to have your presence which we all will never forget in our life. I am very proud of this moment sir. We all will cherish these sweet memories' He became emotional. 'Sir, wouldn't you be coming to the church?'

To take the opinion Prabhakar looked at his friend.

'All depends on your desire.' He gave a blank approval by a whisper with a smile.

'Ok. We will come.' He looked at Francis and said.

Francis and others moved to the nearby church. After dropping Francis at the church, the same car was taken by a few to bring the bride. After some time the bride and party reached the church. After receiving them everyone moved into the church.

Inside the church, the usual religious formalities started. The wedding ceremony took place. After that, the priest commenced his usual speech. He advised the couple to lead a happy life irrespective of the various hurdles they come across. The sanctity of marriage and the necessity of rowing the boat of life smoothly, irrespective of the difference of opinions that might come up during life, is to be maintained. All advice was felt as most valuable and Prabhakar heard the full with patience. When all formalities were over, it was quite late and all proceeded to the girl's house. There they had food.

Prabhakar went near Francis and said. 'I do not like to spend any more time here. My marriage is fixed for this twentieth. You both should come and attend my marriage. After the card is printed, I will come and invite you both personally.' He could read the rays of happiness on his face and agreed with a nod.

'If you invite, we will surely come sir.'

On their way back, as the car reached the toddy shop, the speed started getting reduced slowly. The toddy shop of Francis's relative was found open. Prabhakar cast a meaningful glance towards his friend as if asking permission for entry to the shop. Though he noticed that, Jayaram preferred to neglect thinking about why being an Air Force officer he was behaving as an ordinary person. He had half mind to ask him not to reduce and maintain the usual speed. Before opening his mouth, the car was turned to the front of the shop.

'Let's find if we can get some fish from here. The fresh fish was liked by everyone at home on that day.' Prabhakar stopped the car and said.

Jayaram preferred to remain silent.

The shop owner saw the approaching car. As no one was coming out, he quickly moved towards that and identified the prospective visitors. 'Aren't you coming inside sir?'

When Jayaram replied in negation, Prabhakar leaned towards him and whispered something in his ears. Casting meaningful gazes, they both reluctantly got out of the vehicle and went close to the shop owner.

'We don't want toddy now. We are interested to get a few fishes.'

Suddenly the shop owner's face turned gloomy. Without hurting the visitor's feelings, he said very affectionately. 'Sir, we do not sell our fish.'

As there was nothing else to talk further, they both turned towards the car and started walking.

'Being the superior officer of Francis, how to send them back empty-handed having come to this place?' That person was thrown into a dilemma and turned back and requested. 'Sirs, please come inside. Take your seats.' He ran to the shop and took out the cloth he had been wearing over his head and cleaned the bench with that for them to sit. Both went inside with smiling faces showing slight uneasiness as few people sitting inside started casting their eyes over the approaching well-dressed visitors.

The worker in the shop placed two full bottles in front of them.

With hesitation Prabhakar said. 'No, we don't want today.' He sounded firm.

The person sitting opposite laughed, noticing the hesitation of visitors and said. 'Having entered the shop, it is not correct to go out without having at least a little. You know sirs, here what is served is pure drink. Without any chemicals or any adulteration. Have sirs. No fears.'

'Whatever may be, we are not interested.' Jayaram looked at him and said harshly.

The worker came and took the bottles to carry away. Prabhakar looked at him. 'Anyway, let this be here. It is not fair to take back.' He opened the bottle and filled two glasses and blinked looking at his friend gesturing him to lift one and drink. He asked the shop owner. 'Today is your relative's marriage and you haven't gone to attend? We are on our way back after attending that.'

That person moved close to them and said in low voice. 'Today is the day we get good business. If I go for that, this boy here will do all humbug and create all possible confusions. I wanted to avoid that. Last night I had visited them. For marriage, I have sent my wife and children.'

'Wouldn't Francis feel bad?'

'For what? He is a very sensible person. He knows us very well. This is not like any other shop. If a slight issue rises, that will become serious. Few people coming here for drinking might be having animosity with some. In case they get into arguments, my presence is a must to control and contain them. The majority of people coming here might have some problems or other, personal or otherwise, and after consuming a few glasses those feelings with grudges and grievances might raise its hood. I generally do not allow that to happen. This boy is not grown up sufficiently to contain such things.' That person turned talkative.

After completing one bottle each, they got up. They, along with the shop owner went behind the shop and as per Prabhakar's choice, fishes were caught and put in a polythene bag. Prabhakar handed over the cost of both toddy and fish to the owner. That person walked with them to the car and kept the cover inside the car.

-10-

When the phone started ringing, Kishanlal who was busy writing the list of relatives and friends for sending the marriage invitation cards sitting along with others around the dining table, got up and walked in hurry to the sitting room. He could hear the exchange operator's voice. 'Sir, your call to Punjab, Kalpi. The party is on the line.'

He took the call.

'Baiji, this is me, Kishanlal from Kochi.' He shouted, as on the other side he was not audible enough. 'Our son's marriage is fixed. I called you to inform you that.'

Prabhakar who was in the dining hall commented. 'Father's sound will be heard by everyone in this Kochi.'

Mother Bharati smiled. 'The STD facility to that place is still not established. Your father had booked the call early in the morning and now only that is matured.'

'Earlier days if we book a call in the morning, that will get matured sometimes during the night only.' Uncle said with a smile looking at others. 'After the new facility is established, making a call has become very simple. To call a person in Delhi or Chandigarh, lift the phone and just dial the number, adding the STD code. And that person will be straight available there to talk. But this facility has not reached certain villages.'

'That will come throughout India soon.' Prabhakar said expressing optimism.

Uncle gave the list of his guests to Prabhakar to write their addresses on the invitation card.

Looking at that list, he turned to Deepthi who was sitting opposite and he asked. 'Don't you have any of your friends to be invited?'

She tried to smile but failed. 'My friends will not come here all the way.' Her face suddenly turned gloomy. 'Would have come. But…'

He could read the meaning of what she meant by that. He could not help but sympathize with her. 'I realize your mental agony.' He said in his maid.

When father came back after telephoning, he was found to be perspiring and Prabhakar said. 'You look tired as though coming after the one-mile walk. If you make a few such calls, you will go tired too fast.' He smiled.

'You are making fun of that?' He tapped oh his son's head. 'I am quite used to this. Earlier days, you would not believe, making a call from here to Ambala or Amritsar was a really big job. It was terrific. The mouth will go dry. It used to be a nuisance to the neighbors. Shouting was such.' Looking at uncle he asked. 'Isn't it brother-in-law.'

The uncle nodded in affirmation.

Kishanlal looked at everyone and inquired. 'All of your guest lists are ready?'

Everyone pushed the guest list they made towards him, expressing the contentment of completing the assigned work.

After looking at the list Kishanlal said. 'If we consider all these lists, the total guest will not exceed more than a hundred.' From the bundle of invitation cards, he took out the required number as per each one's guest's list and handed over to them one by one.' Now, your entire job is to write the names and addresses of your invitees on these cards. If you can finish the job today itself, we can post them all without delay. Similarly, it will be the job of each one of you to invite personally your guests, where ever required, without much delay. I will look after my friends. Similarly, Prabhakar should personally invite his friends. In the same fashion, others too.' He turned to Prabhakar. 'You may post these cards today itself.'

'Ok.' Prabhakar said.

Everyone got busy with writing the addresses on the cards. After a while, when the pandal contractor came, Kishanlal and Prabhakar went outside to give guidance and direction to that person.

'I am erecting pandal in the next house also.' That person said.

Showing happiness Kishanlal said. 'That's good. See, both these house's compounds are of the same dimensions. Hence, the pandals of both these houses should look similar. Then that will be very good to look at.' Looking at the other compound he asked. 'What those people had told?'

'They also said the same. Both should look identical.'

'Then there is nothing more to say. Another thing. The chairs and table you bring should be of good quality. If you bring any broken or damaged chairs or tables, I will not permit you to arrange them.'

'On sixteenth we will come with all materials to erect the pandals and for decoration work.'

'No problems.' Kishanlal gave the clearance.

After breakfast, Prabhakar and Bharati took a few cards and got into the car. They planned to visit the nearby friends and hand them over the invitation. As decided, they visited houses and invited them for the marriage. They did not forget to inform them that as the marriage was decided quickly and that would be very simple without much pomp and show.

Toward the evening, Prabhakar accompanied by friend Jayaram visited many houses of their friends. They did not leave anyone who had studied with them. Among his classmates, few were holding good government posts and influential positions, and many were poor. But Prabhakar liked to consider all on the same scale and requested each one of them to attend the function and convey their blessings. When they went to Flight Lieutenant Unnikrishnan's house, there the first birthday celebration of his daughter was going on. Prabhakar felt sorry for not carrying any gift for the child. Jayaram consoled him by saying that their arrival was without knowing about the birthday celebrations and there was nothing to feel bad about that. After handing over the card, when they tried to escape out from there, Unnikrishnan did not permit. After the celebrations when the invitees cleared off they were made to be seated in the sitting room and he opened the whiskey bottle.

'Usually, I do not consume liquor like this, excepting on some special occasions.' Jayaram said as if he was committing some mistake.

'What?' Unnikrishnan asked.

'After his arrival, I am having this very often.' Looking at Prabhakar he said. 'I am scared of getting into this habit.'

Unnikrishnan laughed. 'My dear friend, these are just for fun. These are the moments that we could cherish even after many years. Can you imagine the sweetness of these thoughts after, say, sixty years or so? There used to be a saying. During our wealthy days if we plant few fruit plants, during the weak days we could enjoy the fruits from that. Similarly, if we enjoy life during our healthy days, we can cherish the sweet memories during our old days.' He laughed aloud.

Though his saying did not usher laughter, they also joined him and laughed mechanically.

Unnikrishnan looked at them. "I think, you did not fully understand me. See, these days most of the people have good pay and pension. So financially most of us are well off.' He sipped the drink. 'Hence, what I said is correct, isn't it?' He talked as if he was slightly drunk.

Prabhakar looked at him with raised brows. 'I think you started drinking earlier.'

Unnikrishnan laughed. 'You are right. I had two pegs earlier.' He went inside and instructed his wife to bring some snacks and came back quickly. After sitting he said. 'Friends, these are the enjoyments one should not miss. Today is my only daughter's birthday. That will come again only after a year. So, enjoy this day with whatever way you find.' He leaned towards Prabhakar and asked. 'We being defense personnel, this is the best way we can afford to celebrate. Am I not correct?'

'As you say.' Prabhakar reluctantly agreed.

Hearing Prabhakar, Jayaram laughed.

The wife came with a plate of cashew nuts fried and kept on the table. Looking at her husband, she said 'Don't drink anymore.' When Unnikrishnan did not react, she looked at Prabhakar and said. 'He started this since morning.'

Those words were full of worries.

Instead of showering pacifying words, he said. 'Today is my only daughter's first birthday. If I don't drink and enjoy what will she feel? Not correct. I will drink.'

She became annoyed. 'Don't talk like that. Always you will find some excuse for drinking.' She kept her hands over the head and said. 'Whenever the Air Force stops issuing liquor bottles to its people, then onwards only this person will stop drinking. For drinking, he is cleaver to find reasons. Even some difference of opinion between us will do for him to have a reason to get drunk.' Her words were full of grief.

'That happens often.' Unnikrishnan nodded. His sarcasm filled words pained her. With a swollen face, she withdrew quickly.

Her concern for the husband was touching and Prabhakar stared at Unnikrishnan. 'Why to make her unhappy like this? Only two years have passed after your marriage. These are the days you should spend with maximum adjustment. Why do you drink daily if she doesn't like it? Just refrain from such habits.' That was a piece of advice.

Unnikrishnan's face turned sad. 'We have a good understanding and I don't purposely do this. Even if I am slightly upset mentally, she is right in saying that I resort to the help of this damp thing. But what to do? This is the habit I formed right from my bachelor days. If squadron commander or flight commander says something which hurts my feelings or whenever I realize that my flying was not up to the mark, I used to take the help of a bottle. Many a time, my superiors have warned me to refrain from this. But, it happens without my control. Not that I am doing this to offend her or out of vengeance.' His voice was full of regrets.

Jayaram said seriously. 'Sometimes your liver will stop functioning.'

Unnikrishnan smiled. 'No. That will not happen. My liver is very strong. Had I had some problems of that sort, the doctors would have advised me to stop drinking. So far, nothing of that sort had happened. That means so far, my system is perfectly normal and functioning well. If the liver misbehaves, I will be medically advised to refrain from this good habit. Then I will think of what should be done further. Will stop drinking' He laughed. 'As I said earlier, then I will brood over these hay days and enjoy.'

Prabhakar looked at the watch and got up. He gestured Jayaram to follow him.

'You people are going?' Unnikrishnan showed unhappiness. 'One more drink?' He offered.

'No friend. We have to visit many houses more to give cards.'

Unnikrishnan turned his head towards the kitchen and shouted. 'See, they are going.'

When she came, Prabhakar repeated his request for both of their presence in the marriage. When they moved outside, Unnikrishnan and his wife followed them to the car. When Prabhakar opened the car, Unnikrishnan asked.

'You are on how many days leave?'

'Up to this twenty-fifth.'

'After marriage on twentieth, to reach the unit on twenty-fifth, you will have to start at least on twenty-second'. Unnikrishnan said.

'Prabhakar shook his head in affirmation. 'Yes. You are right." Thinking he continued. 'I have sent a telegram requesting for an extension of my leave for another ten days because of marriage. I am sure they will give.'

'Will you take the wife along with?'

Prabhakar smiled. 'Is it proper for a gentleman like us to leave behind the wife immediately after marriage, friend?'

'Yes. Should not be done. Still, I just asked.' Unnikrishnan said with a tinge of hesitation. 'You both are known since childhood and have been very close since then, except you haven't lived as husband and wife. That is the reason for my question.'

War Hero

Prabhakar did not answer. He satisfied him with a smile.

Entering the car Prabhakar closed the door. Holding the door Unnikrishnan said. 'Something is happening on the border. I am sure, you must have read in the newspapers.'

'I read. In eastern Pakistan, the problem is of Mukthibahini. That is their internal problem. Such things keep happening. I don't think we need to worry about that.' He sounded casual.

Unnikrishnan suddenly became serious. 'No. You can't just ignore that. When their internal problems go out of control, they might do something unexpected. I am scared.'

Prabhakar sat thinking. 'They are not capable to have a face to face confrontation with us. They will not dare. And they are not capable of an open confrontation with us. Hence, I don't think they will dare for an all-out war with us.'

'You can't rule out anything friend.'

'If so, that will be bad for both these countries. In case of a war, both these countries will economically go backward by years.'

Listening to their conversation, Jayaram said in low voice. 'That's right.'

Looking at both Jayaram and Unnikrishnan he expressed his doubt. 'Will my unit refuse to give the extension of leave when the reason shown is my marriage?'

'I don't think. As you have mentioned of the marriage, I am sure that will not be rejected.' Unnikrishnan expressed confidence.

'If they refuse, I will travel back as planned on the twenty-second. I have done reservation for that.'

'If so will you take her also with you?'

'Surely. After marriage, without wife how to undertake the first journey alone? Without her, being along, what will be the thrill?' He shook his head and laughed. 'If some problem arises, she could be sent home back. If I go alone, my friends will cut me into pieces.'

'You are right. 'Unnikrishnan paused. 'Still, you may think well and make a wise decision.'

'Ok'

They started the car and moved forward saying bye.

-11-

Though the muhurta was between eleven and eleven-thirty, invitees started pouring in from ten o'clock onwards. Few of them were not aware of the distance between the two houses of the bride and groom and were under the wrong impression that they have to travel few kilometers from the groom's house to the bride's house and arrived much before muhurta giving allowance for the journey time. After coming there only, they could understand that the journey time is only a few minutes by walking. It was understood that they had not read the invitation card properly.

Inside the pandal, Prabhakar's father, mother, uncle and aunty were busy receiving the invitees. Few were busy distributing lemon water to them and kept moving hither-thither. The gramophone was playing a few old Malayalam songs in low volume. The pandal and surroundings were of festive mood and look. The total environment wore a cheerful mood.

Along with Jayaram, Prabhakar came out of his room in white dhoti and Jubba. Few relatives and some girls, who had studied with him, flocked around him with jubilant admirations.

'When you tie the thali, ensure your hands do not tremble.'

He laughed hearing the jovial advice of a girl there.

'No, that will not happen. His hands which fly huge planes will never shake.' Another girl commented.

Yet another girl quipped. 'To tie thali is not that simple as flying an aircraft. Hands will shake.'

Prabhakar looked around to see that girl but could not locate her.

At ten forty-five grooms party moved as a flock to the adjacent house of the bride. To Prabhakar's left and right, both uncle and aunt walked along. He noticed the absence of Deepthi in the marriage party. He was curious to find out why she was not with them and aunt tried to satisfy him saying that she would join after a while.

There were girls with a lighted oil lamp in metal trays containing rice, in two rows at the pandal entrance to receive the groom's party. As they entered, Sujatha's father and others received and ushered them to be seated. They served aerated soft drinks. Before eleven, a boy came and took the hand and led Prabhakar to the platform that was beautifully decorated with jasmine and other flowers for the ceremony. Sitting on the decorated chair, Prabhakar looked into the pandal. The hall was found full. He could not find Deepthi anywhere in the pandal. Many doubts had crept into his mind and that made him slightly uncomfortable. Many thoughts disturbed him. Was she trying to avoid the marriage ceremony? Thinking about various probabilities, he sat looking at the entrance expecting her at any moment. He imagined the presence of many political leaders in that pandal. His eyes were glued to the entrance for Deepthi.

The Poojary started doing his job of chanting few mantras.

Within minutes, many white dressed people entered the pandal and a total commotion was observed. Prabhakar thought that was the indication of the arrival of some important ministers or chief minister himself. He was right. The chief Minister entered the hall with folded hands looking around whispering good wishes followed by his close party associates. Rajesh ran to receive him with all humbleness and broad smile. The atmosphere inside the pandal suddenly changed. Everywhere silence prevailed. Everyone's eyes turned towards the Chief Minister.

After a while, Sujatha was sighted being escorted by many girls with lighted lamps in trays and walking to the platform. Sujatha was made to be seated on the chair by the side of Prabhakar.

Poojary started his ritual with more vigor and chanted mantras aloud. He asked both the bride and groom to stand up and made them repeat a few mantras he prompted. After a few other formalities, the Poojary gave the golden chain with thali to Prabhakar asking him to tie that around her neck. That was the prime nuptial formality after which the groom and bride get into the wedlock; the inseparable bond. The insignia of a marriage recognized and accepted by others in society! Without shake of the hand, as few girls had cautioned, he tied the holy thali with a smiling face. When a lady tried to help him in putting the chain, he gently moved her hand away and did all by himself. That moment was a memorable one in one's life and few ladies made sound by mouth to draw the attention of everyone in the pandal.

One lady came forward to the platform and read out a poem showering blessing to the newly wedded. It was very clear that she was a politician and she had been passing her gaze frequently towards the Chief Minister as if to read his reactions. When the reading was over, she bent forward and folded hands and thanked everyone. When someone shouted out from the crowd appreciating the poem, she cared to look at him and folded the hands again and thanked them. She moved quickly to the Chief Minister and said something to him and took a seat adjacent to him.

Once the ceremonies were over, the Chief Minister got and walked down to the couple and blessed them and sought everyone's permission to leave. Though Rajesh requested him to wait for the feast which was about to commence and taste the food, he politely expressed his inevitable urgency and walked towards the gate by waving his hand continuously with a broad smile. As he started moving, the crowd who came along with him also moved out behind him seeking formal permission from Rajesh.

Few people who were arranged earlier brought metal tables and chairs and filled the pandals very fast. The arrangements for the feast were being done. Everything went on with precision. Prabhakar and Sujatha were taken to the sitting room. Many people came there and introduced to the newly wedded couple and few even invited them to visit their home to share their hospitality. But, Prabhakar's mind was full of Deepthi and he did not bother the blessings and invitations. Whenever he met aunt, he cared to find out about her, but could not get a satisfactory reply. From the replies of the aunt, he concluded that probably Deepthi would have decided not to attend the function and that decision would have been communicated to an aunt which could be the reason for her cool behavior and absence of anxiety. Still, his thoughts were about her.

When both were invited for food, they moved to the pandal and sat in the front row. Spreading plantain leaves in front of them on the table, the volunteers engaged in serving, came, and served them all curries and *pappad*. Rice and sambar followed. Having feast in the plantain leaf was a favorite thing for him, but he could not consume much, but little rice and sambar. His mind was getting disturbed with the thoughts of Deepthi. He wondered, why the girl who was cutting jokes and passing comments, provoking him at times, during the last evening, sitting around with others in the pandal, had behaved like that.

War Hero

Why hasn't she come? His thoughts kept wandering for answers.

Observing him brooding over, Sujatha showed concern. 'What happened? You are not eating anything.'

'He did not want the tell her about the absence of Deepthi and said. 'Nothing.'

'You did not like the food preparation?'

By forcing a smile on his face, he said. 'Preparations are supreme.'

One person came and asked them. 'You want *payasam* in glass or in the leaf itself?'

Both demanded in a glass. First was *palada* and then wheat *payasam*. They had both little quantities.

When everyone's food was over, the uncle went and talked to Kishanlal about going back home with the couple. He said that the marriage party should move out of that pandal before one o'clock.

After bidding farewell to all, uncle and aunt moved towards their home flanked by Prabhakar and Sujatha. While walking down, Prabhakar inquired about father and mother and it was told that they had already gone earlier to receive the newly wedded.

When they reached home, they were received by his mother with a lighted coconut oil lamp. After handing over that lamp to Sujatha, she asked her to enter the house with that. With care, Sujatha ensured to take the first step with the right foot and walked ahead with little coy, usually seen, in newly wedded girls. She looked at everyone there and walked slowly and entered the sitting room. When asked by Ramani, she sat on the sofa and Prabhakar stood by her side.

Looking at Prabhakar one lady said. 'You can also sit by her side.'

Passing a smile towards her, he went to Deepthi's room and found her lying on the bed with bleeding left arm. He saw a pool of blood on the floor. He called her many times, but there was no response. Scared of her condition, he ran to the sitting room and held Sujatha's arm and dragged to that bedroom without uttering anything. Looking at that, the people around stood perplexed and some even closed their mouths and laughed with a different meaning.

Sujatha tapped on her shoulders and called Deepthi repeatedly. When she realized that Deepthi was lying unconscious, she did not make a further attempt. She passed her glances around for a piece of cloth. Finding none, she tore Prabhakar's dhoti with her teeth and made a bandage to tie the wound. By then, more people came to know of this and rushed to the room. Uncle and aunt rushed in and started crying seeing her condition.

'Nothing serious has happened.' Sujatha tried to console everyone, especially the uncle and aunt.

Both Prabhakar and Sujatha lifted her and took her to the car. In order not to be noticed by anyone, the arm with the bandage was hidden by Sujatha with her sari. Whosoever saw Deepthi being carried, inquired what had happened to her, and to everyone's query, Sujatha kept saying that she felt giddiness suddenly and fell. Without informing anyone about what had happened, they proceeded with uncle and aunt to the hospital where Sujatha worked.

Sooner, they reached the hospital; Deepthi was taken to the operation theatre. Everybody was slightly at ease as Sujatha was also in the theatre.

After a while, Sujatha came out and informed Prabhakar. 'She has lost a lot of blood. She needs to be administered a blood transfusion. 'O' negative is the group.'

'Mine is 'O' negative. You can take mine.' Prabhakar volunteered.

'Needs more blood. Now we are giving her blood taking from our blood bank. That needs to be replaced. You may organize one or two more.'

Thinking for a second, he said.' No problems. I will arrange that. If I inform our air force unit, many will come for giving blood. I will speak to Unnikrishnan.'

'That is to be replaced today itself.'

Prabhakar nodded in affirmation. He moved close to Sujatha. 'How is Deepthi?'

'Nothing could be said. She has not gained consciousness yet.'

Prabhakar looked at uncle and aunt who were anxiously sitting in front of the operation theatre beaming their eyes to the door expecting the latest news of their daughter. Their faces were gloomy with no tinge of blood. His eyes met that of the aunt. He felt as if she was murmuring looking at him. He could see her efforts to bring on her face the anger on him. He could perceive her painful feelings blaming him for the critical situation which her daughter was going through, inside the theatre, fighting with death. It was meaningless to blame her for deciding to end her life itself, as she could not succeed in getting fulfilled her long-cherished desire, that was watered and nourished by the elders. That can't be called childishness. The sudden death of the desire might have caused uncertainties and further life might be thought of as useless which could lead to such decisions. That was what had happened in her case. But he found no reason to console himself. Mother and uncle had talked and took decisions that were not with his knowledge and for that he was not responsible. Though he was totally upset and worried, he felt not guilty. His thoughts kept moving fast from one thread to the other without his control and kept trying to pacify himself.

    Sujatha opened the door of the theatre and announced it. 'Deepthi has gained consciousness. She is out of danger,'

    The long sighs of relief were heard.

    'Can I see my daughter?' The aunt expressed her anxiety.

    'Just wait. I will let you know.' Sujatha again went inside.

    After some time, she came out. She took Deepthi's father and mother inside.

    Sujatha cautioned them when entered inside. 'You should not ask or suggest anything to cause unhappiness or anxiety in her.'

    Mother stood by her side and asked without shedding tears. 'How are you now?' Her throat was choked.

    Deepthi looked at everyone. 'I am ok.' She was seen passing her gaze around as if looking for someone. 'Where is brother.?'

    Her father could read her mind. 'Prabhakar is outside.'

    They did not spend much time inside. They went out and sat on the same chairs they had occupied earlier.

    Looking towards the ceiling, the aunt was heard whispering. 'Poor Deepthi. Since the day Prabhakar joined the air force, we had been saying that she is for him. Probably she couldn't have controlled her emotions when the dreams were not coming through. That is the only reason that led her to take this wrong step.' She turned her head towards her husband. 'We should not blame her alone. We are also responsible for leading her to this unfortunate situation. Hadn't we all nurtured such possessive feeling in her, probably this wouldn't have happened.' Stream of tears rolled down her cheeks.

The uncle's lugubrious face mechanically moved towards her. He expressed his melancholy and nodded in affirmation. 'One can't find who is to be blamed. It is her fate. She had to undergo this agony as per her destiny and she is through that. Otherwise, the blame game has no meaning.'

Their conversation created a deep wound in Prabhakar's mind. He felt like crying aloud expressing his innocence and beg for mercy requesting not to be blamed for what had happened.'
Then, who is to be blamed? Is it poor Deepthi? Or the uncle or aunt?' What was the use of the blame game? He could not reach any conclusion, though that was of insignificance. The serious matter, which was not even thought of by him was made a concern of everyone. Without even consulting him and finalizing without his consent was a vehement lapse on the part of elders. The after-effect of that was a volcanic eruption that would have probably ended in the demise of that feeble-minded girl. Taking for granted and giving high hopes to the tender heart paving way for high dreams was the Himalayan blunder of the elders. He was scared of the public tagging his name as a villain cheating girl by giving false promises and withdrawing later. Such thoughts created immeasurable wounds in his heart and sat looking down by the side of relatives with a sullen face.

As time passed Prabhakar got up and paced up and down on the corridor with a mind full of different thoughts. As he did not expect her sudden discharge from the hospital considering the present condition, he decided to take a room in the hospital. He went and made the request to the hospital authorities and easily got one being the husband of the hospital's doctor, Sujatha.

With lots of coaxing and consoling, he tried to take uncle and aunt to that room from the front side of the operation theatre. He assured them. 'You both can go and sit in the room comfortably and relax. I and Sujatha would be here to find her progress. Don't worry, nothing will happen to her. As and when I get some information on her progress, I will immediately come and inform you.'

Uncle felt sorry for him. 'That is not required. Being your wedding day, it is better if you both go home.' He repeated. 'Both of you may go home. Here, I and aunt will sit. Sitting here or in the room is the same.'

The aunt was found wiping her swollen face with the kerchief. She turned her face towards him. 'Whatever the uncle is telling is correct. We will continue to stay here. That's enough. You both please go home. Many visitors will be coming there to see both of you. If you are staying away from home, that is not right. What will they feel?'

But Prabhakar preferred to stay there at least until Deepthi was declared out of danger. 'That's is ok aunty. At home, the father and mother will handle the guests.'

Time passed. They saw Kishanlal and Bharati coming towards them with bloodless faces. When they learned that Deepthi was out of danger and recuperating well, their anxiety got mellowed down. Bharati sat by the side of her brother and looked at him without uttering anything. Their eyes exchanged many meaningful signals, with blames and regret, and finally accepting total failure on their part. Those eyes exchanged their helplessness and requests for not blaming each other.

Sujatha came out of the theatre and declared. 'Deepthi is normal and happy now.'

Those ever-expecting words reverberated in the ears of everyone spreading the joy of contentment overthrowing the causes of anxiety, ushering the smile that had disappeared for a long time.

Prabhakar and Sujatha sat adjacent to the operation theatre door. When Kishanlal and Bharati moved towards them along with their uncle, they got up.

'Now, you both go home. Sunanda is alone there.' Kishanlal said.

'If you are absent on the day of marriage from home, it is not correct. Here we are there to look into the needs of Deepthi.' The uncle supported him.

Prabhakar passed his gaze around towards everybody. He saw everyone with a smile concurring the elder's opinions.

'Ok.' Though reluctantly he also realized, that was the right move.

-12-

On the following day, While Prabhakar and Sujatha were ready to proceed to the hospital, Sunanda went near them and said. 'I am also coming with you. I am carrying breakfast for uncle and aunty.'

'Welcome.' Prabhakar said. After thinking, he suggested. 'Isn't it better to send them home after we reach the hospital? I think we will not carry breakfast for them. If we carry, they will prefer to remain there.' He looked at Sujatha to take her opinion. 'What do you say?'

She agreed with a nod. 'Yes, that will be better.'

'That is what the mother had told.' Sunanda said.

'It's ok. I will speak to my mother.' He went to the kitchen and informed her of his opinion. 'Let them come here. After bath and breakfast, let them go again. I think that will be better. What do you say?'

'She will be discharged today.' Sujatha said. 'Uncle and aunty are not required again to go there. We will bring her back after discharge.'

When Bharati was not opening her mouth after hearing their suggestions, Prabhakar said. 'Why don't you say something?'

She showed reluctance. 'What should I say?' After thinking she said. 'You talk to uncle.' She paused. 'Do anything as per uncle and aunt decide. Let's not have any difference of opinion on that issue at least.' She expressed fear.

Looking at both ladies he said. 'I will do so.'

Prabhakar along with Sujatha and Sunanda went to the car. They directly went and visited Deepthi. She was found perfectly normal and the hospital authorities were contemplating to shift her to the room and later discharge on the same day. They went to the room and Sujatha informed both uncle and aunt of her progress and the immediate discharge.

Prabhakar looked at their faces. The appearance of a heartfelt smile that bloomed on aunt's face generated happiness in him. Reluctantly he slowly moved towards her and sat by her side. She raised her hand and caressed the back of his head slowly. Suddenly, overwhelmed by different thoughts, her face changed. Without knowing how to react to her present mental condition, he looked at uncle. Seeing his gloomy face, uncle gestured not to mind for her reactions, by closing his eyes. Without opening his mouth, he kept looking downwards.
Total silence prevailed in the room.
The arrival of a nurse with Deepthi to the room was quite unexpected. Deepthi looked at everyone in the room. She could imagine the cause of the prevailing silence. She also joined in their silence and took a vacant chair.
The nurse said Sujatha. 'The patient can go home after paying the bill.' She went out in a hurry without waiting for Sujatha to speak.
Sujatha said, Prabhakar. 'It will take some more time for the bill to get readied.'
'In that case, why don't you both go home?' He asked
the uncle. 'After discharge, we will bring Deepthi.'
Uncle nodded and turned his head towards his wife and asked. 'That is better, isn't it?'
Aunt agreed with a grunt.
XXX
After leaving both uncle and aunt home, Prabhakar came back to the hospital.

When they got the information that the hospital superintendent was calling them to his room, both Prabhakar and Sujatha went there wondering what the reason for such a summon could be. They have ushered inside his office and offered seat opposite to him.

He looked at them and said with a smile. 'Yesterday I had come to attend your marriage.'

'I saw you there, sir.' Sujatha said showing her gratitude for his gesture.

'I couldn't stay there for long. I did not take part in the feast. Without eating I had to return. I had some urgent work.' He looked at both, alternately. 'That girl who attempted suicide is your cousin, isn't it?' He looked at Prabhakar.

Attempting suicide words ringed in his ears. Prabhakar knew that was a punishable offense. He sat mum as if he got an unexpected shock. A sudden doubt and fear arose in his mind about the intention of the hospital of trying to make a police case of that issue. 'Yes, doctor. She is the daughter of my mother's brother. My cousin.'

Showing little hesitation, he said. 'As that was a suicide attempt, we had to report to the police. Sujatha is a staff of this hospital. Still, if some problem crops up tomorrow, which one can't rule out, the establishment should not get a bad name and blame. Considering that the duty doctor reported to the police. Had he asked me before doing that, I should have objected to.' He heaved a sigh and continued. 'Anyway, that had happened.' He observed the facial expression of both. 'In the evening, the police had come. They came in plain clothes and no one noticed. When they asked that girl, she had said she was cutting the cloth and the scissors slipped and the wrist was injured. It is not required to investigate whether what she said is true or untrue. And, the police have not believed what she had said. I have requested the police not to proceed with the case further. I thought you should know about what had happened on this here. Hence, I just called you and informed. If that girl has any mental problems, please take special interest and try to get that solved.'

Sujatha looked at Prabhakar 'Yes, sir.'

'Surely doctor.' Prabhakar also said, though clearly, he knew he can do nothing to solve her problem.

While they came out of that office, they saw the doctor who attended Deepthi on the previous day. That doctor on many occasions had expressed his interest in Sujatha, but she used to avoid him, whenever met. He even had threatened her once that if she did not give her consent to marry him, he would commit suicide. She used to always avoid him. When he realized that nothing was working out on her, he automatically withdrew from his futile efforts.

"I had specifically mentioned not to report the case to the police. Then why did you do that?' She raised her voice stopping in front of him.

That doctor expressed helplessness. 'Oh, no. I did not report it. You know, from the time you brought the case until everything was over, I was inside the theatre only. I don't know who reported the case. Sometimes, the superintendent himself would have done that.' He smiled and proceeded further.

After crossing him, Prabhakar said. 'It is difficult to understand from his talk who reported. Anyway, that should be treated as a closed chapter.' Prabhakar looked at her. 'Will he create any naughty problems?'

'In this case, he can just do anything.' She said confidently.

'That I could understand. But, considering his madness towards you....?'

She stopped for a while and looked up to his face. 'Nothing.' With contempt she said. 'Everyone will have a lot of desires but getting that materialized will be difficult.' She heaved a sigh. 'Everyone who desires something should never forget about what others think about that. If either one of them dislikes, that desire will never get fulfilled. If I like to marry one person, that doesn't need to get materialized. It is not like the case where two persons of the opposite sex like each other and parents do not give permission. Since the day I came and joined the hospital, his madness started. I could sense that and I had been purposely avoiding him. But, he could not understand that. He kept moving behind me. On one occasion, I had even mentioned to him that I am not interested to marry him. Then on, he had been moving after me saying his expectations will not die and will pray for my change of mind.'

'Poor doctor. He is another Deepthi.' He said with mock sympathy.

After paying the bill in the counter, Prabhakar got onto the car with others.

The car moved.

When no one was opening the mouth, Sujatha asked. 'Why such silence? I just do not like such silence.'

'I also.' Deepthi opened her mouth.

Hearing her, all laughed. But, then again everyone observed silence.

Prabhakar thought that the reason for silence could be to avoid reminding Deepthi of the last days' incidence by any word inadvertently coming out of their mouth.

XXX

As the car approached the house, Deepthi said with regret. 'Because of me, you people had to undergo a lot of problems. I am sorry.'

Prabhakar turned back and said as if casually. 'Forget about that. Don't think of that and spoil your mood. Think that a great bad time has gone with that.'

'Yes, you are right. A bad time is over.' Sunanda said.

After reaching home, Deepthi quickly came out of the car and went in a hurry to her room without even looking at anyone who was waiting for her arrival on the verandah. Her father and mother, who were also waiting outside, wondered seeing her unusual behavior and moved behind her to the room with anxiety.

They sat on the cot and asked her to sit by their side.

Deepthi's countenance suddenly changed. Her eyes got filled and tears rolled down over the cheeks. Gently wiped the face and sobbed like a child. She clung to her mother like a child and mourned. 'I was foolish enough to do that. All of you may forgive me.'

'To err is human. Everyone commits mistakes. Forget about the past and think of only the present and future.' Her father tried to be philosophical, attempting to pacify her. Gently he stroked her back and showed deep affection.

She sat, taking hands off her mother, and looked at both with mercy, with pleading eyes.

Her mother wiped her face with hand and whispered. 'Forget everything. Just think, that was a very horrifying dream.'

Those words worked and they could observe a mild smile blooming over her otherwise withered face.

When Prabhakar entered the verandah after parking the car, father Kishanlal went near him and handed over a paper saying 'this telegram was received by me.' Enthusiastically he opened that expecting to be the information containing permission of the commanding officer to avail the requested additional ten days leave. But that was an atom bomb. The extension of leave was not agreed to. He read, 'On twenty-fifth itself to report back to the unit'. Quite an unexpected message!

'Did you read it?' He asked the father.

'I read it.' He sounded gloomy. 'Probably you wouldn't have stated the reason properly. Why don't you send another request mentioning the reason for demanding additional leave with a brief?'

Hearing his father's innocent advice, he chuckled.

'Father, I am working in the Indian air force. Defense force. One can't keep sending requests as in civil. There would be some proper genuine reason for not granting additional leave.'

Kishanlal suddenly turned serious. 'What genuine reason? There is no war now.'

Prabhakar smiled. 'Sometimes, I would have been detailed for some course which would be better for my career. Usually, no details are shown in telegrams.'

Kishanlal realized his ignorance. He knew his son was not in a mood to take his suggestions. 'Then, what is the next course of action in your mind?'

'Have to go.' The words were full of unhappiness. 'When the marriage date was decided, I had done reservation for both of us. Luckily, we both have reservations. From Madras, the reservation is confirmed in GT express.'

Prabhakar with Sujatha went to her house and exploded the news. When it was told that, they both would be proceeding to their place of work on the twenty-second, her father Rajesh expressed his unhappiness. 'What nonsense? This is a democratic nation. Who can order to get back to the place of work just after two days of marriage? Forget about that. You just go only after a few days thinking that you are granted additional leave.'

'Our reservation is for twenty-second. If I change the date, we will face difficulty.' Prabhakar showed his helplessness.

'I will take care of that. Being in politics, if I can't do that, what is the use?'

'That will create problems for me. I am asked to report to the unit on the twenty-fifth itself, as planned earlier. If I fail, they can consider me absent without leave and that is a serious offense.'

He laughed. 'Agreed. I will do one thing. I will ask our chief minister to speak to your defense minister about this. I will ask him to phone him up.'

Prabhakar was not interested to prolong that conversation. He kept thinking wondering over the ignorance of these local politicians about our defense system and its rules and regulations. 'How to convince him?' He wondered.

Sujatha could read the dilemma on his face and come for his rescue. 'Father, this is military. If he fails to report on a particular date, they would initiate action against him. You talk like this as you are not aware of the air force rules.'

Her words struck on the right point of his mind. 'If so, you may proceed with what is appropriate. You plan to leave Sujatha behind here, isn't it?'

With a smiling face, he replied. 'No. We both have a reservation.'

'Would not it be inconvenient for you, if she is taken along? Especially if you are detailed for a course somewhere else?'

Father's question created uneasiness in her. She was scared, whether she would be compelled to stay back home by Rajesh sensing the urgency of his requirement in the unit. 'Nothing like that father. Even if detailed for course, he can take me to that place. There will not be any restrictions of that sort.' She said looking at her husband with a mock nod and smile.

Rajesh was sensible enough to realize his daughter's interest to accompany him on twenty-second itself. He smiled mildly and shook head as if understood the whole.

-13-

There was a huge crowd on the railway station to send off Prabhakar and Sujatha by Madras mail. Both of them faced difficulty in bidding farewell to each one of them before boarding the train. They occupied the two-berthed first-class coupe and looked outside through the window.

Jayaram came near them and asked. 'When can we expect you next?'

'Only after few months. Not immediately.' Prabhakar said slightly aloud so that others also could hear.

Observing the two-berthed coupe, he said with mock jealousy. 'Oh, purposely the railways have allotted to you this for you to enjoy your honeymoon on travel. Instead of going and enjoying the honeymoon, you can enjoy while traveling through different states of the country. Good. Lucky'

Prabhakar joined others in laughter. He said. 'This is up to Madras only. From there on, if we get a similar coupe, that will be nice.'

As the train slowly rolled out, everybody raised their hands and waved.

Sujatha could not control her emotions of leaving her parents. Her lips quivered. Looking at her, Prabhakar sat speechless realizing her mental condition. Leaving the parents for the first time, except during college days, and moving away to an unknown place with another person could cause anxiety, however, known that person would be. He kept looking at her with sympathy. Feeling shy for not behaving like a grown-up, she looked outside with controlled laughter. Earlier days, while going back after leave, he too had been experiencing such feelings and he remembered those scenes. Later that became routine and the departures were without many emotions. He could imagine the condition of her mind and tried to console by making faces and smiling. Whispering in mind, he thanked the railways for giving a chance to travel comfortably without any disturbances, in a two-berthed coupe. He kept looking towards the farthest, through the open window of the first-class coupe, without opening his mouth.

Sujatha wondered why he was maintaining silence. She fondly held him by shoulders and pulled him towards her 'Why are you silent?'

'No. Nothing. I thought of leaving you alone without disturbing. 'Grabbing her hand from his shoulder, he fondled. 'Now the feelings of leaving home, I mean the homesickness, has reduced; isn't it?'

Casting a glance at him with a smile, she leaned on to his shoulder and mumbled. 'When I am with you, there is no cause for any worry.' Very sweet words!

'Still?' He held her chin and shook with love.

Looking towards him she smiled with shy.

'Your mind is disturbed because of the frequent thought of parents creeping in.'

'That can't be avoided. But...'

That might not be the cause of her present thoughts, he guessed. 'Could you please tell, what is the cause of present worry and mood off?

With hesitation, she asked in a low voice. 'Will you get offended if I open my mind?'

He grunted. 'Never. For what?'

She showed vehement hesitation. With coy, she held his hand and caressed fondly. 'I just thought of Deepthi. I could not control my mind. To be frank enough, I feel sympathy for her. One can think of her mental condition when she realized that the dreams she had been hatching for years are just got blown out. Poor girl!' She frowned.

With a big head shake, he whispered. 'I have no part in that.'

'Let it be anything. I find pity for her and she is really innocent. No one should blame her.'

Showing little aversion to such topics he said without hurting her. 'During our journey, should we continue that topic? Can't we find some other topic which could cool our minds?'

Leaning on him she said. 'There is no question of impending happiness. I said as my mind suddenly went into that direction. Often my mind whispers in my ears blaming me to be the root cause of her misfortune. To be frank enough, I feel slight guilt too.'

Pushing her away from him gently, he raised his voice. 'What are you talking about? Why should you feel guilty? I too will not feel. Because, none ever mentioned of such an intention at any point in time, to me about that. She had been very much free with me. What does that mean? She is my cousin and such behavior could be expected. The freedom between sister and brother. A brother-sister relationship. Nothing else was ever thought of.' Frowning, he said scornfully. 'You are unnecessarily getting into the wild.'

Realizing the realities of facts, she kept mum. 'Ok. Let's talk something else.'

'That will be better.' He looked towards her. When he saw she was smiling, he expressed happiness. Pulling her towards him, he made her lay on his lap. Holding the bangles and the chains she was wearing, he asked. 'Why didn't you keep all these ornaments at home?'

She suddenly got up and looked into his face. 'Whenever I accompany you without these ornaments to mess parties or visiting some of your friends what they will think of you and me? I don't want to downgrade you. You should be proud of having more ornaments with me. People will think that both of us are from rich families.' An innocent smile appeared on her face. "I don't want people to think that your newly wedded bride is without sufficient ornaments.'

He could not control his laughter. 'Best... Even after having so much of education, I wonder why you talk like some country girls. Now I feel pity for you.' He held her ears and pulled lightly. 'In our circle, there is no such thing as wearing ornaments. If you go to the mess or anyone's house with all these, people will think, either you are trying to show off or you are slightly out of balance.' He laughed again. 'Here ladies wear at the most a chain with the *mangalsoothra;* that is thali. Wearing more ornaments and parading is the fashion of few ladies of our small Kerala state. Only here, the feelings of getting more attention and adoration by exhibiting all ornaments prevail. Out of Kerala, especially in our defense crowd, that will be viewed with mockery. In our place in Kerala, this is the only way to show one's financial position and social superiority.'

'Then, when we go for parties?'

'Then also no one will wear so costly ornaments.' He tried to pacify her. 'These gold ornaments are real culprits for inviting crime. Because of this, one may invite injuries and probably even loss of life.'

Showing helplessness, she asked. 'Then, what could we do with these?'

'Now, you remove and keep inside the suitcase.'

Immediately, she removed all bangles and chains. By holding the thali chain, she asked. 'I will not remove this. That is auspicious.'

He opened the suitcase and kept gold ornaments inside and pushed that underneath the berth. Looking at the thali chain he said. 'That is made of ten sovereigns.' He forced her to lie on his lap again.

After hearing her husband, realizing the problems that could lead to due to gold ornaments, she said. 'Had I known of this, I would have bought an imitation thali chain, at least for the journey.'

He laughed. 'There is a hidden risk in that also. The thieves will not know that it is imitation gold and snatch. Later, when they realize their futile effort, they will curse you and might even attack if possible.'

Hearing the knocking sound, Prabhakar gently moved her from his lap and opened the door. The ticket examiner entered the cabin. He examined their tickets. When that person left the cabin, a person with tea and snacks came inside. They bought tea a Vada.

'Can I get one bottle of water?' Prabhakar asked that person.

With alacrity, Sujatha was quick to say. 'Not required. I have brought water.' She opened the airbag and took out two water bottles.

'You are clever. Having traveled for years, I didn't think it necessary to carry water.' He blamed himself.

'That is the difference between male and female.' She uttered with scorn.

When that person went away, he closed the cabin.
'Anything else you have brought?'
'Yes.' Wicket smile appeared on her face.
'What?'
'Chapatti and chicken fry.'
Laughing, he hugged her.

'No. Someone might see.'

'Who will see? Except for the trees and grass outside.'

As the train was to approach Palakkad station, the passengers flocked near the entrance.

'You pull down the shutters. On this station platform, there will be several beggars and they will come here if the windows are found open. They are not supposed to enter the platform for begging. What could be done? Nobody can stop. There will be many. They keep crying for food saying they are hungry.'

Hesitating to pull down the shutter, she said. 'We will pretend as if we haven't seen them. Ignore them.'

He agreed with her. 'Then, you take out the food packets you brought. Here the train will stop for twenty minutes for food.'

She took out two packets from the bag and gave one to
him. Looking at her palm, she said. 'I want to wash the hand.'

'You go and wash.'

She opened the door and went out looking on either side. She went to the toilet and came back after some time.

'Which toilet you visited?

''On the left.'

'Is it neat?'

Expressing hatred, she said with hesitation. 'Just ok.'

'I too will go and come.' He too went to the toilet. After a while, he came back.

The train came to the platform. As Prabhakar had said, there were many beggars on the platform. Looking at the approaching beggars, she brought down the glass shutter. While they were opening the food packet, a woman with a crying child approached the window and started begging for food to feed the child. The very sight of that crying child with that shabby woman irritated his senses. Looking at Sujatha he said. 'We did the mistake of opening this here now. We should have opened after Palakkad only.

He observed Sujatha closing her food packet. 'Your packet can be opened later. I am going to hand over this packet to that woman.' He opened the shutter and gave the food packet to her. It was very satisfying to see the happiness and the hundred-watt bulb smile on her face when she got the food packet.

When the train pulled out of that platform, they opened the other food packet. The food was sufficient for two persons. The quantity was such that as if Sujaatha's mother had put enough food even to cater for one or two extra passengers in the compartment.

'That woman came in front of us on time. Otherwise after eating from each packet, the extra food we would have thrown outside without being used by any.' Prabhakar felt what she did was right.

In the morning, the train reached Madras central station. Engaging a porter, they carried the luggage to the clock room and deposited there for safe custody. He went to the reservation counter and confirmed their onward reservation. Their names were seen in the Grant Trunk express train chart. Then what next? The question was raised in their minds. The GT express was at five in the evening. How to spend so much time? Going to the cinema hall or Marina Beach was sheer wastage of time. He thought. Why not take a trip to the Air Force station Thambaram, which is slightly over thirty kilometers from there? There were many of his course mates in the Flying

Training Unit, located inside that Air Force station. His suggestion was accepted by Sujatha.

Coming out of the railway station, while searching for a cab, he saw the bus of Air Force Station, Tambaram at the parking bay. They walked down to that bus and on inquiry, they could find out, that bus was the posting vehicle from Air Force Station, Tambaram, and was about to start. They both got into that and alighted in front of the flying unit inside the air force station. Prabhakar went into the adjutant's office and inquired about his course mate Kulkarni and Yadav. Both were available in the unit. The adjutant informed both those officers and asked to come immediately to his office.

Both came without delay.

Sujatha kept watching their expression of happiness on meeting after a gap of few years. They shook hands and hugged whispering what others could not hear. She could not help laughing seeing their gestures and various expressions exhibiting happiness at the meeting. When she was introduced, they moved slowly towards her and with utmost courtesy shook hands welcoming her to the small family of the air force. They escorted them to the flying crew room and introduced it to everyone present there. Meanwhile, one person came with a bread omelet sandwich and served. While they were having that, Squadron Leader Verma who was present there, asked.

'When was your marriage?'

'Just two days before.' Prabhakar looked at him.

'Didn't you try for extension of leave?'

'I had applied. But, I received a telegram asking to report on twenty-fifth itself.'

Shaking head, he asked. 'Had they mentioned any reasons for that?'

'No.'

'What you thought the reason could be?'

'I might have been detailed for some course or other.'

Verma smiled. 'Why did you think so?'

Wondering what to reply, he looked around and said. 'I couldn't think of any other reasons.'

Verma laughed. 'Good.' He looked at Sujatha. 'But, things are not as you guessed. You might have read of the skirmishes on the border. The situation is slightly bad there. That is what I could know.'

'These sorts of things happen often there on the border.' One officer said.

'You are right. But, it can't be laughed off every time. There is a general feeling that something might happen this time. Not that it could be correct. However, in all defense forces, the leave is not being given unless on extreme compassionate grounds. In some stations, they are recalling the personnel back from leave.'

Prabhakar looked at Sujatha. He closed his eyes and made face gesturing there was nothing to worry about.

'To be frank enough, there should be a war. And we should destroy our enemy entirely. The existence of Pakistan will always be a headache for us.' One officer said.

'Don't talk nonsense. Then, our enemies will be China and other neighbors. As long as we have neighbors, there will be border issues.' Another officer corrected him.

They were taken to the officer's mess by friends. Sitting in the guest room, they had been. Observing Sujatha's unhappiness over his drinking, Prabhakar showed contentment with just one glass of beer. Having relaxed for some time after food, they proceeded to the railway station by three-thirty.

-14-

After taking the luggage from the Madras central station, both Prabhakar and Sujatha walked towards the platform. The GT express train was lying there as if waiting for them. Entering the first-class compartment, they occupied the reserved berths. The porter kept the luggage under the berths. Prabhakar gave the demanded amount to the porter. Leaving a long sigh of relief, Prabhakar looked outside and saw people running up and down on the platform. There were crowds in front of the reserved compartments, waiting for the arrival of the ticket examiner to check the possibilities of allotting seats by him. Even after so many years of independence, the freedom to travel to any place without difficulty has not been achieved by us and Prabhakar felt sorry for that. The population is increasing and also the passengers, but the railways were unable to increase the travel facilities as per that. That was the only reason.

'When this will start?' Sujatha asked.

Prabhakar looked at his watch. 'In five minutes.'

There were two berths in that four-berthed cabin and looking at them Sujatha said. 'If nobody comes for occupying these berths, our journey would be quite comfortable.'

He laughed. 'That will never happen. There would be some passengers coming at the last moment. Otherwise, these will be allotted to some needy ones by the ticket examiners. Berth will not remain vacant, especially from the starting station.'

Within a minute one young person entered the cabin and looked at the berth numbers and kept his luggage on the upper berth and sat opposite to Prabhakar. He kept whispering something looking at Prabhakar suspiciously. Then, he turned his head away as if he was wrong in his decision. Again, he looked at Prabhakar, brooding over something.

'Is your name Prabhakar?' He asked in English.

Prabhakar looked at that person and nodded in affirmation.

As if won in a match, he smiled and again asked. 'Flight Lieutenant Prabhakar?'

'Yes.'

Their conversation was in English only. 'Have you ever met me?'

Thinking for a while he said. 'No. I don't think.'

That person smiled. 'I am Flying Officer John. I am working in the Station Signals section.'

Prabhakar tickled his brain for a while and then accepted defeat. 'No. I don't remember to have seen you.'

An elderly person was seen entering that cabin. The person accompanied him was seen pushing the suitcase under the seat and moving out in a hurry bidding farewell.

Without considering that person's presence, they continued their conversation.

'On that day's belly landing, you just got escaped. Thank god.'

Prabhakar did not say anything but smiled.

John fished out the cigarette packet from the pocket and kept one in between his lips and offered one to Prabhakar.

'No, Thanks. I don't smoke.'

John looked at others and humbly asked. 'Will you mind if I smoke?'

'Not at all.'

After looking at Sujatha he inquired. 'You might have come on leave to visit south India. Which place did you visit now? Ootty or Kodaikanal?'

The ticket examiner entered and checked everyone's tickets.

When he left, Prabhakar asked. 'You are coming back from leave?'

'Yes. I could not complete my full leave.'

'Why?'

'I got the message that the leave is curtailed and to report back to the unit immediately. I received a telegram. As soon as I received, without thinking about anything I started my journey.'

Showing sympathy, he asked. 'You are from which place?'

'Trichur.'

'Which place in Trichur?'

John smiled wondering what he would know of small villages in Trichur. 'A small village you wouldn't have heard of. Vadanappally. Probably you wouldn't have even heard of this village.'

'Who says so?' He said in Malayalam. 'John, I am also a Malayali.'

He opened his mouth in surprise. 'We are under the impression that you are from North India.' He looked at him carefully. 'Someone said you are from Punjab. No one would believe that you are a Malayali.' They laughed.

'I think, Malayali pilots are rarely seen. I doubt if there is another Malayali pilot in our station. Till now, I was thinking there is none other than me as Malayali. But that is clarified.'

'You are right. In totality, Malayali officers are seldom seen. But, among airmen, there are plenty of

Malayalees. That is why; Indian Air Force is jokingly referred to as India Nair Force.' He laughed aloud.

'In Kerala, where do you live?'

'Kochi.'

'I think, you are newly wedded.'

'You are right. Only two days back we got married. I asked for an extension of leave but was not granted.'

'At least your marriage is over.' John turned pensive. 'My marriage was fixed for this twenty-fifth. When I received the telegram, I could not stay home further. Some exigencies would be there. Otherwise, they would not recall. Everyone at home compelled me to stay for marriage and go afterward. But, I could not get peace of mind. I too felt like staying for a few more days and start back after the ceremony. But, the very thought of committing such a mistake when called by the country, pulled me out from my home. I know without any serious reasons they will never call back a person who went on leave. Immediately I went to the district collector and got one berth released in emergency quota. That's how I got the reservation done.' His face shone as if he could achieve something great when he talked about the reservation.

'In the morning I had been to the flying unit at Tambaram. From there I learned that the leave is stopped and the personnel gone on leave are being recalled. Till then I was under the impression that I am recalled for some course or so. At the most, I expected this could be due to my posting out.' He smiled.

'Is there any problem on the border?'

Prabhakar sounded casual. 'That happens frequently. There is nothing new. But this time, there is something, which we do not know.'

'Will this end up in a war?' John sounded exposing his fear. He was seen slightly shaky.

Prabhakar was mused to his panic. 'Nothing could be told. If anything happens like that, it would not be like as had happened earlier. Our Prime Minister is strong. The strongest and capable Prime Minister India ever saw. Madam Indira Gandhi. Once she decides, she will not leave them just like that. They will be caused maximum damage which they will ever remember.' Prabhakar sounded cynical.

Prabhakar realized that their conversation was being overheard by the fourth person. He controlled his further talk on the subject.

One person entered the cabin with a can of tea.

Prabhakar looked at the fourth person in the cabin and asked. 'Sir, tea?'

When he nodded his head in affirmation, Prabhakar asked for four teas and took the tea filled plastic cups from tea vendor and gave it to each one. He gave money for four teas. The fourth person opened the purse and took out a ten-rupee note and gave him.

'No sir.' He refused to accept.

That person forcefully slipped that note into Prabhakar's pocket and said. "You must accept this. Otherwise, I will not allow you to take anything from the vendors for me.'

When he heard that, he took money for the tea and gave back the balance.

'After hearing your conversation, I could understand that you both are from the air force.' He sounded very polite.

Both nodded. 'Yes. You are right.'

'Where do you work?'

John looked at Prabhakar. They did not like to divulge the location. Prabhakar said. 'We are not supposed to reveal that to anyone. It is somewhere in north India; close to the border.'

That person admired them by his looks and facial expression. 'My name is Thankavelu. From Salem, in Tamil Nadu. My son has done his BE and is very keen on joining the Indian Air Force. I and wife are not in favor of him joining any armed forces. He has got the appointment order from the State Electricity Board. But he is not keen on joining.' Thinking, he continued. 'He had been to Services Selection Board. There also he is selected. We are totally in confusion. What is to be done? I am lucky to meet you both on this train unexpectedly.' He looked at both and asked very sincerely. 'What is your opinion? You are sincere.'

Prabhakar turned his head to John. 'You joined after taking an engineering degree, isn't it? You will be the right person to give him advice.'

With a broad smile, John said. 'I am also an electrical engineer. Immediately after graduation, I applied for this job. I too would have got a job in Kerala State Electricity Board. Many of my relatives advised me to apply for that. But, I preferred this. In Air Force, I got Tech Signals branch.' After thinking he continued. 'In the electricity board, one can make a lot of money. As bribe and pay. That is not possible in the air force. In the electricity board, one could get promotions and reach the top position. That is possible in the Air Force also. If an officer is sincere and hardworking he could reach the top post of Air Marshal. The job and position of every defense officer are much better than any other class one officers. In pay and position also. Their pay is much better than any other class one officers. They get seventy percent of basic pay as a pension, whereas others get only thirty percent. That is a great difference.' He chuckled. 'One more thing I would like to highlight. All officers in defense need not hear the usual shouts and abuses of the uneducated politicians. Here in this force, everyone right from the lowest to the top, all are well educated.'

Thangavelu paid full attention to him. 'Is it so?'

John continued with a smile. 'In the Army, Navy, and Air Force, all officers are well educated. In the army, the soldiers may not be well educated. That is not required. Implicit obedience without questioning the authorities is the requirement there. Their job is such. If an order is received to shoot, he should do that without any further clarification or questions. That sort of discipline is taught there. In the other two forces, it is not like that. New technologies are applied in the types of equipment we procure and those we have. The technicians of these forces have to learn to service and maintain these types of equipment. For that, they should have a relatively good education.'

Thangavelu smiled. 'I think, these uneducated ones are experts in exaggerating all their deeds like pushing the bombs by hand and guiding away from the bullets by hand etc.'

Prabhakar laughed. 'Though their work is of great importance and nobility, they have a misunderstanding that they are not much respected in society. To counter that, they keep boasting whenever get a chance. That irritates some, but many appreciate and encourage. One can't blame them for that. We should take that in the right spirit. Their experiences are multifarious. Those boastings and exaggerations should be taken as entertainment.'

'You are right.' Thangavelu said. 'Think of our country without these forces and jawans. It would have been impossible for all of us to live comfortably without fear or malice. The defense personnel is doing the noblest and praiseworthy job. That is the reason the country gives all awards and honors to the defense personnel.'

Prabhakar was anxious to know that person. 'Even after talking so much, you have not identified yourself.'

He felt guilty. 'Oh, sorry. I am the Vice-Chancellor of Madras University. I am going up to New Delhi. I will give you company up to that place.' He paused. 'As per your advice, we will honor our son's desire and send him to the Air Force.'

'You must.' Both of them said in the chorus.

Looking at everyone Sujatha smiled.

After food at night, they wished a good night to everyone and prepared to sleep.

At midnight, one person opened the door with the help of a knife and entered the cabin. In the dim light, he found the long chain on Sujatha's neck. While he was trying to cut that with scissors, his hand touched her body and she opened her eyes. She saw the thief trying to take out the long-chain slowly from the neck. She quickly raised her foot and kicked on his naval. With pain, he covered his front bottom with both hands and screamed and sat on the floor. Hearing the scream, when everyone woke up, they saw a person being held by Sujatha around his neck. Prabhakar came down in a jiffy and reached for her help. He caught hold of the thief and the other two joined him. The thief was tied on to the window metal bar using a shawl of Sujatha. Immediately John went outside and informed the conductor and he was handed over to the police at the next station.

All the three in that cabin praised the courage and alertness of Sujatha.

-15-

From Old Delhi railway station, Prabhakar, Sujatha, and John boarded the train to their place of destination. The first-class compartment was almost empty. They occupied a four-berthed cabin. After the arrival of GT express at New Delhi in the morning, they had enough time to move around and they were all very tired. They decided to retire wishing good night. Before lying down, Prabhakar ensured the door to the cabin was well secured by the latch.

XXX

The train was late to reach its destination station. The sun was already up. They moved out of the platform and went out and saw the Air Force station's posting truck parked outside. As that had to wait for another train, they decided to engage a taxi. John joined them.

When the taxi reached the main gate of the air force station, the guard on duty there checked the complete identity of all three and then the gate was opened. Noticeable changes were observed inside the camp. Much uniformed personnel was seen with rifles patrolling on the road, at different points, keenly observing the taxi. They directly went to the officer's mess. Prabhakar and Sujatha got down in front of his room and with the assistance of John, their luggage was carted to that room. John took leave from them saying he would meet them later.

After the bath, Prabhakar and Sujatha changed their dress and went to the mess. Entered the dining hall and sat for breakfast. He tried to teach her the basic table manners to be observed in the mess. As she was already aware of them, it was just a reminder. Still, he thought it was his duty to remind her certain important points. He told her how to use the spoon, fork, and knife without making a sound. After a while, John walked into the dining hall in uniform and took a seat by his side.

After their breakfast, before getting up, Prabhakar looked at Sujatha and said. 'I have to go to the unit. If you are sitting alone in the room, that will be boring. I will leave you to one of my friend's house. You can spend time there without boring.'

Thinking, Sujatha said. 'Not required. I will remain in the room. I can spend time reading some magazines or books.'

They went to the room. He took out a few magazines and books from the almirah. After wearing the uniform, he went out and started the scooter. 'I think, we should think of buying one car'. Looking at her he said affectionately. 'You go inside the room and relax. Though you will be alone in the room, there is nothing to be scared of. This is a military camp.' He smiled.

In the unit, he parked the scooter in the parking area and directly went to the aircrew room. Excepting the officers already flying, all were there. Though the additionally demanded leave was not granted, as he could marry within few available days, everyone appreciated him and moved forward to congratulate showering their sincere affection.

'At lunchtime, all will assemble in the officer's mess bar to welcome Prabhakar and his wife to this family. We will welcome the newly wedded with a beer party.' One officer said. And others agreed to that.

When he walked down to the office of Flight Commander, Squadron Leader K N Singh, few others also joined him. One of them informed K N Singh of the marriage of Prabhakar and of the proposed beer party in the mess on that day.

'Should we leave it at that? Just a beer party?' He asked curiously.

'No sir. We should give a grand party. But, this is just a starter.' One officer quipped.

K N Singh laughed. 'I will speak to the Squadron Commander.' After thinking he amended. 'I think, you go and tell him.'

Prabhakar looked at the officer standing by his side and inquired. 'Hasn't Mukerji sir left the unit?'

'No. All postings and promotions have been kept in abeyance. It might take time.'

The news was not desirable and Prabhakar's face suddenly turned gloomy.

'Shall all of us go and see him in his office?' One officer took the lead.

They all moved into the Commanding Officer, Wing Commander Mukerji's office, after taking his permission. When he knew all about Prabhakar's marriage and the beer party, he said.

'After marriage, you could not stay in your house for more days, and for that, we all feel hurt. But what can be done? We were helpless, as we got the instructions from the Command Headquarters to recall everyone back from leave. I came to know of your telegram asking for a few more days' leave. The adjutant also came to me and discussed this. With much mental difficulty, I had to ask him to recall' He looked at Prabhakar. 'Please don't feel bad.'

'Never sir. That was the right decision you took. When airmen were being recalled, leaving me alone would have been bad.'

He kept looking at him without saying anything.

When he was informed of the day's beer party, he said. 'You may go ahead with the beer party. I do not wish to take part in that.' He smiled. 'This Saturday, let us have a grand dinner dance party. We require to welcome his wife to the Air Force family and to get acquainted with her. If all of our families also join, then only that will be a welcome party. As far as the beer party is concerned, go ahead. Enjoy.' He smiled.

Before one o'clock, all officers of that unit assembled in the mess main hall. They opened beer bottles and kept enjoying the drink. After some time, Sujatha walked into the hall exhibiting a slight coy. Prabhakar ran towards her and by holding her hand moved around the hall introducing her to one and everyone. K N Singh, on coming to know that she was a doctor, advised her to take up the appointment, if interested, in the Family Wing as there was one vacancy existing.

When an officer tried to cut a non-veg. joke, K N Singh expressed his dislike.

One officer, who heard K N Singh's prohibiting order to non-veg. jokes said. 'That is why ladies are not permitted to attend the beer parties. We will not be able to shoot any masala jokes.'

Looking at Sujatha one officer said. 'I think you sing well. I could read that on your face. Please sing a song.'

Suddenly the silence was brought in. All eyes were glued to that beautiful face.

Exhibiting surprise, she kept casting her gaze all around and muttered. 'No, I don't sing.'

'That is a lie. Whatever written on face can't be wrong. If you are not gifted with that talent, I am ready to shave off my half mustache.'

That officer had no mustache and looking at him another officer commended. 'There is nothing on his face to shave off.'

With sympathy, another officer said sarcastically. 'He is too young to get mustache growth.'

Looking at Prabhakar one officer said. 'Kindly tell her to sing. Otherwise, these people are not going to leave her. This is some sort of ragging in the officer's mess style.' He laughed closing his mouth.

Prabhakar nodded looking at her as if requesting to obey them.

After thinking for a while, she sang an old Hindi song sung by Latha Mangeshkar. The environment suddenly changed. There was pin-drop silence and everyone's ears were focused on her beautiful voice.

Even after the song, the silence continued to prevail.

'That was very good.' K N Singh applauded. 'But for the absence of background music, it was as good as the original song sung by our nightingale. Very good. She will remain an asset to our crowd. Being a Malayali lady, singing Hindi song with such word clarity is commendable. I again say it was very good.'

Everyone there applauded and showered their praises on her.

-16-

Usually, the officers arriving on posting or after marriage with their families are permitted to stay in the bachelor accommodation only for a limited period of ten days. Before that period, the officer should find some other accommodation. Either should fix up a house outside the camp or make arrangements to share with some other officer temporarily. In the case of Prabhakar even after twenty days, as he continued to stay in his room, the subject was discussed by many in the station. He had registered for family quarters inside the camp. Had the officers whose posting orders were released were to vacate the quarters and move out to their new locations, he would have got one. But in the prevailing scenario, as the situation was explosive on the border, all movements were withheld. Without the improvement of the border situation, there was no feasibility of those orders removed. That might take considerable time. No one would permit him, till such time, to continue to occupy the room. Even if he desired to move out of the camp after fixing a house temporarily, that would not be permitted by the authorities. As per the orders, all pilots should be available in the unit, to meet any urgent requirement. Hence, even if he fixed one house outside, the authorities would not permit to shift

One day, Squadron Leader K N Singh called Prabhakar to his office and made him be seated opposite.

'You know the mess administration has been taken over by our squadron, as per the roaster. Our Commanding Officer is the President Mess Committee and I am the Mess Secretary.'

'These are the facts known to me and why does he repeat this to me.' He thought.

'We should not violate any regulations of the mess.'

Those words apprised him of the preamble of his talk. When the bull was raising its tail, he could guess for what. 'I could understand what you are struggling to convey.' With little discomfort he said. 'I should vacate the room.' To decode your facial expression and your concern, a person doesn't need to be too intelligent; he whispered. 'Sir, I have found a house outside. But, there is no telephone. Hence, I am double-minded to fix that up. If the unit wants me after working hours, that would be difficult to contact me.' He showed his helplessness on his face.

K N Singh opened the cigarette packet and lit one. Blowing the smoke out, he beamed his gaze on him critically and said in his usual tough voice. 'No. Don't do that. In the present scenario, it is not advisable. The situation will not permit you to do that. Our Commanding Officer will not permit that.' He drew smoke again and looked at him with knitted brows. 'If so critical, why don't you think of sending her home?'

Prabhakar felt annoyed. Marriage was only a few days earlier and such an opinion was not expected from him. What sort of person he was, to suggest such move without realizing the mental uncomfortable condition of a newly married couple? 'I never expected you to be merciless without considering the agonies of separation of newly wedded.' He mentally assessed him. He looked outside embracing silence.

'I am made to understand that two or three people have reported to Wing Commander Mukerji about this. It seems they had pointed out the impropricty of permitting our squadron officers to stay in the mess with families beyond the permitted duration. If tomorrow officers of other units or stations bring their families and occupy the room, we will have no voice to curb that. We will have to keep mum. If Air Office Commanding comes to know of this, our squadron Commander will be questioned of the veracity and will order to take the corrective step.' He examined the facial expression of Prabhakar and continued showing his mental agony. 'Today he had called me to his office and advised me to instruct you to get this sorted out immediately. 'He drew smoke and extinguished the cigarette butt in the ashtray. 'As mess secretary, I can close my eyes. But, others may not.' Those words conveyed his helplessness.

The subject was creating a lot of worries and sometimes sleeplessness. But, Prabhakar found no solution so far and after hearing the sermons of the Flight Commander, he decided that he had to do something urgently, or that may become a discipline case in Air Force parlance. 'Sir, I will do something appropriately within two or three days.' There was no way out in his mind when he uttered that. Ultimately the only way in front of him was to dispose of the family back to Kerala. That should be the last resort as far as he was concerned. Pacing slowly, he entered the crew room and watching his change of mood, all sitting there inquired of the reason. Reluctantly, he disclosed the ultimatum he was issued with for occupying the room with the family. Everyone there looked at each other for finding a solution and Flight Lieutenant Ahluwalia moved towards him and pacified him.

'I don't mind giving one room in my quarter to you. There is only one kitchen and that could be common. If you don't mind sharing my accommodation, you are welcome.' He cast his glance at everyone there showing pride in his broadmindedness.

All aircrews supported the offer and nodded looking at Ahluwalia and appreciated him.

'That is an ideal move.' One officer supported vehemently. 'You can stay in camp till the situation improves and will be independent also.'

Prabhakar accepted the offer with a pinch of salt. Will Sujatha accept such an offer? Sharing the house with someone not known well and that too with a Sardar? He was not sure of acceptance by her. Using the same kitchen will be cumbersome. As everyone there has appreciated the idea, he did not want to reject the offer. He showed his gratitude with a smile and said politely. 'I will discuss with Sujatha and inform you.'

One officer did not like that attitude. 'Bad. These sorts of decisions are to be exclusively taken by gents. If too much of liberty is assigned to them, later on, you may have to repent.'

One officer made a casual comment. 'We are the pilots of life. We lead and they will follow.'

Another officer who heard him commented. 'So long as your mentality is not changed, you should not get married. Even after marriage, you will not change.'

Ahluwalia smiled. "Prabhakar is right. In this case, the wives are to decide. They are the ones who spend maximum time at home. He is right.' He asserted.

At noon, while Prabhakar was walking down to the mess for lunch with Sujatha, he bundled out the suggestion expressed by Ahluwalia. The very proposal was not liked by her. When she thought of the interest shown by that officer on that Saturday's party to dance with her and when she moved to the floor with him the way his body was made to rub hers was not liked by her and she preferred to stay away from such officers. On that night, she felt that he was behaving like a mental patient. He was trying to tell something, bringing his face too close to her, but he was inaudible as the music was in high volume. When she thought of the smell of liquor when he brought his face too close, she felt like vomiting. But at the same time, she knew the difficulties they have to face once the accommodation was not found out within three days, as agreed to the Flight Commander.

'Can't we avoid that?'

The main reason for putting forward that question was understood. 'Ahluwalia is a fine gentleman. Not a bad person, as you think. Dancing with other ladies is very common and usual.' He smiled. 'Before marriage, I have danced with many ladies here. There is nothing wrong. Depending on the music, sometimes while moving fast, the bodies may touch. That should not be considered to assess a person.'

'But, on that night, the majority of officers danced with their wives only. Why did he come and invite me to dance with him?'

He preferred to keep mum.

While having food, Sneha, the daughter of Air Commodore Sinha, was seen entering the dining hall and talking something to an officer and walking out briskly. Prabhakar was certain that she would come to his table, as she had seen them. That did not happen. As he was continuously tracking her movements, Sujatha became anxious.

'Who is that girl?'

Without pulling out his gaze from Sneha, he said. 'That is Sneha.'

'Oh, I see. This is that girl with whom you are very friendly.' With surprise, she asked. 'Then why didn't she even bother to look at you now?'

He could not find a satisfactory reply to give her. 'Probably she wouldn't have seen me.'

'She was absent from our welcome party also.' She remembered.

'That was our squadron party. She wouldn't have been invited.'

She snapped a meaningful look. 'Or is that due to some despair. I mean, love despair?'

Concealing his mental disturbance, he contained the reply in a mild smile. Sneha was sure to have observed him sitting by the side of a lady around the dining table. Purposely, she would have avoided him due to some unknown cause. What could be the reason? He started scratching his brain. Would have been in a hurry? Or would it be due to some misunderstanding? For that, as per the best of his knowledge, he had not given a chance. His mind started moving haywire. 'I am sure, there have to be some serious reasons, otherwise, she wouldn't have avoided me'. He concluded himself.

Sujatha could guess of the undercurrent of disturbances in his mind from his gestures and face. 'Are you thinking of that and worried?'

Suddenly he pulled out from his thoughts and acted energetically with a wild smile. 'I was thinking of what I should reply to Ahluwalia.' A totally different track.

Looking at his face she could judge, what was said was not correct. But, she refrained from continuing with the subject and decided to change the track.

XXX

On that evening, while Sujatha and Prabhakar were sitting in the mess lawn, Flight Lieutenant Sudhir came and took a chair adjacent. Sudhir yelled for the bearer and ordered their drinks. Whiskey with soda. In spite of repeated compulsions, Sujatha refused to have hot drinks and Sudhir had to surrender and ordered for coco cola for her.

During drinking, Prabhakar brought out the topic of Ahluwalia's offer and sought the opinion of Sudhir.

Suddenly Sudhir turned jubilant. 'That's a good idea.' He took a sip of whiskey. ', being so close, I should have offered this to you much earlier. But, I didn't. You know the reason. You definitely would have thought of why such an offer was not projected from my side. There is a reason. If you happen to stay there at my house for one day and night, sometimes, there is every probability of you going mad. Every day we fight. Her mandate is to oppose anything said or suggested by me. That is as if she has taken a vow. If I say, it is night time now, she will argue saying it is day time. Such is her character. Then, the arguments will start. That is the only reason; I didn't offer you to share my accommodation.' He was too apologetic.

Prabhakar looked at him sympathetically.

Sudhir looked at the soft drink bottle in her hand and said. 'There is nothing wrong with ladies taking little wine.'

'No. I don't like it.' Respectfully she refused.

Sudhir smiled. 'Ok accepted.' Looking at Prabhakar he inquired. 'Did you meet Sneha?'

Such a question was not expected from him at that point in time. 'What happened?'

'Just asked.'

With slight hesitation he said. 'While having our lunch, I saw her coming inside the dining hall and going out. Probably she wouldn't have. Other than that, after leave, I haven't met her.'

After sipping from the glass, Sudhir hesitated and said. 'Two days before, I heard something from an associate. Knowing well that I am close to you, he opened the topic. It seems that girl is in shambles. I mean worried.'

With curiosity, Prabhakar inquired. 'For what?'

Tapping the glass with his fingers he asked. 'Is that to be mentioned by me?'

Raising eyebrows, he became more alarming. 'I couldn't follow you.'

As if taking an excuse from Sujatha, he looked at her and asked him. 'Was she not after you all these days?'

He could not control his anger. 'See, don't talk shit. I don't like this.'

Sudhir could not say anything but laughed aloud. 'Not that I am telling. It is talk of the station, among officers. You and I also knew of her madness towards you. I too have seen her flirting with you.'

Prabhakar looked at both sides. 'Please don't talk rubbish and make Sujatha feel bad about me.'

'We know that. What I said was, she was too much interested in you.' He emphasized the last words.

He wondered. 'But, I have never shown such an affection or love, whatever you may name, towards her. She was very free and friendly with me and I too was. Nothing over and above that.' He looked at Sujatha and winked indicating that whatever he was talking carry no meaning.

'Might be. But she had taken everything differently. That is the reason for her avoiding you.' Sudhir continued thinking. 'Sometimes, she might have entered the dining hall after seeing you show her annoyance and indirectly convey her feelings to you.' He smiled. 'After all girls! They are too cunning.'

Sitting for some more time, Sudhir got up to take leave. 'I feel, you better shift to Ahluwalia's house. He is a nice person. He will entertain you both with his jokes.'

'That's is right.'

-17-

Prabhakar and Sujatha moved to Ahluwalia's house. Two rooms were given to them. The study room adjoining the bedroom could be used as the kitchen. But, Ahluwalia was not in favor of that idea and requested them to use their kitchen. Cooking both Punjabi and Keralite food was to be done from the same kitchen. They had to reconcile and concede. Paramjit Kaur, wife of Ahluwalia was an expert in culinary art, and her interest to learn south Indian food preparation was welcomed by Sujatha. She was curious to get appreciations for her capabilities and the presence of Sujatha for getting on the spot positive response was welcome. Both had decided to learn each other's preparations with utmost interest.

If Ahluwalia went near the kitchen for want of anything, Sujatha cared to stay away from him, because of fear, without outwardly exhibiting. The scare of coming too close or touching her body was always alive in her. Many times she had expressed that to Prabhakar, but he had not taken that seriously. He even tried to make fun, saying irrespective of the modernity and higher education attained by the south Indian girls, they remain suspicious of all gents. She could not help, but to make faces to show her disagreement.

Days passed very pleasantly. Both Prabhakar and Sujatha soon became a part of that house and enjoyed their stay by sharing accommodation. The only difficulty faced by Sujatha was to keep an arms distance from Ahluwalia to thwart her fear. Her firm belief was that the ladies should always be careful to look after her to avoid unpleasant situations. Within a few days of staying together, she could master various north Indian preparations and she was proud of that. The interest in north Indian dishes grew in her and she gave full credit to Paramjit Kaur for that. Similarly, Paramjit also widened her culinary area of interest and specialization

XXX

The situation on the border was getting worse and the instructions were issued by the air force authorities to dispose of their families so that they can concentrate on defense matters and their duties, without the diversion of attention. All airmen took that seriously and send their wives and children home and made free themselves, but few officers preferred to keep their families with them, at their own risk and promise of not deterring their duties.

By the beginning of November, the border was on the verge of the warlike situation and the words started moving of impending unwanted situation; the war. Instructions were floating drawing everyone's attention to be alert to meet any eventualities with all might. Everyone was instructed to be available at their place of work at short notice. Two teams of officers and airmen were made and one team remained on duty at a time and got relieved by the other team, once their period of duty was over. But, if the situation warranted, irrespective of which group one belonged to, all were to be present and that remained to stay as the standing order. Everything was under strict control and the whole station was ready to face any situation at any time. With all this, the morale was very high and there was never a panic among anyone, officers, or airmen, and everyone's visualization remained to face the all-round victory. Their only intension was to give their life and blood for maintaining the integrity of the nation with their all might. With determination, they remained on duty without rest or sleep and waited for the D-day if that was inevitable.

Every morning and evening fighter planes, fully loaded with essential weapons, kept flying around the aerodrome guarding the vital locations and installations. With the available modern equipment, they remained in the sky over the airfield intending to attack the intruding enemy aircraft with all might. Once the allotted flying time of one set of two aircraft was over, another set got airborne to replace them. The roaring sound of those flying overhead aircraft and other capacious arrangements generated a great sense of security and feeling of one-upmanship among everyone in the station.

While having lunch, Sujatha said.

'Most of the items in the kitchen got exhausted. Many days have passed since the market was visited. The main thing we need is rice. Paramjit has no rice in her stock. You know, they do not use rice. In case the items are not bought, tomorrow onwards we may have to depend on mess food.'

Thinking, Prabhakar tried to satisfy his wife. 'I will ask for a one-hour break from the squadron. Ok?'

'Vegetables are also to be bought. And there are no fruits also.'

He smiled. 'No problem. We will buy everything. More quantity we will buy so that frequent running to market can be avoided.'

'If you buy more, there is no fridge with us to store. That will get spoiled.'

'Can't you keep in their fridge?'

She laughed. 'Paramjit herself finds difficulty to keep what they buy in their fridge. Then, how can I ask her to keep our things also?'

He stared into her eyes. 'Why not we buy one?'

'Then, where will you keep? We will think of that once a house is allotted to us.'

As if realizing his folly, he laughed. 'Yes, you are right.'

After reaching the squadron, he went to K N Singh's office and sought a one-hour break from the unit citing the home requirements. He was pleased to grant.

With a long list of items to be bought from outside, Prabhakar proceeded to the outside market on the scooter with Sujatha on the pillion. As they had acquaintance with certain chosen shops, they could procure all items of provision, vegetables, and fruits without much delay and loaded the scooter carrier and the front hook just below the seat. During their journey back, hearing the scooter horn, Prabhakar turned his head back and saw his friend Sudhir on his scooter. He reduced the speed and made his friend come parallel to him. He observed Sudhir was without a helmet and gestured why riding a two-wheeler without that. Riding two-wheelers without a helmet, in Air Force, is considered as a great crime and invited punishment if caught. Hence some people used to make fun of that by saying; one can afford to forget the head, but not the helmet. There were ample reasons for making that practice very strict. It was found out that many the air force ace pilots lost their valuable lives in road accidents as compared to flying accidents. The courts of inquiries after every accident invariably concluded in their findings that the main and only culprit responsible for the death was a head injury which could have been avoided, had they worn a helmet. The life of an experienced pilot was very precious and to replace one, the country had to shell out an enormous amount for the training and further up-gradation by continuous flying efforts to attain enough experience. Hence the Air Force has made it compulsory to wear a helmet while riding two-wheelers and many lives were saved by this order by avoiding head injuries in accidents.

'Where is your helmet?'

Suddenly his hand went up and felt his helmet missing. He turned his head back and found his wife was also not on the pillion. He suddenly became panic wondering where he had gone wrong.

'I thought she is on the pillion.' Expressing fear, he said. 'She would be waiting in front of that shop.' Saying so suddenly turned the scooter and a motorcycle that was just behind his scooter collided. Sudhir suddenly fell with the scooter. Blood started oozing out from his head and Prabhakar though that could be a head injury. The motorcyclist escaped without any injury from the fall. He briskly parked his motorcycle on the roadside and moved to help the uniformed officer.

Prabhakar kept his scooter on the roadside and moved fast with Sujatha to help him. Sujatha examined him and said firmly. 'He needs to be taken to the hospital immediately. He is bleeding profusely. She pressed a cloth piece over the head injury and said looking at Sudhir who was in perfect senses. 'Nothing to worry. The injury is minor.'

To avoid traffic congestion, Prabhakar lifted the fallen scooter and kept on the roadside.

Prabhakar kept looking at either side of the road to request if any car passed that way to take him to the hospital. Luckily, a car was seen coming and he stopped. Seeing an officer in uniform on the road in blood, he suddenly stopped and showed his willingness to help. With the help of Prabhakar and the motorcyclist, Sudhir was carried to the car and he was made to lie on the rear seat. Before starting the car, Sudhir requested his friend.

'Prabhakar, she will be waiting for me in front of the shop. Just go and bring her.'

'Which shop?'

Sudhir said the name of the shop.

Prabhakar asked Sujatha to accompany Sudhir and requested the car owner to take him to the army hospital.

He followed the car on his scooter for a certain distance. At a diversion, he took the road leading to the town. He straight rode to the shop identified by his friend. There he saw Sudhir's wife in tears standing waiting with her eyes glued to the road. Seeing him at a distance, she moved fast towards him with a bag in one hand and the helmet in the other.

With tears, her face was swollen. 'He asked me to sit on the pillion. Before I took the seat, he moved the scooter and proceeded.' She sobbed wiping her face. 'Even forgot to keep the helmet on. This is his habit. For everything, he is in a hurry. Wouldn't do anything perfectly and properly. Is this his habit in his office also?' She expressed anger. 'If I say anything, he gets upset and shows annoyance.'

Prabhakar did not know how to start with. He has to somehow inform her of the accident. How to open the subject? He searched for proper words. In a mellowed voice, he opened. 'Sudhir has met with a minor accident.' He saw her face suddenly change. 'To check whether you were on the pillion or not, he turned his head back and collided with a motorcyclist. By the grace of God, nothing had happened. But, for a medical check-up and further medical care, if required, he has been taken to the hospital. Sujatha has gone with him.'

Tears were found streaming down her cheek and she was on the verge of breaking down. 'What happened to my Sudhir?' She yelled.

'I told you. Nothing. Just for the sake of check-up, he is taken to the hospital. There is nothing to worry about.' He tried to pacify her.

'I want to see him.'

'We will go to the hospital.'

She sat on the pillion.

In the hospital, when she saw Sudhir, she got cooled down and wiped off her face.

'There is nothing to worry about. He lost little blood. Nothing else. If after head injury had he lost consciousness, there was cause for worries. In this case, it is a minor scratch. Nothing to worry.' Sujatha went near her and pacified.

As it was a head injury, the hospital doctor advised getting the head scan done. Hearing of the head scan, Sudhir's wife became worried. But, when Sujatha, being a doctor explained the circumstances under which that was advised, she became convinced.

When Prabhakar expressed his desire to go back to the unit urgently, Sujatha preferred to stay in the hospital giving company to Mrs. Sudhir. She did not like to leave her alone pondering over unhealthy thoughts connecting to the head injury. Her decision to stay with her was hailed by Sudhir and his wife.

-18-

The unprecedented and unexpected sudden attack of Pakistan by air, at five-thirty, on the third of December 1971 took everyone by surprise. Their aircrafts entered Indian Territory and attacked the airfields near the Indo-Pak border. A simultaneous attack on a few Indian airfields near the border created little surprise among everyone. They intended to cause heavy damage to Indian airfields, to incapacitate their fighter aircraft from taking off using those runways. But, as their pilots were not efficient enough, none of the airfields were damaged and they all went back after showering the weapons such as bombs and missiles on either side of the runway. No damage was caused by them to any property or the lives on the Indian side. All Air Force installations were intact. Though any sort of attack was predicted from the Pakistan side, the sudden bombing and shelling caused little psychological setback momentarily which was got over by the high morale prevailed. As no damage was caused by that, the courage and the morale of all personnel further got a tremendous boost. Before the attack came, the red wavy siren was sounded and all had taken shelter in the trenches, dug much earlier, and no one was hurt even with a minor scratch. They all remained there inside the trench till all-clear siren was sounded - a continuous long siren.

    The war had started. The time to exhibit the capabilities of every soldier had arrived. Immediately after the all-clear siren, everyone got onto their assigned jobs sincerely and meticulously. Sitting inside the trenches, our personnel enjoyed seeing the anti-aircraft gun firing aiming Pakistani bombers. The anti-aircraft gunfire created a cover of fireballs by the burning shells over the airfield due to which their aircraft could not even approach the runways accurately. The sight of those shells going high aiming their aircraft like balls of fire was a sight to watch from the ground. It was like the great festival Deepavali firework. Due to the constant shelter to the airfield provided by this gunfire, they had to drop their bomb and missiles somewhere near their target and had to escape, causing no damage to the Indian side.

Evening at seven, the Squadron Commander, Wing Commander Mukerji called all officers of the unit to the conference hall. When he saw an exceptional enthusiasm on everyone's face he could not control his smile. 'This is what I wanted. When I see this confidence in you, I feel proud and horripilate.' In the dim and subdued light of the hall, he could see everyone's face and said passing his gaze to all. 'That day has come. The day to prove our capability and to show the whole world what we could, has arrived. This is the opportunity to prove the worth of continuous training you received. Every one of us is responsible to prove our worth in safeguarding the country's integrity and security. Our country is calling you for its security. It is time we have to respond positively and do our best to safeguard the country. Since Pakistan has attacked us, we cannot keep quiet. This pre-emptive attack will have to be adequately retaliated. The decisions on that regard are being taken at a higher level in New Delhi and we expect to receive the directions and instructions shortly. Having received such a blow, we are not going to keep quiet. We know how to retaliate with maximum pressure. That blow, they would never forget in their whole life. We can do that. My earnest request is that the opportunity we get should be most effectively utilized to cause maximum damage to their defense potential and all vital infrastructures.' He looked at everyone with a positive note. 'The aircraft which is allotted to you must be maintained in top condition. If any snag is observed, that should be immediately reported and ensure the rectifications are done immediately. All airmen technicians working on the aircraft should be given adequate support; both material and morale. Even minor snags should not be neglected. The attitude of getting corrected later-on should be avoided. Get everything attended to and get rectified immediately, however trivial it is. That should be your attitude.' He looked at everyone and asked. 'Are there any questions? You may ask.'

'Sir, when can we expect the retaliation?'

The restlessness of that officer brought a broad smile on his face. 'Let's wait. You might receive without much delay.'

Early morning on fourth December 1971, Wing Commander Mukerji addressed all officers of the Squadron. 'We are instructed to take action. We will be retaliating in the most befitting manner. We will cross in three groups of four aircrafts each and cause them enough damage. Our targets will be their strategic locations. Aerodromes, ammunition depots, signals units, army convoys, radar stations, missile units, and tanks. Each one of you will be assigned to the targets. And any other targets you feel vulnerable should be destroyed.' He scanned everyone's face. All faces were seen with glows of confidence adorning a smile. The craze to achieve the maximum result was seen on their face. That alone boosted his confidence over the surety of achieving the specific task allotted to the squadron.

He called out the names of officers in each group and specifically mentioned the names of batch leaders. Also, he gave details of targets for each batch and group. 'You all should be alert always. The counter-attack from their side can be expected from anywhere. You should be aware that the danger could be in any direction. If you fly very high, your aircraft will be caught on their radar screen. To destroy, they will deploy their missiles. The missiles coming from your front could be detected by your aircraft radar and you should do whatever you could to avoid them. When that approaches, you will see and should do whatever possible, such as duck, dive, or any other usual maneuvers. To avoid their radar, you may fly low. But then their anti-aircraft guns will be active. These all warfare and tactics are known to you and have learned at various stages of your career. But, I have to remind you all once more.' He looked at everyone.

He continued. 'You all should perform your duty with utmost care and perfection. No one should ever think of somewhere dropping their bomb or launch missiles at any target. Each such action will be photographed by the inbuilt camera and that will be studied at the base to assess their damage. You will be caught. Whatever you do, we get the proof. When you drop a bomb, the place it falls will be photographed by the inbuilt camera. Similarly, when you get in a dog fight with enemy aircraft the gunfire will be photographed. That will be seen by all of us. If anyone does any foul play, that will be found out. That should be in your brain always.'

Few officers looked at Ahluwalia and smiled.

He continued. 'Till the last drop of blood in our body we must fight. That is our duty and mandate. One brave will die only once. But, a timid person dies many times. People will try to emulate a brave. They will talk highly about him. But people will make fun of timidity. They will laugh at you.'

When he was very confident that he had imparted enough courage to one and all, he passed on the list of pilots detailed for the day's task. They all saw that. In the first batch, Wing Commander Mukerji was the leader. Prabhakar and Ahluwalia and one other officer were to follow him. The tasks to be performed were also listed in detail.

As per the standing instructions, the essentials like medicines, few hand weapons, and preserved eatables containing survival kits were carried by everyone, and with flying, helmet officers moved to the tarmac. All were in high spirits. Their minds were full of varying strategies to be adopted during their mission over the enemy sky. None had an iota of fear or apprehension of what would arise of pessimism. The smiling warriors moved to their allotted aircraft smiling keeping the morale high.

Ahluwalia, who usually avoided flying for fear, never showed any signs of such unwanted thoughts and moved along with Prabhakar to his aircraft. Prabhakar was surprised to observe the enthusiasm his partner possessed during his conversation of the duties to be performed after take-off and on entry to the enemy territory. His morale was very high. A firm determination to cause maximum damage to the enemy by him was predominant in his talks. A real Sardar with manly traits predominating! Prabhakar before peeling off to his aircraft wished him all the best and all success in the mission. Ahluwalia wished him back on the same coin exposing his full teeth.

'You are not scared of entering the Pakistan territory?'

While peeling off, Prabhakar asked casually showing reluctance.

Ahluwalia turned towards him. 'Never. When the nation is calling me, showing reluctance and keeping away from my duties is unwarranted and un-officer-like.' He said with pride.

War Hero

'I shouldn't have asked such stupid question to him' He thought. To satisfy himself, he decided to offer clarification. 'Usually, to avoid flying, you used to back out citing silly excuses. That's why I asked. Please don't feel bad.'

He smiled. 'For what? Prabhakar, you are right. I am scared of flying. But, it is not correct to back out now. If I seek an excuse, someone else will be detailed. By chance, if something happens to him, I will be cursed. And that curse will ever follow me.' He smiled. 'I am not a coward. I avoid flying; don't ask me why. Now there is a vital need for my flying skills.' He moved close. 'You should know, a real Sardar never buckle under any adverse circumstances. And I am one. Sardars will not run away from war. He will fight with all his might until the end. That is how we are bought up. That is what we have been doing from our earlier generations to generations. The tradition will never change. Valor is foremost in our life. From war, they will never run away.' He sounded firm. The determination seen on his face was like a burning fire.

Prabhakar was surprised to see his courage and felt that was worth emulating. With a smile, he patted at his back.

'See, I am not alone. You are all there with me. Especially our Commanding Officer with umpteen number of flying hours and well experienced. Then why should I be worried?'

'Once more, wish you all the best.'

'Same to you too.'

Prabhakar moved to his aircraft and carried out the mandatory checks and got satisfied himself. Removed the pitot headcover. Checked the bombs and missiles fitted onto the aircraft. With an eagle's eye, he moved around the aircraft and ensured everything was in proper order. With the help of the side ladder, he went up and got into the cockpit. The technician briskly moved towards the plane and climbed up the ladder and closed the hood of the aircraft. He came down and moved out the ladder and waited at a distance. Prabhakar started the engine and carried out the routine checks and having satisfied, looked outside. The technician moved out the chocks from under the undercarriage and again took his position. When Prabhakar again looked at him, he raised his right-hand thumb indicating that everything was in order. When the pilot moved the plane out slowly, the technician saluted wishing the pilot all the best in the mission and safe return.

Prabhakar established contact with flying control. The flying control gave complete information regarding the climatic condition and atmospheric pressure and permission to form. Everyone started taxiing out. The first aircraft to enter the runway was that of Wing Commander Mukerji. Following him was that of the other three of his group; Prabhakar, Ahluwalia, and the other. Prabhakar was the third in the line.

After entering the runway, each one of them ensured the proper functioning of the engine and monitored other parameters and after getting permission to take off from the flying control, one by one took off.

Throughout the journey from takeoff, the pilots maintained constant contact with the leader.

Before crossing the boundary, many had little apprehensions and a slight increase in pulse rate. But once they crossed the border their fear disappeared and only the thoughts of ways to cause maximum damage to the enemy popped up and prevailed. Soon after crossing the air territory, Prabhakar saw a convoy of army vehicles. With the permission of the leader, he destroyed the whole army vehicles with gunfire and missiles. Looking at the massive

War Hero

fire on the road, he expressed his satisfaction and reported that to his leader.

Reaching the destination and targets in sight, Prabhakar reduced his altitude and flew very low. Dropped bombs exactly on the target and fired continuously on a few other targets. The damage caused by his unblemished valor was beyond his expectations. To report on his successful mission, he called his leader on VHF (very high-frequency wireless). There was no response. The plane that was right in front of him was seen engulfed in flames hit from ground anti-aircraft gunfire. That was of Wing Commander Mukerji. The sight gave him a momentary jolt, but he could succeed in recovering back to normalcy in seconds. He looked at that falling ball of flames. He pulled his eyes out immediately, lest he got scared the sentimental feelings might draw out his attention. Sighting the huge radar aerials, he aimed a missile onto that and observed that to getting gutted. Having completed the assigned task very successfully, he decided to return to the Indian base. The very thought of his leader Mukerji kept propping up involuntarily and made unwarranted sensational feelings, but he kept pulling out from such disturbances for fear of still being in the enemy territory. During those moments, he felt few of his pulses were missing and the heart behaved erratically. He wished and prayed to God for the safety of his leader. But he could not imagine any scope for his safe return. There was no chance for Mukerji to escape from that plane that was turned into a ball of fire. He wouldn't have got time to bail out. Everything might have happened in a fraction of second. He tried maximum to reign in his thoughts from going out of control and gave complete attention to flying.

There were only three of his team to fly back home.

Prabhakar called Ahluwalia on wireless. 'Our Mukerji sir.'

'I saw everything. He was just in front of me. This is not the time to think of that. Let us concentrate on our flying now. These are all part of our job. Today it was Mukerji. It could happen to anyone. Now just forget about that.' Ahluwalia was courageous enough to express such a strong opinion.

Then, no one spoke of that subject.

After reducing the speed, Prabhakar landed the aircraft. He deployed the drag parachute to reduce the speed. Moved slowly to the tarmac and stopped it at the spot guided and marshaled by the technician. When the engine was stopped, the technician brought the ladder and placed on the aircraft and he climbed up and opened the hood.

Prabhakar remained inside motionless and the technician was alarmed. 'Sir, any problems? Should I call for the ambulance?'

As if not heard, whatever was asked by the technician, he kept mum and remained there inside.

The technician got worried and shook him and again asked. 'Sir, anything wrong? I will call the ambulance.'

Still, Prabhakar was motionless.

In a hurry, the technician got down and took a water bottle and again climbed up. Holding the water bottle towards him he said. 'Have water, sir.'

Prabhakar turned his head and looked at him. He removed the helmet. 'I am ok. There is nothing wrong with me. Perfectly fit.' He took the bottle from him and drank water. 'Thank you.' He came out of the plane and moved around to inspect to find out if any damage had happened in the ground fire. Nothing was seen.

He straight walked to the aircrew room. Ahluwalia, who was behind, accompanied him.

'I think, the sudden disappearance of Mukerji has given a shock to you.' Ahluwalia looked at him and said.

Prabhakar looked at him and tried to smile. 'He was a good officer. A good person. Poor man, he was to put his next rank of Group Captain and sit in the Western Air Command Headquarters.' He sighed.

'That is his fate.' Without showing a speck of mental disturbance Ahluwalia said.

Prabhakar was really surprised to observe the stubborn attitude of his friend. He had an idea of asking him from where he could muster so much of courage but refrained.

Within a few minutes, all other planes also returned.

From the information gathered by various sources of the air force, the disappearance and death of Mukerji were established. All pilots who were behind him had seen the unfortunate sight and they all had vouched for the death of their Commanding Officer.

Around one o'clock, Air Commodore Sinha and Officer in Charge Flying along with their wives went to the quarters of Wing Commander Mukerji. The unexpected visit of the station luminaries raised many doubts and questions in the mind of Mrs. Mukerji, but she did not open her mouth and ushered them warmly. The countenance of visitors was lugubrious and it contained the wild message of some unpleasant news, but she never thought that could be something that would break her heart. When the visitors remained silent, the doubts climbed high beyond her imagination. She kept looking at their faces one by one and her heart started beating at a faster rate.

Only silence prevailed. Even the inhaling sound of visitors was feebly audible. She wondered why everyone was observing such silence in her house. 'Has anything happened to my husband?' She broke the silence.

Air Commodore Sinha looked at everyone and saw the bloodless faces. He fixed his eyes on her and said in an almost inaudible voice. 'Mukherjee's plane has not come back yet. Nothing is known about that. Probably he would have bailed out.'

He did not reveal the versions of Prabhakar or Ahluwalia. 'We expect him to come back. The aircraft got disappeared from the radar screen and hasn't come back yet.'

The news broke the heart of that lady. She started shedding tears. She felt as if the whole world was shrinking leaving her alone. The soil under her feet was felt to be eroding. The world was coming to an end. She opened her mouth and cried aloud. Seeing her going out of control, Mrs. Sinha moved towards her and tried to console with pacifying words. Mukerji's daughters also went out of control and cried aloud.

The villainous intrusions of such bad news of the loss of a dear and near one's strangle the much happier life of air force ladies. The maladies of unwanted war!

-19-

In the evening, both Prabhakar and Ahluwalia came back home from the unit. After the bath, they decided to go to the mess and spend some time there. They needed relief from the tedious routine and have liquor with friends, without brooding over the great losses. Just for a change! They took permission from the higher command at home, their wives, and went out. With a smiling face, Paramjit hurried to Prabhakar and stood in front of him and said.

'After getting your company, I find hell a lot of changes in my husband'. Her face was luminous with happiness.

Wondering over her such a remark, Prabhakar looked at her with a pinch of surprise. 'What is that? Whatever it might be, shall I expect that to be a positive one?' He smiled.

'Yes. It is positive.' Looking at her husband who was about to be with them soon, she continued. 'The person, who used to avoid even the daily practice flying with some excuse or the other, is said to have done bombing in the enemy territory. That is the thing.' Moving closer to him she whispered in his ears.' Can this be believed? Or has he dropped all bombs over our territory and came back cool?' She was skeptical.

With mock anger Prabhakar said. 'What is the cause of your doubt?' He chuckled. 'It is a bad thing to doubt your husband's capability.'

As approached, Ahluwalia saw them looking at each other and laughing. 'Has my wife cut some jokes?'

Prabhakar replied with an expression of negation.

She suddenly changed her face to be serious and asked. 'What for you both are going to the mess now?'

'To drink. What else?' Ahluwalia said.

Expressing dissatisfaction, she asked. 'Why don't you sit at home and drink?' She smiled. 'Then, we can also have a little.'

Giving a contemptuous look, he said. 'Sitting over the lawn there with the legs up on the side table and sipping a whiskey with soda and ice cubes gives a different ecstasy which you can't appreciate sitting at home. That is a real blessing, especially when one is under tension. The cool breeze caressing the lawn grass and moving touching the body gives tremendous pleasure and that can't be derived sitting at home.' He suddenly turned poetic and romantic equally and touched her cheeks expressing fond love.

Turning her face with shy she said. 'What are you doing? Aren't you ashamed to do like this in front of others?'

Showing innocence, Ahluwalia said. 'I haven't shown anything. If you want I will show.' He moved further close to her and tried to embrace.

She moved away making faces to show her disapproval. 'Aren't you ashamed?'

As if not interested in their talk, Prabhakar started the scooter without casting any remark.

Looking at his friend Ahluwalia expressed his opinion. 'Can't we walk? The mess is so nearby.'

'While coming back, if snakes are on the road, we will not be able to see. They are worse than Pakistanis. I don't want to be hospitalized with a snake bite.'

'So long as they are not disturbed or threatened of their life, they usually do not cause any harm.' Ahluwalia said.

War Hero

''That's true. But if unintentionally we stamp over them?'

Paramjit who was hearing them with patience gave the ruling. 'You go on the scooter only. I don't want anyone to get admitted to the hospital.' She sounded firm.

Ahluwalia agreed with her and said. 'My Commanding Officer desires that we go on the scooter. Now, there is no other choice.' He sat on the pillion.

They went to the mess and found two chairs on the wide lawn to sit. Pulling a cane table near those chairs, they sat and enjoyed the evening breeze embedded with attractive fragrance. They yelled for the bearer and he came without delay.

'Whiskey- soda with ice.' Ahluwalia gave the order.

When the bearer left, Prabhakar said seriously. 'We should stop at one drink. Not more. Morning again we have to fly. If the hangover persists, the missiles coming towards us will be misinterpreted as lightning.'

Ahluwalia decided to fully agree with that suggestion and he raised his right-hand thump upward and said 'Ok.' He moved his head towards his friend. 'Now we are drinking to dispel the grievances caused by the untimely departure of our beloved Wing Commander Mukerji.' He looked up. 'At that time, I didn't show any emotional change, because I knew that would affect my performance. Sudden grief might cause severe uneasiness and sometime that could be uncontrollable. Hence, purposely I remained courageous. That is the real fact. Separation is always unbearable. More so, if the affected one is loved by one and all. That is the case with Mukerji sir. He was a very good person, a good leader, and over and above, he was a very good human being; a real humanitarian. The loss is irreparable.' He became too sentimental.

Prabhakar was surprised to hear such dialogue from him. He wondered, if he talks so much before taking liquor, what will be his sentimental feeling and expression after consuming a peg or two. He advised him. 'Don't be so concerned. If we get involved in that subject, our present mood might get spoiled.'

The bearer came with two glasses of what they asked for and kept on the table. Ahluwalia said cheers and sipped the drink. Similarly, another person also.

In the dim light of the moon and glowing color bulbs on the hedges, Prabhakar saw Sneha walking towards the mess in a hurry with another girl. He called her aloud. Though she turned her head towards that direction, she did not care to have seen him or respond by words.

'Probably she would not have heard you.' Ahluwalia said. 'I stand corrected. She will not hear you.'

'Why?'

'She might be annoyed with you. She loved you so much and you did not honor her love. She liked it so much.'

Taking a sip from the glass Prabhakar said. 'I haven't felt so. We were good friends. And that will continue to be like that forever.'

With sarcasm he said. 'She was not for your friendship. Everyone in this station knew about that. When you came with your wife after marriage, everyone here was surprised. If that was what we had felt, you just imagine her mental condition when seen you with your wife.'

Prabhakar became speechless. He sat thinking. 'I was too close to her, but I never even thought of having such a relation with her. I didn't have even an iota of a hint of her such intentions. I have had a friendship with a few other girls too. But never with such an intention.'

War Hero

Seeing them enter the bar, one officer asked them to join him. That person kept two glasses in front of them and ordered the barman to pour drinks of their choice. 'Today's their drinks will be on me.'

'What is the occasion?' Prabhakar became curious.

'Today I am very happy.' That officer said.

Everyone's attention turned to that side.

'Today, while I was proceeding to destroy Lahore, I saw one missile cruising towards me. Without the loss of the presence of mind, I acted wisely and ducked immediately and the missile went overhead. I could see the disgruntled missile roaring with shame and going away. And, after that, I could damage several aircraft on the ground.'

Encouraged by those words, another officer opened his mouth with pride. 'I could destroy a large number of army vehicles. Few tanks and a water tank come to my credit. The huge water tank I destroyed with the missile.' He laughed. 'I could stop their drinking water supply. That is sure to affect their morale.'

All those who were in the bar kept saying about their valor and kept receiving other's appreciations.

One officer turned to Ahluwalia. 'I heard you were flying. A wonder of the year. But, I didn't find any crows flying *Ulta*. Usually, that is the indicator of unusual happenings.' He laughed aloud.

Ahluwalia could digest his joke. 'I think you are over drunk. Bottom it up and have your food and go to the room and sleep. Early in the morning, you have to go on the mission. Don't get further drunk.' That was a piece of advice.

Observing Prabhakar keeping mum holding a filled glass, one officer showed inquisitiveness to find out the cause.' What happened? Dreaming?'

Looking at that officer he said very gently. 'No. Nothing.'

Not being satisfied by that casual reply, he turned to Ahluwalia. 'What is the reason of his silence which we have never seen earlier. Did he have any misunderstanding with you? Or you picked up a quarrel?'

Ahluwalia smiled. 'No. Nothing of that sort. He met Sneha outside. They had talked something, after which he is out of the mood.'

'To be frank enough, she is the one to be out of the mood. Not he.' Another officer passed a comment.

'Love failure.' Another mockery.

Feeling pity, one officer moved towards Prabhakar and said. 'You need not have to worry about this. Maintaining friendship is a common thing. It is ruthless to think that all girlfriends should be married. If so, how many I have to satisfy like that. I have many girlfriends.' He laughed sarcastically. 'You just ignore such talks or comments.' He supported him.

After reaching home, both sat for dinner with their wives. Prabhakar was off mood and he ate little for the sake of not missing the dinner. Sujatha had been observing him right from the time he came back from the mess and showed inquisitiveness to find out the reason for that. He remained silent and preferred to be left alone. She doubted the cause of change of mood could be due to overdrinking.

After going to the bed, Prabhakar cared to apprise his wife of the meeting with Sneha and the subject they talked about. She tried to pacify him saying, that was a minor matter which should not be encouraged to get into his mind to create mental disturbances. When he tried to exhibit his innocence, she could not gulp everything as per his thoughts and blamed him for his imbecility.

'It is a must to keep a certain distance when you come close to someone, especially the girls. Too much closeness will brew a lot of unnecessary desires and expectations. That has what had happened in this case and that of Deepthi. Because of frankness and too much closeness, they expected that the relationship would end up in a marriage. And the damage caused by that in both these cases is evidence of your mistakes.' She looked at him and felt pity for seeing him lying lost in thoughts. 'Both these girls can't be blamed. The over expectations pushed them to the stages where they are now. Though your conversations at any stage wouldn't have carried a hint of marriage, they would have presumed of that. That is the weakness of the majority of girls. One can't blame them for that. It is not necessary to tell everything by words. From our behavior and doings, one may misinterpret the way which you might have even dreamt of.' She patted him. 'Anyway, forget about everything. Think that such things have not taken place. Consider all were some dreams.'

With slight guilt, he asked her.' Do you think that I have done any mistake in both cases?'

She felt pity and thought why she said all those words as if trying to educate him. 'No. Never. You haven't done anything wrong. Those girls are fools. The imbecility of those girls created all these confusions. Just because someone is free with a girl, it is the foolishness of that girl to conclude, that will end up in marriage. Utter foolishness.'

Those words were a good therapy to retrieve him from the unwanted thoughts.

The night was full of disturbances and unnecessary thoughts. He could not sleep properly. A feeling of blaming himself for the unwarranted mental condition of both Deepthi and Sneha kept haunting him and he kept taking bail himself. A sense of realization of his mistake of giving them wild hope kept whirling in his brain making him restless.

-20-

On fifth December, as on the earlier day, the officiating Squadron Commander Squadron Leader K N Singh, after the daily briefing, gave the detailed list of tasks and targets allotted to each officer. The names of officers in each batch and the team were also given. There was total silence throughout the entire procedure and there was not a word mentioned of the loss of the earlier Commanding Officer Wing Commander Mukerji by anyone. That sort of conversation was known to affect the mental strength of flyers and purposely avoided. On such occasions, everyone's thoughts should be only about the enemy and any other thoughts, if made to get generated, might seriously affect their courage. Their topics of conversations also should be such that their thoughts remain fixed on to the enemy and only about the enemy. Any deviations of thoughts about the death or accidents of near and dear ones were sure to affect the concentration and such deviations are purposely avoided when moving with firm determinations; such as in war.

Prabhakar was in the team of Squadron Leader K N Singh. Third in position. Each one of them, with the permission of the flying control, took off and gained sufficient height and crossed the border with firm determination.

After flying for some time, Prabhakar saw one enemy missile coming towards him. He suddenly ducked and escaped from its attack. That escape gave him enormous courage and confidence. He was very happy with that escape and smiled unknowingly.

War Hero

A huge conglomeration of army vehicles and mortars and other lethal weapons fell into his sight and he went for that. With firm decision to destroy that, he reduced the altitude. He destroyed most of them with accurate bombing and missile launching. The anti-aircraft guns of the enemy kept showering bullets onto his aircraft. Without caring for the extent of damage to the aircraft or self-injury, he continued with his job of causing maximum destruction to the enemy's war potential. He determined to cause maximum damage even without caring for his safety. He was fully satisfied with his action, but when he sensed fire at the rear of the aircraft, he got a shock. When that was reported to the leader, he was advised to return to base immediately. But, he did move around over the territory until all his lethal stock was exhausted causing unimaginable destruction to Pakistan's fighting capacity. Satisfied, he decided to return to the Indian Territory. The fire at the back was raging and when he was sure of an impending explosion, he bailed out.

With a thundering sound, the hood on top went up. Then the second explosion with which he was thrown upwards along with the seat. A parachute was opened and the whole thing came down slowly and got stabilized. With another explosion, the seat was separated and he was with another parachute and started coming down. The parachute was deployed and speed at which he was coming down retarded. With the wind speed, the parachute kept drifting and when he looked down, he saw a huge wild forest beneath. Without losing his sense of balance, he controlled the chute with the strings but got stuck on top of a huge tree. He looked down. There were no branches sighted underneath on which he could step on and he kept hanging. After a while, he started feeling body pain due to hanging and he kept thinking of ways to get down.

Holding firmly on to the ropes he tried to climb up, but he could not get a branch to step on. Though many times he tried to get the help of any branch but had to retreat with despair and failure. Suddenly struck an idea and with difficulty, he reached for the survival kit and took out the knife and cut the string on one side of the hanging chute. That came down slowly and again got stuck on one side rope. But he could get help from one strong branch to step on. Keeping both feet on that branch, he pulled the parachute and brought down. He came down the tree.

He kept the feet on the ground. He felt as if they were getting buried as in slush. So much damp was the ground. He could not remain without shock when a huge snake was sighted crawling on the ground by his side. He jumped aside with fear and a sudden howl came out. The huge snake looked at him and moved away with the shyness of meeting the coward and probably with a smile wondering why the human is so scared of them. He kept looking at it till vanished out of sight. As it was too damp, there was an ocean of leaches around. He stood perplexed. Where to go? He kept looking around. All directions looked like. There was no way found to find out which was east and north.

Praying for a ray of sun to judge the direction, he looked up and found one huge python on the branch he was standing earlier. His body quivered slightly. That giant creature was seen looking at him and wondered what its intention would be. Though he was certain that snakes generally do not attack anyone unless provoked, he was scared to continue to stay there; horrified of its look. Normally, he was not scared of snakes, and during the commando training at Kashmir; the mandatory requirement of catching one snake was performed by him to his credit. But, being alone, he felt as if little scare was creeping into his mind. Though he was certain that snakes are harmless and do not attack, he decided to drift away slowly from there.

Pulling down the whole parachute, he bundled that up and slowly dragging that and moved to the nearby tree. Attention was drawn by shrilled sounds; he looked up and saw a few monkeys of enormous size looking at him. When he tried to scare them away by making sounds and moving hands, the monkeys started making funny sounds. Probably by responding to that sound, many monkeys came from somewhere and flocked around.

They are behaving like the Pakistan army; he thought. The shrilled sounds and grinning of those animals generated laughter in him. He took the knife and kept in hand, to protect himself, if any attack from that army was to be faced. He sat leaning onto that tree.

Different varieties of creatures were seen coming out from the bottom of leaves around. The idea to tie the chute to the tree and take rest for some time came to his mind. Once dark, it would not be safe to move around, he thought. Spreading the parachute on the ground, he tied one side with the rope to the tree trunk and threw the other end of the rope to the branch and pulling that again tied the other side of the chute to make a hammock. He ensured that no reptiles would climb up as the height from the ground and that was sufficient enough.

He felt thirst. He took out the water bottle and drank. 'Now, I should try to escape from here somehow.' He mumbled. Since the forest was dense and even a ray of sunlight was not dropping on the ground, there was no way to judge in which direction he should walk. In which direction, the border was or what was the distance to the border was not known to him. Total darkness prevailed in his mind and all-around.

Deciding to rest for a while, he jumped into the cradle made of the parachute. The December cold and the breeze made his unease. The weariness took over all other thoughts from his mind and he slipped into slumber slowly.

The deep sleep slowly dragged him into a dream.

Sujatha was busy cooking in the kitchen and Ahluwalia was standing enjoying her beauty and curves. Seeing that, his wife Paramjit came there. Instead of shouting at him for his indecency, she was seen encouraging him in his enjoyment.

'You love her so much to enjoy her curves?'

He was seen shaking head with a smile in affirmation.

Biting nail, she pretended shy and asked. 'Then, why don't you catch hold of her?'

Soon after her permission, Ahluwalia hurried to grab her expressing his sincere desire to spend time with her and tried to embrace. Sujatha resisted and tried to run away from the kitchen, but she had to yield to his powerful hands. With a smile, Paramjit was seen pacifying her with cajoling words and compelling her to satisfy her husband. Sujatha was seen expressing her hesitation and protest and after some time she had to accept forcefully his demands. His hands ran over her body, though she was trying to wriggle out. He brought his lips close to her and to avoid forceful kiss, she turned her face aside.

As Sujatha was still not yielding to satisfy her husband's desires, Paramjit moved close to Sujatha and tapped on her shoulder and said. 'These things he does to me too. Don't worry.'

Somehow Sujatha got escaped from his grip and ran away. Ahluwalia followed her. On her way, there was a swamp and she fell into that. Slowly she started going down and cried aloud for help.

'Your destiny is to die there in this deep swamp.' Ahluwalia said with hatred.

Only her face was visible. Raising her hands, she again begged him to save her with tears.' Please save me.'

Ahluwalia kept watching her precarious condition. 'If you are willing to satisfy me, I will save you.' He shouted.

She begged to look at Paramjit also. 'Please don't let me die. Save me.'

'My only desire in life is to fulfill the desires of my husband. I don't like anyone coming against. You should die. Or get my husband's desire fulfilled.' She yelled.

'Never. I will not lose my valuable chastity.' Sujatha cried out.

'If so, it is better you die.' Ahluwalia said as his last words.

Some unknown force lifted Sujatha out of the swamp in split seconds. Sujatha herself showed surprise over the unexpected happening. She turned her head and eyes to find that unseen force.

Everyone heard that divine power. 'Paramjit, let you become a window, for having sided the devilish and heinous desires of your husband.'

The curse made Paramjit cry aloud. Seeing that, Sujatha looked around as if to look for that divine power and begged like a child. 'Oh no. Don't give such a curse. Please pardon her from her misdoings and get her relieved from the curse.'

That divine power laughed. 'You being a real female with chastity, I am obliged to consider your request. I respect your demand and give her relief.'

Prabhakar who had been watching the whole episode from far off place smiled with contentment and appreciated her courage and desire to keep up her chastity.

He could not refrain from appreciating her attitude of helping even the enemies. He laughed aloud.

'This dog is dreaming and laughing. He doesn't know that end of his life is in our hands' Hearing that, Prabhakar opened his eyes and saw four Pakistani soldiers in uniform standing in front of him with loaded rifles with open bayonets pointing towards him. Though the sight shook his mind terribly, he did not lose his courage and faced them squarely. Momentarily, he thought that the dream was continuing.

-21-

Prabhakar forgot all of the dreams. In the present condition, all about Ahluwalia's indecent behavior and Sujatha's courage and fight against his demands to maintain her chastity got faded away in seconds. He opened his eyes fully and realized that he had fallen into the clutches of the enemies. Showing scant surprise, he passed his gaze towards all four of them, one after the other. Four strong army men were seen standing in front of his swing with pointed bayonets. For a moment, his mind suddenly went blank. An experience, which can't be explained. He closed his eyes for a few seconds. Heartbeat was rising slowly to a point of palpitation. He opened the eyes fully to establish the reality of what was happening. The army had located him and at last, they had taken him to be a prisoner. And that was the end of everything, he concluded. Now, his fate was to remain as a prisoner under the custody of the enemy for umpteen amount of time. The most demoralizing period of a prisoner, he was destined to face has arrived, he thought.

'It is better to kill him.' One Pakistani was heard saying.

'Let's not do that.' Another soldier said. 'We have to take out a lot of valuable information and secrets from him. Sometimes there could be a treasure of information. We will take him to our bunker. From there they will come and take him. In case we kill him, we will have to carry his dead body to give an account of Indians we caught. We will let him live and his destiny is decided by them.'

Whom were these soldiers mentioning as 'they'? He thought. When they decided not to shoot and kill him, he was put at peace. They will be trying to extract whatever informations they could get from him if he knew. Then they would keep him as a prisoner of war. He sighed. Pakistan is a nation that does not respect the Geneva Convention and they may keep the prisoners as long as they want. That might even extend to years. They might even cause body torture. He decided to go through everything as destined. And he had no other choice, but to accept everything as it came. He sat up in the cradle and prepared mentally for any eventuality.

One person tied his hands and covered the eyes with long black cloth. By the most inhuman way, he was pulled down from the parachute cradle and made to stand surrounded by them. He did not show any protest or cry. For him, that was felt to be nothing compared to what he could foresee. They dragged him and threw it to a vehicle. Though he felt terrible body pain due to their ruthless handling, he refrained from howling or making sounds of grief or pain. With a firm belief that if any way out was there, his favorite God, Lord Ayyappa would pave way for his escape. Until then, he decided to undergo whatever torture or ill-treatment he was subjected to.

'Why not we take him to the headquarters?' One person said.

'Shut up.' A powerful voice, as if overruling him was heard. 'I will decide what's to be done. I don't need anyone's suggestions.' The voice was very authoritative and seemed that he was the senior of the lot and he did not permit others to give their opinions. Others kept quiet. No one gave any suggestions after that.

After driving for more than an hour, the vehicle was stopped. Everyone got down. While pondering what they were going to do with him, a person came and dragged him down and slowly made to walk into to a guided place. He removed the black cloth from over his eyes. The hands were still tied.

That was a bunker. A huge bunker was made by digging the earth for over six feet, with overhead covering by metal sheets. Even if a bomb or missile fell in adjacent areas the possibility of damage to the people or equipment inside would be remote. He saw much wireless equipments inside that bunker. But he could not understand what the function of so many equipment would be. There were only six army personnel there. He was surprised to see two beautiful teenaged girls inside. They were in civilian dress and presumed they would be assisting the soldiers in their duties. Otherwise, the soldiers would have brought them for their entertainment. The possibilities are for the latter. The Pakistan officers and soldiers are very fond of girls and liquor. Those are their weaknesses. That was what Prabhakar had read and was told by others. They need all comforts and pleasures where ever they are, as a source of encouragement.

Messages kept coming on the wireless equipment. The men were writing down those messages as it was and recording on the tape recorder. Prabhakar could understand that those messages were from the Indian side. Hence, he concluded, that unit was for monitoring and deciphering our communications on wireless and forwarding them to the higher-ups for timely action.

He heard one soldier reporting on the wireless about the capture of an Indian pilot from the jungle and Prabhakar could understand, that was about him. He could not hear the reply received as that was heard by the operator on the headset.

One person with a big mustache came near him and asked in the harshest voice. 'What was your aim?'

Prabhakar preferred to remain silent.

That person with anger repeated the question, but he remained silent. When again he embraced silence, that person started harming him bodily. Still, he did not open his mouth.

With anger, he grunted and kept his knee on his naval and asked harshly. 'If you co-operate with us, you will be treated gently. Otherwise, you will be tortured.' He lowered his voice. 'What was your mission?'

Thinking Prabhakar said.' To destroy your country.'

That person pressed his knee against his naval and with pain, Prabhakar yelled 'Ayyo'. He started receiving blows on his face and head simultaneously. 'You bloody dog. You or even your grandfather can't do anything to cause any damage to this country. Pakistan is very strong.'

'You are right. Our grandfathers aren't alive.' Sarcasm predominating words came out from his mouth and he spat on his face.

'You dog.' He started hammering on his face and other parts of his body.

'In your squadron, how many aircraft are serviceable?'

'All are serviceable.'

'What we're all the targets assigned to you?'

'All your airfields and radar stations.'

Many questions they had put forward, but he refused to divulge any secret information by saying he did not know. Then they kept torturing him in different methods.

'He is a soldier like anyone of us. He may not know.' One Pakistani came for his help. 'What is the use of torturing him like this. It is their job. They know how to extract all these secrets. Even if we get, what are we going to do with that?'

War Hero

With blood oozing out from the face Prabhakar looked at him. 'Even among Pakistanis, there are good human beings.' He mumbled. Through his gaze, he conveyed his thanks to him.

Without considering that person's opinion, everyone there tortured him one after the other. Still, he refused to divulge any vulnerable information saying the same words, 'I do not know.' He did not know any of the information he was asked, and even if he knew he would not have divulged. Feeling sad, seeing the inhuman behavior of his colleagues, the person who showed him sympathy earlier went near them and requested to behave humanely and refrain from further torture.

'Don't hammer him anymore. He will die. This is not the way to extract secrets. They know that. They will come in the morning and pick him up from here. Probably, as he is telling, he may not be aware of what you are asking.'

Everyone looked at him harshly and withdrew.

Throwing Prabhakar to a corner with legs and hands tied, they got engaged in their drinking session. The girls poured them drinks.

'Please do not drink more.' One person advised.

'Why?' Another person questioned him.

'We are responsible to pass any information received on the wireless. We should be alert.'

'You shut up. At this night who is going to attack? No message will come. That never happened during the night. The night is only to enjoy. Had we been near the border, we have to be careful. We are far away from the border.'

'But'

'What but? You enjoy. Today we have caught a prisoner. That is a great job. Let's celebrate that. Enjoy friends. You enjoy.'

After some time, one person opened the dinner packets. Chapati and chicken fry. Those girls served them drink and food.

One person looked at Prabhakar and asked. 'Shouldn't we give him? After all, he is our guest today.'

Hearing that one person sitting by his side lifted his booted foot and gave a kick on his thigh. 'You just keep quiet. Who is our guest? He is our enemy. He crossed the territory with the intention to destroy us and our country. And you say, he is our guest. Shit! He should be killed. And you say he is our guest! Shame on you. He should be killed. We will not give him anything. Let him starve and die.' He shouted.' And you say he is our guest!' He kicked him again. 'If I hear you saying so again, I will kill you.' He became too furious.

After hearing their conversation, Prabhakar concluded that there are kind-hearted people among the Pakistanis also. He was very hungry and wished he could get something to munch. But had decided not to accept any food from them even if offered. The smell of chicken fry and the aroma of liquor was something he had liked, but to avoid the very sight of that, he turned his to the other side with hatred.

All personnel were under the influence of liquor and they started to dance and sing loudly. All sang Hindi film songs. The girls kept on pouring the liquor and serving them food. Whenever the girls went close to each one of them they caressed and hugged them with delight and the girls never exhibited hatred. The longer time the girls spent with a person, the larger the quantity of liquor he had to consume. Some even treated the girls by pouring liquor and shoving chicken and chapati in their mouth which they accepted with pleasure. They also danced to entertain the soldiers. When one soldier ran his hands over the forbidden body areas of a girl she smiled and peeled off, without offending him, avoiding such acts further.

Everybody in the bunker enjoyed the night with dances and songs; of course, with the inseparable intoxicating liquid.

One Pakistan soldier looked at Prabhakar with wicked eyes and moved close to him. He gently lifted him from his sitting position and slowly dragged him to a corner of the bunker. Prabhakar was scared of his intentions which he thought would be to cause further bodily harm to the already battered body. The corner was like a room covered all sides with blankets. After entering that area, Prabhakar was made to stand near a pole of the bunker and he tied his hands to that pole with a cloth that he picked up from that area. He wiped off dirt and blood stains from Prabhakar's face. That soldier started cajoling him. Wondering over that method of the enemy, he stared at him. What was he aiming at? He could not conceive. But he never buckled and mentally prepared to face any sort of torture he was going to be subjected to. Suddenly he felt his 'G' suit was cut from the back with a knife. That soldier pulled his woolen inner down below the buttocks. As Prabhakar could guess his further intentions, he started showing his protests. There was no use and that soldier caressed his back with laughter and pushed him down to bent position and did the unnatural sexual act. His all protests and hesitations went in vain. Finally, he had to concede and yield to satisfy that filthy soldier's desire.

After him, a few others also did the same.

The inflow of wireless messages ceased.

Those fully intoxicated soldiers started lying here or there and slept off.

After a while silence prevailed. The atmosphere was calm and quiet.

One girl got and walked towards Prabhakar. She cajoled and caressed him. Talked to him very politely. He wondered whether she intended to provoke and make use of him. He showed hesitation and then finally she gave up. His arms and legs were freed and she looked at him sympathetically. 'I will help you to escape from here. I like you so much that I don't want you to get tortured any further.'

Those words were very consoling. He could not help but look at her passionately with a smile. Those words started ringing in his ears as the blessing of some unknown power. 'Really?' He wanted to hear her again.

She looked at the sleeping soldiers to confirm they are all in deep sleep and said in a mellowed voice. 'They are all in deep sleep. This is the right time to escape.' She looked at him to see his happiness. 'These people brought both of us hereby force. I don't think, we can think of an escape from here unless we are freed by these ruthless buggers. This is our fate.' She looked helpless. 'Like this, in almost all bunkers there are girls. These soldiers are happy with wine and women. These are their weaknesses. They are not interested in war. Most of the messages received are not sent to the concerned higher authorities by these people. They are living to enjoy life. Scoundrels!' It seemed she was very much angry with those soldiers due to their oppression. 'They are brainless. If the superior officer says to jump, they will do. For everything, they are to be guided.'

When his hands and legs were freed he felt half freedom was achieved. Thankfully he glanced at her with courtesy and decided to escape with her assistance as fast as he could. She moved close to him and embraced saying something very feeble for his ears to understand. He was in no mood to counteract but praised her beauty looking at her face. He was in no mood to enjoy that beauty and the only thought that flashed in his mind was to avail the opportunity to escape as fast as he could. Slowly he tried to get rid of her grip and moved her forcefully away from him. She showed reluctance and hugged him again with more force and tried to kiss on his face. He got pulled out himself from her grip and moved backward with a broad smile so as not to offend her.

Realizing his intentions, she slowly moved away from him. 'The border is quite away from here. This bunker is in a forest. The border will be about a hundred kilometers away. You just walk eastwards to reach the border.

'Aren't you coming?'

He asked with affection.

'Where to? What is the use of escaping? I have only my home to go to. These people will come there and forcefully bring me back again.'

'I will make you free.' He held her hand and said with confidence.

She glanced at him courteously. 'No. That will even put your life at risk. You escape. Don't delay further. Once these people get up, everything will be doomed.'

He had no words to praise her humanity. 'She is also a Pakistani. But see how sincere her intentions are?' He thought. 'Even an Indian might not show that much of affection'.

Many blankets were seen stalked on one corner. He, with her permission, took two of them for the further journey. Without her being noticed, he took one grenade and held underneath the blankets.

Bidding farewell to that angel, he walked out of that bunker after repeatedly expressing his gratitude for the magnanimity shown to the prisoner. After coming out and walking to a comfortable distance, he removed the safety pin of the grenade and hurled that into the bunker. With a huge sound, the grenade exploded. 'Sorry baby.' His lips quivered. He could not forget that girl. 'You are the one who helped me escape from there. But I had to do that. I could not help. I am very sorry.' He yelled. The sound that came out from his throat with the confidence of no one nearby to hear him.

-22-

He turned back and stood looking at the burning inferno. It was like a ball of fire. Feeling guilty for not saving the girl who helped to escape, he stood motionless for a while. Had she wished to walk away with him, she would not have had such an end. Suddenly the thought of someone might be noticing him in the light of the burning bunker flashed in his mind and he dared not to stand there anymore. But, in which direction he should walk? A big question mark raised in his mind. Everywhere he found only darkness. She has asked him to walk eastwards. But which was east? With an extreme dilemma, he looked upwards. The sky was full of stars and he found them making fun of him by blinking rapidly. No idea of directions!

Closing the eyes, he walked aimlessly. With both blankets, he covered the body tightly. So long as the blankets are on his body, he thought, nobody would be able to recognize him to be an Indian. Once they are taken out, the real picture will be known to others. Once he thought of removing the 'G' suite and throwing out. But the December cold prevented him from doing so. Then he corrected himself that the blankets were there for protection.

After walking for some distance, few funny thoughts popped up in his mind. Ghost stories. The stories told by his grandmother. When a person dies, the soul of the person will take shelter in the person whom the dead person liked most. The very thought dragged him to a pool of fear and momentarily he quivered. Those stories had made him, during childhood, to refrain from visiting the houses if someone was dead or even avoided seeing the dead bodies. A fear prevailed during those days of those souls entering into his body, by chance. He knew such saying and belief had no substance, but once the darkness set in with aloofness those fearful thoughts haunted him often. Even after growing up, that weakness never faded out.

In the moonlight, he looked at the watch. The time was one o'clock. He craved to take rest lying down somewhere if found safe. When he saw one rivulet, he stood wondering what should be done next. He thought of ways to cross and move forward. If the dress gets wet, he had nothing else to change and moving in the wet cloth for long, he was sure to fall sick. He removed his complete dress. Examined the 'G' suit which was cut by the Pakistani and after realizing that, that was of no further use and if seen in that by anyone, easily they could judge him to be an Indian pilot, he threw that out. After realizing, that would be of some use later, he picked up that and folded neatly. He stood on the bank for a few minutes enjoying the night's cold breeze and prayed his favorite power; Lord Ayyappa.

The rivulet contained only a little water. He dipped his feet in the water and felt the real coldness of the winter water and waded through quickly. Though he had half mind to wash the whole body with the cold water, he was scared of falling sick and refrained from doing so. Pulling the undergarments and the woolen inner over the quivering body he slowly walked forward in the same direction with the blankets covered over the entire body. He was too tired and hungry. He turned back and drank water from that rivulet. Mentally he was prepared to walk further but the body refused to function as per the desires. A large tree was seen at a distance and decided to lean onto that and rest for a while and moved fast.

The roar of the tiger was heard. 'Oh, my lord, have I to fight for survival with that too?' Emotion filled words came out of his mouth with depression. Slowly he climbed that tree and took a place on a branch and sat motionlessly and looked around for the wild animal. In the moonlight nothing was clear, but he presumed there was no immediate danger. He decided to lie on that branch and sleep. To ensure he would not fall from there, he tied himself onto the branch with the 'G' suite. After ensuring his safety by pulling that again and again, he decided to sleep. After usual night prayer, he closed the eyes and tried to sleep. His only wish was not to present any dream as shown during the day nap.

Different thoughts kept creeping into his mind. The thought of destroying the bunker and the soldiers of the enemy offered immeasurable contentment. The enemy who had captured him for questioning and gathering secret information had perished leaving only traces of their destruction. Suddenly the girl who paved way for his escape entered into his brain. Felt sorry for being a cause for her death. Even in that agony filled condition, he could not avoid wild laughter with the satisfaction he gained by destroying whatever he could do before the escape.

The thoughts of Sujatha kept regurgitating in his mind even during his busy planning of ways to escape from there, without further getting caught by the Pakistanis. He kept praying for there should not be even an iota truth in the dream he had about Sujatha's effort to get away from the attack of Ahluwalia. If such an attack would ever take place, during her worries of his disappearance, mentally she would get crumbled into pieces, he thought. If ever such an incident had taken place, he decided to kill him without mercy. Grinding his teeth, he kept mumbling something.

The doubts regarding his safety on the tree brank often bothered him. He doubly ensured, by pulling the 'G' suit repeatedly, that the knot on the branch was sufficiently secured. Hoping all good in life, he slept off. Though frequently he kept opening his eyes, unknowingly fell prey to the uncontrollable sleep.

When heard the rumbling and chirping sounds of little birds he opened the eyes and realized the day had broken out. When he could not see any sun rays, he wondered why and kept spreading his sight around. Realized he was inside the wild forest and wondered why so many jungles in Pakistan. Had a feeling of not confident of the direction in which he had to undertake the further journey to reach the border.

Thinking of what the next course of action was, he looked up and found a few monkeys on the top eating some fruits. He knew all items ate by monkeys could be eaten by human beings also. The stomach was empty and it started rumblings irritating him. Had he had the survival kit he could have taken a few dry fruits and eaten. Courtesy the soldiers who were killed, that was left in the exploded bunker. He avoided the thought about that unpleasant episode.

He untied himself and came down the tree. Saw a large number of fallen fruits on the ground. Reluctantly he picked up one and ate with apprehension. It tasted sweet and sour. Most of the fallen fruits were either decayed or bitten by monkeys. He collected few and ate with greed to kill the hunger. He wished he could get a few good ones and looked up and found many such fruits of the tree. Replicating the story, he had read as a schoolboy, he decided to get the benefit of the anger of the animals on

War Hero

top. Picking one fruit from the ground, he threw that aiming one monkey. He continued to do that repeatedly. To his surprise, all monkeys started plucking the fruits from branches and throwing that towards him. Though few fell on his body, considering their act as bliss, he smiled thanking them, in his mind, with a glee. Collected as many fruits as he could and leaning on the tree he ate in peace.

He collected all undamaged fruits from the ground and stored inside the 'G' suit. Contented by the monkey's act, he bade farewell to them and ensued his mission of walking forward. On the way found a rivulet and bending to its surface he drank sufficient water like an animal. Many small fishes were seen inside and wished he had the fire to cook and eat. In the water, he could see the reflection of the rising sun. Judging the direction in which he had to proceed further he smiled as having been moving forward so far in the desired direction only, though unknowingly. God is great! He exclaimed; mumbling.

Aircraft's sound was heard overhead and looked up and wondered that was in search of him. No, that could not be, he consoled, as the concerned authorities would have conceded that he too would have perished in the bunker explosion. He was sure that the plane was making low flying; otherwise, so much loud sound was not possible to be heard. Or could be our planes aiming at targets so vulnerable. There was no limit for his imaginations and conclusions.

Suddenly he heard the sound of a helicopter. That was also flying low. That could be in search of him, he imagined, but immediately corrected with the conclusion he had made earlier of the explosion of the bunker. If so, the possibilities of reconnaissance to locate him could be ruled out.

Crossing the rivulet, he continued walking in the direction dictated by the rising sun. After a distance, he felt tired and the wounds on the body started experiencing pain. In Ayurveda, he had heard of few leaves juice, if dropped over the wounds getting cured faster than any modern medicines. But, he did not know what that leaves are and of the availability of that in that jungle. Deciding to have a bath and to clean the wounds in the next rivulet or river coming across, he walked fast with all the uneasiness and discomfort.

Some sort of uneasiness he started feeling in the stomach. Gurgle and griping pain incapacitated him from further walking. The fruit could have done the damage to his stomach, he doubted and regretted having had so much without knowing the edibility. Pressing the stomach to contain pain, he continued walking to reach the border area as early as possible. He kept praying for that without being fallen into the sight of enemies.

Suddenly felt his stomach was creating terrific trouble and wanted to relieve himself. Loose motion!

When the stomach was emptied, he felt comfortable. Due to weariness, he decided to relax a bit. Leaving on to a tree he relaxed closing the eyes. The sudden commotion of monkeys made him open the eyes and saw a herd of elephants walking past without noticing him. They were walking, without looking at on either side, with certain fixed destinations and he believed there would be a river or rivulet nearby and they were on their usual track for drinking water and bath.

Thought of throwing out all fruits left in the 'G-suit' and opened the bundle he had made. With an afterthought, he decided not to and felt like having few more. Took out two fruits and ate deliciously. Again, the remaining fruits he secured in the suit. With the ingested fruits, he could satisfy his thirst and hunger to a certain extent. He prayed to God not to further damage his stomach.

Elephants, monkeys, bison, different varieties of snakes and deer were seen en route and he prayed for not to show dangerous animals like tigers or lions during impeding further journey. A huge snake creeping by his side was noticed. He sat motionless, lest that might get provoked. He watched that reptile moving away with its head raised.

A large scorpion was seen approaching him from underneath the pile of dry leaves. Though, he pushed that away with feet that again with vengeance moved towards him. He thought that was the right time to get up and walk away from there. He kept walking eastwards.

When he started feeling excruciating pain on his legs, he was compelled to sit again. The time was six in the evening and he decided not to walk further. The tiredness had overtaken his willpower. He pulled a few creepers from the jungle and tied on two nearby trees and made a cradle. Climbing into that, he relaxed in a horizontal position. Taking out a few fruits from his store, he ate two and felt hunger had vanished. The strong wind was blowing and he prayed for not to rain. Opening the blankets, he covered himself nicely and kept lying looking upwards into the unseen sky. Without knowing he dozed off into sleep.

During sleep, he felt something was moving over his body. He opened his eyes and moved the eyeballs around. In the darkness, nothing was visible. While moving his hands, he could feel something was moving under the blanket, lying by his side. Jumped out from the fabricated cradle and looked into that carefully and realized that the creature giving him company was a python. Realizing his non-cooperative movement, that creature slowly moved away from there gently. Again, he had no sufficient courage to take shelter in that cradle and kept standing with the puzzle. He looked around and showed hesitation to walk in the darkness with the leg pain and body weakness. But, what to do? The question mark appeared in front of him. Consoling himself that the animals and all creatures of Pakistan, as far as the experience concerned so far, are friendly and non-harming, he gathered courage and decided to take shelter in the same cradle. Again, he climbed into that cradle and covered the full body with a blanket and prepared to sleep.

As the morning broke out, he jumped out and started his walking session. By noon he had covered a considerable distance. The body was paining, apart from the leg pain that he had been suffering from since the last day. The fruits he had gathered were over and the next question was what to eat to kill the hunger. For some time, he lied on the ground. Though the weariness and pain commanded him to take more rest, he refrained from doing so and got up to walk slowly. A river came across and he thought of ways to cross that wide obstruction. Few wooden logs were seen lying here and there and he decided to collect them and make use of to fabricate a vehicle to carry him across. Moved around and collected a few and tied them together with the creepers available nearby. Dragging that slowly, he pushed to the river. When that floated he smiled unknowingly. Getting over that he slowly moved that forward aiming the opposite bank by rowing by hands. Propelling forward to the desired direction was cumbersome as the current was strong. However, with the constant struggle, he succeeded in his effort and reached the opposite bank.

While tried to come out from that he felt his limbs were not moving as per desire. They trembled and felt weak as if he was on the verge of collapse. Realized that he was running temperature. Remembered someone's saying that the short sicknesses such as fever and cold usually get cured without medicines and he decided to bank on that. Even if he thought otherwise, there was no other go. Pulled the boat he made with wooden logs to the shore and lied down on that and covered the whole body with blankets. His firm belief that no wild animals would disturb him or cause any harm coming over there gave confidence and that waded off all fears. He curled himself under the blankets submitting himself to his Lord Ayyappa who had saved him from different difficult situations so far. He took a vow that provided he was saved from the current situation and taken back to his unit without any harm, he would visit the Sabarimala shrine where the temple of Lord Ayyappa is located and offer his prayers and poojas.

-23-

In Kochi, Prabhakar's father Kishanlal, and mother Bharati were tensed up from the day the war broke out. On fourth December when the paper news came about the attack describing the way the Pakistani aircrafts entered our territory and bombed different airfields, they guessed that the war was broken out. Skirmishes on the border were a usual affair and they never thought that such a drastic action by the enemy Air Forces would have taken place. The frequent letters of Prabhakar had never mentioned the possibilities of ending up with a declared war. There was no hint of such drastic action by the enemy and their impression was that the same would get withered off with dialogue and agreement. The uneasiness undergoing over the border was never highlighted in any of his letters.

Kishanlal was quite regular in hearing the radio news. In that, the details of what had been happening on the border were not described. From the newspapers, he could read and understand what had happened on the third evening and was happy to know that no damage was caused by the aerial bombing by the enemy aircraft. After reading the whole in detail Kishanlal was certain that our side would not keep quiet and our powerful Prime Minister was sure to retaliate in a most befitting manner. If our Air Force gets into the action, he knew Prabhakar also would have to take part in such a move. Being a fighter pilot, he knew, Prabhakar cannot avoid being a part of the retaliatory work. If so, he was certain that his son would give a most befitting replies to them causing heavy damage to their lives and property. He was certain that his son being a Punjabi by birth would carry out any task assigned to him, especially when that comes for safeguarding the integrity and security of the nation. He was very confident of the sincere determined action by his son. It was an unwritten practice of every Punjabi family to send at least one son to armed forces, army, navy, or air force, for safeguarding the nation's security. They feel proud of that and take that as their duty to the nation. From certain families even, all sons were seen joining the armed forces and such families were honored by society. The head of such families was respected by all in society. Apart from being getting to a most secured job, they give prime importance to the security of the country. They often ask others, if the nation is not secured, how others could live peacefully.

In the newspaper of December fifth, the war news was read. We were fighting well and in certain regions, our army could surge forward into their territory without much casualty and difficulty. That was interesting news. To give ground support to the surging army, the part played by the Indian Air Force was also given in much-glorifying words. The part played by the Air Force in destroying the enemy's army supply lines was specifically highlighted in the paper. Destruction of supply lines was the most tactical method in any warfare to make the enemy handicapped. Once the arms and ammunition supply and ration distribution were disrupted, the enemy's morale and fighting capability would be drastically destroyed and they might have to doubly think of continuing with the aggression. Hence, in the majority of warfare, the prime importance was given to the disruption of supply lines.

'When our Air Force planes cross their area, wouldn't they try all methods to destroy them?' Prabhakar's mother Bharati raised doubt after reading the newspaper.

Kishanlal who was sitting outside in the verandah and reading the newspaper looked at her face keeping the newspaper aside wondering what should be replied. 'No. They wouldn't be able to do anything. Our aircraft would be flying at a very higher altitude, above thirty-forty thousand feet or so, and at that height, they can't do anything.' He brought back the paper to his front. 'From the ground, how can they fire an object at that height? Impossible.' Though he knew that they would use their ground to air missiles to destroy the intruder aircraft, he did not mention that. He also knew that the aircraft's flying so high can't bomb or strafe the enemy areas and they had to come down to attack accurately. If such facts were told, she was sure to be left in deep morose. Purposely, he refrained from revealing such known facts.

The reply consoled her.

Through the corner of the eyes, he glanced at her countenance. She was found still not at ease. He continued. 'Our planes go at speed greater than that of sound waves – above one thousand two hundred kilometers. In such high speed, they just can't do anything.'

She stood thinking. 'From that height, is it possible to bomb the enemy targets? Will our pilots be able to see anything from that height?'

Kishanlal never expected his wife to be so educated about the warfare tactics and wondered what to reply. Folding the newspaper, he kept that aside. He decided to answer her genuine query with whatever knowledge he had. 'You are right. They will not be able to see the ground from that height. Hence, they have to come down to, say one to two hundred feet, and carry out the destruction process, such as bombing and strafing. But as the speed of aircraft would be high at that height also, they wouldn't be able to do anything.' He turned his head towards her. 'Over and above everything, our aircraft are much superior to theirs's.'

She heard everything very attentively. 'But, our son has to fly in that enemy's territory and will not try to harm him and the aircraft? However high he flew, wouldn't they have missiles to attack?' Her sound got cracked.

He was confused. How to console her? He searched for words. 'See, the speed of their missiles is only less than one thousand kilometers. How can they catch an aircraft flying at more speed than that?' He did not know whether what he was talking about was correct or not. But, he found no other way to console her. 'As the missile comes near, our aircraft will increase the speed and escape. Our planes can do all sorts of maneuvers to escape from the incoming missiles. Our pilots are trained on that.' He tried to smile looking at her. He wished if there was someone to console him and eradicate his fears and doubts.

After dressing up, Kishanlal had his breakfast and came out and found his car inside the garage itself.

'Where is our driver?' He shouted.

Bharati came out and said. 'He hasn't come yet.'

'Why hasn't come? Had he told anything before he left last night?'

'No'. She said. Still, to confirm, she rushed to the kitchen to find out from the maidservant. After some time, she came out and said. 'Before going back home last night, he had not mentioned anything to anybody.'

He was found perturbed. He took out the car from the garage and drove to his shop. While driving, his mind was full of thoughts regarding Prabhakar. The thought of what the Pakistani's would do to the war prisoners if someone was caught, disturbed him. He did not know why such thoughts kept popping up and causing disturbance to his mind. As per the Geneva Convention, they are supposed to behave properly with the prisoners. But, will those cruel people of Pakistan treat the prisoners with respect, at least considering being human beings. His thoughts went wild. The car he was driving was hit by the truck coming in the opposite direction, purely due to his mistake. Though the car was completely damaged, luckily, he escaped unhurt. He came out morose and looked at the car. That was completely damaged. As the truck was not damaged, the driver did not have any complaints and was not interested in the police complaints. With the help of bystanders, he pushed the car to one side of the road for not to cause traffic disturbance.

In a taxi, Kishanlal went to his shop. By then, all employees in the shop had come to know of the accident. Sooner he reached, all flocked around him and inquired of the accident and prayed God for nothing untoward had happened; not even minor injuries. They showed their interest to know of the cause of the accident.

'While driving the vehicle on the road, if the full concentration is not on the road, this is what happens.' Jokingly with a smile, he said. 'My mind suddenly went to Pakistan. This was the result of that.'

One employee heaved a sigh looking at him. 'Something big which were to happen had gone off with minor incidence. Let's console thinking so.'

Kishanlal was amused by that saying. Looking at that person he asked. 'If a person walks on the road and if some accident takes place, will you say the same?' With a forced smile, he looked at everyone. 'For everything, there is a saying!'

That person showed little embarrassment and moved to hide behind another employee thinking he should not have told that.

War Hero

Seeing the approaching driver panting, Kishanlal asked aloud. 'Where you had been so far?'

Expressing guilt, he stood in front of him biting nail. 'Sir, my cycle got punctured while coming and all the way I came pushing that.'

With anger, he mumbled. 'What a day for the cycle to get punctured? Nonsense.'

After choosing the gold ornament, one person approached Kishanlal who was sitting at the cash counter. He gave the bill given by the salesperson at the counter. The amount mentioned on that was one thousand three hundred thirty. He gave currency notes for fourteen hundred rupees and waited for the balance amount. After counting the notes, Kishanlal deposited that inside the drawer, and instead of giving back seven ten-rupee notes, he took out seven hundred rupees notes and gave. Receiving the notes, the buyer looked at Kishanlal and put that inside his pocket and moved out of the shop with the item in a bag. A salesman, who had been observing this, moved near the counter and informed Kishanlal of the mistake he committed.

'No. I gave only seven ten-rupee notes back.' He insisted.

'No sir.' He disagreed and sought his permission. 'Shall I go and ask that person.' Looking at that person moving towards his bike he asked.

'Ok.'

That salesman ran to the buyer and appraised of the mistake committed by the shop owner. That person came back to the counter and said.

'I never expected that to be a mistake. I thought you have given me that much discount. How can I take it as a mistake.? I am giving fourteen and you are giving back seven hundred-rupee notes.' He chuckled. Giving the amount back he muttered. 'If you do business like this, very soon this will have to be closed.'

The driver moved towards the salesmen and showed surprise. 'What has happened to our sir?'

'Everyone commits mistakes.' One person said. 'I think, he hasn't got over the shock he received from that accident.'

The driver kept his finger over the nose and said. 'If you see the condition of that car no one would ever believe that the person who was driving would be alive. The front side of the car is completely damaged.'

'Our sir is a very good person. Hence, God will always be kind to him.' Another person said.

'That's right.' Another person supported.

A person who was listening to the conversation went near them and said. 'Sir is worried about his son. These are the signs of that. Mistakes after mistake! Otherwise, a person who had been driving all these years without even a scratch on the car, how would smash his car against the truck head-on?

'You are right.' The driver agreed to that. 'Something is happening on the border.' He looked up and prayed. 'Hope nothing will happen.'

Responding to Kishanlal's call, the driver moved towards him.

'I have spoken to the workshop. You take and leave that car there. Otherwise, you ask the workshop people to take by towing.

'Ok, sir.'

-24-

On December fifth morning eight o'clock, Ahluwalia's wife's father Sukhdev Singh and his wife reached the guard room of Air Force Station. Without getting down from the car, he asked the guard at the gate to open the gate. When the guard remained there like a rock without opening the door, he got out and went near and again asked to open disclosing his identity. When that person said he can't open the gate for any new person without the permission of the authorities sitting inside the guard room, he went into the guard room and repeated his request.

'I am the father of Flight Lieutenant Ahluwalia's wife. Along with me my wife also is there sitting inside the car. We have come to meet them. It will be very nice if you can permit us to go inside.' He said very humbly.

The Air Force policeman looked at him and said politely. 'We can't permit you to go inside. Your relative officer has to come here and identify you first and then only we can permit.'

Sukhdev Singh became slightly disturbed. 'Then, call my son-in-law and inform him of our arrival. Let him come and take us.'

The policeman looked confused. 'I do not know this officer. I don't know in which unit he belongs to. Do you know?'

'I don't know anything about that. He is a pilot. Our letters we address to the officer's mess.'

'Then, how can I find out. Here, there are many officers. Before the war commenced, a lot of officers had come from other units also. I don't know anyone of them. I came recently on posting to this station.' He asked another policeman in the guard room. 'Do you know this officer?'

He also raised his hands.

Their attitude was not liked by Sukhdev Singh. 'If so, please connect me to your Station Commander. I will speak to him.'

The policeman suddenly realized that the person who had come was not a simple man; could be highly connected. He asked him to sit down and showed a chair.

'You contact the Security Officer and inform him.' Another policeman suggested.

That person contacted the Security Officer and appraised him.

'Sir, one old person has come here, saying he is the wife's father of Flight Lieutenant Ahluwalia. He is seeking permission to go inside.'

'You ask him to sit there inside. I will contact Ahluwalia and inform him.'

After some time, the Security Officer rang up to the guard room. 'Flight Lieutenant Ahluwalia is flying. I will inform his wife. Let them sit there.'

The Security Officer sent one police airman in the jeep to Ahluwalia's residence. That person directly went to that house and informed Paramjit about the arrival of her parents who were waiting for permission to enter. With her, he went to the guard room. She met her parents and when she had confirmed their identity, the policeman on duty permitted them to go inside. The taxi was not permitted to enter the gate. Instead, the visitors were taken to the house in the jeep.

When they got down from the jeep, the policeman sought Paramjit's permission to leave. He added. 'Madam, please do not mind. These days, as the security has been tightened so much that we do not permit anyone without proper identification.'

'Never.' Sukhdev Singh said. 'Nothing should be done which affects security. Why should we feel bad about that? We will appreciate that. Our security is based on your security. The laxity shown in the security will adversely affect the security of the whole nation. We are proud of you all.' He smiled.

While moving towards the quarters with their luggage, Sukhdev Singh saw Sujatha standing at a distance looking at them.

Looking at Sujatha Sukhdev asked. 'Who is this?'

'She is Sujatha. Newly wedded. Wife of Flight Lieutenant Prabhakar of our unit.'

'Is she a Punjabi?' He folded his hands and greeted her.

'Prabhakar is Punjabi. But, born and bought up in Kerala. He speaks Hindi, English, Punjabi, and Malayalam.' Paramjit said with pride.

'That's good. That means he knows a lot of languages.' Sukhdev Singh smiled.

'She is Malayali. She is a doctor.' Paramjit said.

'Good.' Sukhdev Singh expressed happiness and smiled looking at Sujatha.

After entering the house, the mother and daughter kept the luggage inside the bedroom and came to the sitting room where Sujatha was standing observing the commotion created by the visiting parents.

'Your husband is a pilot or technical officer?'

'Pilot. Prabhakar and your son-in-law are working in the same unit.' She smiled.

'Where they are now?'

'Both have gone in the morning to the unit. They will come for lunch.'

Sukhdev Singh sat thinking. 'Actually, it is luck to become the wife of a defense officer. Anyone can serve the nation in whichever way one can. But the service by a defense officer is praiseworthy. Food, sleep, and even their life itself they sacrifice. Such a noble work where else one could think of? We Punjabis are, from the very early days, more concerned about the nation's security and we usually sacrifice our sons by sending to defense forces. Not only as officers but also as ordinary soldiers. As for actual warriors. We value the IAS and IPS as the second. The parents of defense personnel are respected by everyone in society. We have three children – two sons and one daughter. Both sons we sent to the army. One was a Major. He died in nineteen sixty-five war. The second one is the Colonel now. He is on the border. The third one is Paramjit.' He pointed his daughter and said with great satisfaction.

I am sorry to know of the demise of my eldest son.' Sujatha expressed her concern.

'You are right. At the same time, I feel proud of him. He is a martyr and he died for his country. It is very difficult to explain the sorrow of the parents whose son is lost. But at the same time, when one thinks of the cause for which he lost life, you feel proud. When the news got flashed of the death of my son on the war front, the consoling messages we received from different corners of the nation and the society as a whole were innumerable.' He looked at Sujatha. 'You may think that I am not talking like a father who lost his son, but I have been talking like this from day one. Everyone will die one day or another; has to die. That is certain. The birth is uncertain, but death is certain. One day, one has to succumb to death. Then, why not that be for a noble cause? If one is lost for such a cause, the very thought of the loss will be of mixed feelings. One will be relieved of the great degree of sadness.' He looked at his wife and found her eyes full of the thoughts of the eldest son.

Sujatha observed his eyes also getting filled.

Though one might explain with great words of sacrifice when one is lost in war, the loss for parents will never be reconciled and can't be accepted.

At noon Ahluwalia was seen coming on scooter alone.

'Where is Prabhakar?' Sujatha was anxious to know. Usually, coming from the unit and going to the unit after shifting to that house were always together. That prompted her to inquire with a little suspicion.

With hesitation, he said. 'I didn't find him.' He was seen a little restless. 'I went to some office before coming here. Hasn't he come so far?' The question was dramatic.

The unusual behavior Ahluwalia prompted a few questions in her mind. 'You both went in the morning. Then, where is he?'

With a blank face, he entered the house without answering her. As he had received the information on the arrival of the in-laws from the security section immediately after landing, there was no surprise shown by him after meeting them and he sat mute without looking at anyone.

'We came here in the morning.' Sukhdev Singh said with affection. 'We came to take Paramjit along with us home. When the situation improves, you can come and bring her back.'

He looked at them and kept thinking. 'No. That's not possible. When I go flying, Sujatha will be left alone.' Somehow, he managed to tell that much.

Those words and the way those were delivered, carried lots of meaning and Sukhdev Singh could apprehend some unusual tinge in his talk and keep quiet.

When everyone in the room was seen sitting embracing silence, Sujatha hurried to the kitchen and said. 'You people are sitting as if not knowing what the time is now. Let's have our food.'

The embedded distress of her mind was read by Sukhdev Singh and he whispered. 'Poor girl. I can understand the fire in her mind. Similar feelings I too had years before.' He slipped into deep thoughts.

Paramjit quickly moved to the kitchen and asked Sujatha to sit for food. Sujatha refused to sit and worked with Paramjit to keep the dishes on the dining table.

All sat for food.

No one was prepared to have food. They sat speechless and motionless. No one even cared to put the chapati and curries in their plates.

Sujatha who had been watching that, took the plate of chapatis and put one each into everyone's plates and served them curries. Still, there was no positive action from anyone and she took one chapati and ate attracting their attention. 'I think all of you are lost in some other world. Eat, eat.'

Sukhdev observed tears flowing down her cheeks. But he refused to pacify or console her. As if everything was normal, he started having food without even turning his head towards her.

Ahluwalia who had been sitting looking downwards, got up in a jiffy and moved out of the room.

Sujatha called him aloud. 'Where are you going without eating anything? Come and sit and have food. Otherwise, when Prabhakar comes, he will shout at me.'

Her words made everyone's eyes get filled.

After spending some more time in front of the food, one by one got up.

War Hero

After some time, a car with Air Force flag followed by other cars came and stopped in front of that house. Air Officer Commanding Air Commodore Sinha, followed by the Officer in Charge Flying and Squadron Leader K N Singh along with their lady wives moved into that house with grieved faces. The sight of their presence gave the message of the purpose of their visit.

All were ushered into the sitting room. With morose faces, they walked in and took their seats.

The wife of Air Commodore Sinha got up and moved to Sujatha and said. 'Prabhakar's aircraft has not come back yet.'

She looked at her. 'Though Ahluwalia has not told, I could guess that from his behavior.' She looked quite bold. 'But I am very confident that nothing would happen to him and he will come back.' Her words were full of confidence.

Her courage and confidence were not expected by any of them. They had expected uncontrollable weeping and crying from her. They wondered how the newly wedded could muster so much of courage to withstand the unpleasant news of missing husband.

Mrs. Sinha patted at her back and said. 'You are right. Nothing would ever happen to your husband. He is sure to come back.' She consoled her. 'He would have bailed out and would be somewhere near the border. As you are certain of his coming back, he will come back.'

Sujatha quickly moved to the kitchen and brought a tray with glasses filled with water. The glasses were held against all those who came there to break the news.

While taking the glass from her, Air Commodore Sinha said in low voice. 'Your belief will enhance your confidence further. That alone can give you peace of mind. Let God bless you.'

All others agreed with him and grunted.

-25-

A thick forest. Kishanlal was roaming inside without aim. The surrounding was quite horrifying. Pitch dark. He was not sure in which direction he should walk to come out of that horrifying area. While standing confused, few wild animals moved towards him with the intention of hunting him down. While trying to escape from there, saw a wild elephant with its raised trunk trumpeting looking at him. His efforts to run away and escape from its attack were found futile. The legs were not moving as he desired. Hands and legs suddenly became ineffective and however he tried to get away from there, either by crawling or rolling, could not find success. Loudly he screamed. The whole body suddenly became motionless and he started sweating profusely. The eyes were fading away and suddenly the voice failed to come out. With the imminent death in front, he closed the eyes and waited for the inevitable. Suddenly as a savior, his son Prabhakar was seen approaching and he opened the eyes and saw him climbing over the elephant and controlling that huge animal with his might. The furious giant animal snatched him from the back with trunk and tried to throw him out. Kishanlal wanted to get up and help him but could not move. He wanted to cry aloud to attract someone's attention for help, but the voice remained within the throat only. That did not come out. He kept crying.

'Why do you cry?'

War Hero

When he heard the voice of his wife, he opened the eyes and realized he had a bad scaring dream.

She was found too inquisitive. 'Why did you cry?' Shaking his body, she again asked.

Recovering from the hangover of the dream, he smiled looking at her. 'Oh! I had a bad dream.'

'Like small children.' She pushed him aside and made fun of him.

'When we grow old, childhood returns. Then, there is nothing unusual. Otherwise, also, bad dreams dwell in disturbed minds.' He pulled her towards his body and tried to kiss.

Showing reluctance, she looked towards the door and said with coy. 'You are still like a youngster. Leave me.'

'Age doesn't come on the way of desires. Mentally, I am still very young.' Suddenly his thoughts moved towards his son and eased his hands off her body.

'The bad dream was due to your worries about Prabhakar.' She pulled herself off from his grip and said with a sullen face.

Heaving a long sigh, he looked into her eyes. 'Our only son. Is it possible to keep the thoughts away from him.?'

Suddenly she gained courage and consoled him. 'Just because of war, it is not necessary to keep thinking of him and bring in unnecessary worries and spoil your health. I am observing you being morose and worried always. See, even when there is no war, he daily flies the aircraft. Similarly, now also he flies in the sky and not in Pakistan. Then, what is the cause for worries.?' She looked at him and continued. 'You know how many planes fly on a day. But the air accidents are the least compared to any other mode of conveyance. Don't think of unnecessary things and make your mind sick.'

After daily routine and bath, Kishanlal sat outside on the verandah and started reading the newspaper.

'Good morning uncle'.

Hearing that, he looked towards the gate and found Prabhakar's friend Jayaram walking towards him. 'Good morning Jayaram. After your friend's departure, you have never paid a visit to this house.'

With a broad smile, Jayaram came near him and sat on a chair lying adjacent. Looking at the newspaper in Kishanlal's hand he glanced through the front-page headlines. 'These days, in newspapers there is no news other than that of war.'

Kishanlal folded the paper and kept aside. 'That is what is required. This war might bring a lot of changes in our life. Isn't it? The cost of everything is sure to increase with a war. Everyone's full attention is only towards one thing; the war. Everyone desires that the war should be won by all means. If not, the confidence in our government would be lost.'

Jayaram sat speechlessly. He felt sorry for commenting on the newspaper reports of these days. 'You are right uncle. What is the news of Prabhakar?'

'Apart from the usual letters, nothing unusual. Have you received any letter from him?'

Jayaram smiled. 'After going with his wife, he hasn't written to me.'

Thinking, Kishanlal said. 'He wouldn't have got time to write.'

'I read in the paper that all families of defense personnel are directed to be sent home. Is there any news about Sujatha coming back?' With slight reluctance, he asked.

'That would be for the other ranks; I mean not applicable to the officers. For soldiers, keeping their families with them would be difficult especially when they have to go to the field. As far as the Air Force is concerned, in a unit, there will be only a few officers. All sorts of securities and possible comforts would be given to them even under these circumstances. All Air Force units would be far away from the border. And, the Air Force personnel will never go to the border and take part in the real fighting. Their job is only to safeguard the sky. That they will do from far off places. The responsibility of fighting on the border is of the army. Air Force gives the army the required air support. Also, the Air Force will be sent to the enemy areas, crossing the border, causing heavy damage to their vital installations, and to destroy their fighting capabilities. When the assigned task of officers is completed, they come back home. Some officers might keep their families at the station itself for their convenience.'

'Daddy, the breakfast is ready.' Daughter Sunanda came and announced.

Keeping the paperback on the small table, Kishanlal got up. 'Would you mind if I invite you to join me for breakfast?'

Getting up, Jayaram thought for a while and agreed. 'Is so, I will have today's breakfast with you.' He laughed.

While moving towards the dining hall, Kishanlal asked. 'Today you are on leave?'

'No. I have to go. To be frank enough, breakfast was not ready at home. Hence, I thought of visiting you to know of Prabhakar's news.'

They washed their hands and sat for breakfast.

Looking at Sunanda who was standing there Kishanlal said. 'You can also sit.'

She sat by their side. She served them Chana and Battoora from the dishes kept on the table.

Kishanlal took one Battoora from his plate and tore a small piece from that and said with a sad face. 'Chana-Battoora is the favorite breakfast of Prabhakar. With whatever quantity he might eat, will never get satisfied.'

Jayaram said. 'These items are not made in our kitchen. There, the mother makes, putt-*kadala*, *iddali*, dosa with sambar or *chatni*.'

'That is your eating habits. This is the north Indian style.'

Sunanda wanted to disagree. 'Not so. In my friend's houses, these sorts of preparations are very common. They make poori, chapati, Chana- Battoora and all. Similarly, in north Indian homes, our idli and dosa are made. These days as people move about a lot, all sorts of culinary culture is widely getting spread over the whole of India.'

Kishanlal turned his head towards his daughter. 'That's right. In north India, they like our certain preparations. Our sambar is one such preparation. Some of my relatives, while they are here with us, used to drink sambar. They like it so much.' He chuckled.

Jayaram smiled. 'Slowly our eating habits also might change. Here in Kerala, few houses prepare north Indian dishes.' He waited for someone's support. 'Food habits are based on the availability of grains and other agriculture products. Here we cultivate rice, hence that is our main food. In the north, the main cultivation is wheat and hence they prepare items with that.'

'Yes, yes. You are right.' Kishanlal supported.

They kept eating without talking.

Jayaram broke the silence. 'Even though they like our food and sambar, their behavior towards the south Indians has not changed yet. Isn't it uncle?' He asked with hesitation.

Kishanlal raised his brows.

'Even now, all people from south India are 'Madrasis' for them. Irrespective of which state one is from, that person is referred to as 'Madrasis'.'

Kishanlal laughed. 'That is due to their lack of knowledge. They know only the state they live and the adjacent ones. Don't you think, that is due to their lack of knowledge?'

'I don't think so. It is due to the superiority complex they have. The complex towards the black-skinned south Indians. I have read somewhere that they refer a south Indian as 'Kalu'. Isn't that due to the hatred towards the dark-skinned people?'

Sunanda did not like such conversations on the dining table. 'These talks are unnecessary. Please stop.'

Both looked at Sunanda and laughed.

'You are right.' Jayaram supported her. 'Such topics are unnecessary.'

After breakfast, they got up.

'Shall I make a move uncle. Thanks for the north Indian breakfast.'

'Where you are going now? To school?'

'Yes, uncle.'

'If so, I will drop you on my way to my shop.'

'No uncle. Not required. I will take my scooter and go. Otherwise, coming back will be a problem.'

When they went out, the driver opened the door of the old Morris minor car door.

Looking at the old car, showing surprise, Jayaram asked. 'Uncle, this must be quite old, isn't it?'

With a contented laugh, Kishanlal replied. 'Yes. It is quite old.' Keeping his hand with force on the bonnet he said. 'This is quite reliable than any new car. I can confidently take this to any place. She has not given me any troubles so far.'

'Why don't you sell it, uncle? When you have a Benz, why to keep this old one?'

He was not pleased with that suggestion. 'My dear son, this is the first-ever I car I bought with my own earning. I am too much attached to this.' He tapped on that. 'I will never sell this. After my demise, it is their desire and decision.'

From the adjacent house, Sujatha's father Rajesh shouted. 'Today Jayaram master has come to visit you. Is there anything special?'

'Nothing.' Kishanlal shouted. 'He has come to know if we have received any latest information about Prabhakar.'

Showing hands Rajesh said. 'I will also join you, people.'

When he was seen coming towards them, they waited.

After Rajesh reached, Jayaram looked at both and sought permission to go. 'Then, let me take leave from here. If I get late to reach the school, I will have to listen to the headmaster's scoldings. Why give a chance for that? You both relatives sit and talk.'

As Jayaram walked out of the gate, the telegraph department employee entered on his bicycle. Seeing him, Jayaram stood hesitating to go away.

'Who is Kishanlal here?' That person inquired.

Kishanlal moved forward and said. 'I am.'

'There is one express telegram.'

Kishanlal received the telegram and signed the paper he was shown. While affixing the signature, his hand was shivering. Observing that, Jayaram turned back and walked towards him.

War Hero

Kishanlal opened the telegram and read. Without any expression, he remained silent and handed over that to Jayaram.

'Flight Lieutenant Prabhakar is missing in the war.' He read.

Hearing that, Rajesh kept his hand over his chest and wailed. 'Oh, my God! I am betrayed. My only daughter has become a widow.'

Looking at the wailing Rajesh, Kishanlal bit his lips with sorrow. He remained silent without uttering a word.

Rajesh looked at Jayaram. 'I have only one daughter. I have repeatedly told her not to marry a military person. She was bent on having this relation.' He looked up. 'Let her suffer. What else I can say now.'

When Bharathi came to the main door to confirm the departure of her husband, she saw their assembly at the gate with gloomy faces. 'Aren't you going to the shop today?' She asked aloud. As no one even cared to look towards her, she guessed that there was something wrong and walked towards them quickly. Seeing the paper in Jayaram's hand, she wondered what that could be and took that from him with his permission. Gathering confidence and courage she looked at everyone.

'Are you worried about this message?' She read that once more. 'In this, they have mentioned that he is missing. Probably, when the plane he was flying developed some problems, he would have bailed out. Our forces would not have found him out so far, hence they informed us.' Though her heart was about to burst by the news, she decided to play calm and pray to God to bring him back safely.' He is my son. Nothing will ever happen to him. I am very confident of that.'

Jayaram wondered looking at the courage of the mother. Usually, they are the ones who broke down despite consoling words from different dear and near ones. Here the boldness with which she was ready to face the information received of the calamity was praiseworthy. 'The belief is sure to heal' He whispered. He moved near her and said. 'That would be the fact. By the grace of God, he will be hale and hearty. Missing in war is common. They all have come back also.' He just said to console her with her firm belief.

With some relief, Rajesh took Kishanlal's hand and walked towards the house.

-26-

The day broke. The night was peaceful without any untoward incidents. Hearing the birds chirping sound, Prabhakar slowly removed the blankets off his face and looked around. The first sight that fell into his eyes gave a jolt. A heard of elephants standing by the river bank and drinking water. Few were seen inside the river for their ablution. The scare sent a painful wave from his toe to head and the unbearable shiver of the body practically made him momentarily handicapped. Quickly he covered his whole body again and decided to refrain from making any movements that might attract their attention, culminating in his peril. Tirelessly he kept chanting certain mantras he knew and prayed Lord Ayyappa to rescue him from the agonies he was undergoing. To his surprise, when he looked outside through the small opening he made by lifting the blankets, the sight was favorable; all elephants had disappeared. He called Lord Ayyappa again aloud and thanked for helping.

Slowly he got up after removing the blankets. It was very cold. His body started to shiver. What next? He did not know. With hunger and fever, what could be done next? With courage and determination to reach the destination, he walked willy-nilly. His body was not able to withstand the courageous moves made by him. He was too week to continue to walk further. He wished he could find some herbs of which by eating the leaves or fruits could cure the fever. He touched his forehead. He was running a high fever. The tiredness started overpowering his will power and he wished for the courage to withstand the turmoil. He wanted to cry aloud. But who will hear and console?

With all the discontentment, he pursued his mission of attempt to escape. He walked with all might and saw one plant which was seen used by Ayurveda doctors in Kerala; *'panikoorkka'*, to get relief from fever, especially for the children. He plucked one leaf and smelt and confirmed the herb. Quickly plucked few leaves and chewed them and drank the juice. He ate the residue and that could contain hunger to a certain extent. Wondering over the abundance of the same plant, seen in Kerala, in the enemy territory forests, he plucked a large quantity of them and kept inside the blanket. He firmly believed that the plant was a creation of his favorite Lord and he called that name repeatedly.

The hunger was haunting him. The search for the trees from which he could eat and store fruits on the first day, with the help of monkeys, went in vain. Till noon he continued walking. When the weariness overpowered him, decided to rest and leaned on a huge tree. When a cool wind blew, his body shivered. Opening the blankets, he covered the whole body. Without knowing, he got slipped into slumber.

A huge snake moving by his side was seen. Without any movement, he continued to sit looking to find out its intention. He wanted to run away from there but the weariness held him back. The snake disappeared in the wilderness. After resting for some time, he got up and started walking. The thirst also started alarming him. In the next rivulet, he decided to have water. From a distance, when he saw few monkeys playing jumping from one branch to the other, he was happy. The experience of the first day of gathering fruits came to his mind. When he reached near the tree, there were no fruits seen. The monkeys were seen eating the leaves of the tree instead. He wished he could get a few of the leaves to try, but none was seen at pluckable height. Climbing the tree was beyond imagination as he was tired of fever and hunger and to top it up, the thirst. Disgusted, he decided to walk further forward. Luckily, a small tree of the same leaves was sighted slightly away from that huge tree. Pulling the branch down he plucked one and smelled. There was no smell and he was not able to judge the edibility. However, he put little in the mouth and chewed. That was *karuka* (cinnamon tree) leaves. With slight sweet and hot that tasted nice. Plucked enough leaves and ate with greed. The thirst and hunger were brought down by that. Enough leaves were also stored inside the blankets. While keeping the leaves inside the blanket, he took out one bunch of the leaves he had collected for a cure for fever and ate that also.

He continued with the walk. By evening, his fever had come down. When a rivulet was sighted, he moved towards that. He drank enough water. Saw many small fishes inside that water. Catching one he, with hesitation, put in the mouth and bit the edge. No much of the taste problem was felt. Only the mental block of not cooked created an aversion in him. Notwithstanding, he ate the whole fish and was delighted by its taste. Ate a few more fishes and drank water and felt very comfortable.

After resting for some time, he got up to go. Suddenly, a big fish fell in his vision. With a stick, he could find there, he hit that and caught easily. But, he could not think of eating such a large one without cooking. How to make a fire? He thought of ways. Moved about and collected two round stones and a few dried grasses. Started the trick of ancient men of making fire during the stone age. With continuous efforts, he could succeed and laughed and jumped with joy like a child seeing crackers during

Diwali festival. The smoke and fire generated by the stone and dry grass gave him more self-confidence of survival and he was sure, he could withstand any number of days with the natural supply of fresh fruits, fishes, and water. Collected the dry tree branches littered around and kept over that and made a fire to cook that fish. Keeping the fish over that fire and changing the position up and down, he cooked that well. Once cooled, he started eating that by pulling the flesh little by little. Except for the deficiency of salt and chilly, the flesh was delicious and he consumed the full. He burped indicating that his stomach was almost full. He decided to carry those two stones for future uses. Mentally he became stronger when the hunger vanished.

After walking for a long distance only, he thought of taking rest. By evening, he decided to abandon the walking effort. As he did earlier, collected the creepers from the jungle and made a cradle-like affair tying on tree branches and slept very peacefully. He was sure that there was no likelihood of any Pakistani forces coming in search of him and decided to avoid thoughts of getting apprehended or caught unexpectedly.

In the morning, as usual, he commenced his endless and unknown journey, full of uncertainties. The frequent doubts kept generating in his mind of the result and on the culmination of the journey. He was not certain of the direction in which he was progressing with the journey. The direction dictated by the sun was being followed and he was sure that would never go wrong. India is on the east and he had been walking only in that direction. He kept walking. With no rest, he kept walking. Dependence on leaves, fruits, and fishes, if small without coking otherwise cooked with fire made using the stones and dry grass continued for days together. Drinking water from the wayside rivulets and bath in rivers kept his morale high and as days passed his enthusiasm spiraled up craving to meet his beloved Sujatha. Sometimes the dream he had of the encounter with Ahluwalia burped in his mind causing uneasiness. Her security was of more concern for him and wished such irritating behavior from Ahluwalia never happens at any point in time.

One morning when he saw his reflection in the rivulet while drinking water bending forward, he got scared. Longbeard and undone hair with the dirty dress. Decided to take a bath and wash the dirty inner and undergarment. He undressed removing everything including the undergarments and exposed the naked body to the morning sun. It was cold and he decided not to expose and get the fever bout relapsed. When he heard some sound, he cupped both palms over his genitals with shy forgetting there was none other than few monkeys to watch. The instinct of shyness played a lot even in the jungle. Slipping into the torn 'G' suit he looked around with the confidence in covering his whole body. He washed the inner and undergarments and spread them on the branches of dwarf trees. As the sun rose, he removed the 'G' suit and had a ceremonial bath by rubbing the body with few leaves he had gathered. While he was still inside the rivulet, a huge bear with its baby came there to drink water. The sight of that wild animal created shivers in his mind and body. His mind suddenly became filled with various thoughts. To fight with that, he had no strength and courage. He wanted to run away from there, but the thought of being naked warned him and he decided to stay motionless in the water without making a signal to attract their attention. The huge animal after drinking water looked forward and happened to see him. But, not caring for his presence there, without further passing its gaze towards him, that walked away with the baby. Suddenly he felt of some unnatural power helping him from the attack of that. Looking at retreating boar, he smiled thanking God.

The animals of Pakistan are so friendly with us, then why the people of this country are antagonistic with Indians? He could get the answer. It is not the people, but the leaders are.

As each day passed, the haste to reach the Indian soil kept on increasing. The certainty of each day bringing him closer to the native land kept encouraging him morally. The desire to participate in the war kept growing in his impaired mind, with immeasurable revenge. As each day passed his grudge towards the enemy kept spiraling up. He wished the ongoing war should be a decisive one with a positive result by crippling the opponent's entire fighting capacity.

How many days more the struggle for his freedom would continue? There was no hint or signs of certainty. The only wish he had been begging the almighty was that at no stage, the enemy hands should fall on him. Should be saved from being fallen into their clutches, as a prisoner of war. He was prepared to undergo any agonies and obstacles coming on the way. The desire throughout lingered in mind was, somehow should reach the motherland without the loss of health. He was sure that the almighty would be kind enough to get his desire fulfilled and he kept praying for that repeated many times.

Though various obstacles of wild animals and creatures kept coming across his way, he could easily survive all with ease and determination. As days passed, the weakness started attacking on his health, but the desire to escape kept spiraling up and he remained mentally strong. The aim to step onto the native land prevailed undisturbed. After that, fight with the enemy till the end and show the entire world the valor of a determined soldier.

Irrespective of hot sun or pitch darkness, he did not disrupt his efforts and continued to stride with longer paces. At a distance, a small mountain of about one hundred feet height fell into his sight. Wondering how to cross that, he stood motionless for some time. The possibility of slopping on either side to reduced height could not be ascertained and decided not to take chance for that and waste time. Without hesitation, with the assistance of a long and strong stick, he walked over and reached the top. A dim light fell in his sight. Standing there he started thinking, 'From where that could be?' Found no answer. During the war total blackout was to be adhered to. The enemy pilots coming for night bombing could easily judge the habituated areas and the military camp locations by homing on to the glowing lights. Such changes would not be taken by any villagers. Then, why the light? Was he going away from the border and cursed him for all the efforts going in vain. 'No. I can't be wrong. The sun God would never cheat me so. I had been trekking by the direction shown by the sun.' The assurance made him mentally confident. Without giving weightage to any of his doubts and misapprehensions, he kept walking aiming the source of that light. He threw away the 'G' suit that he had been using for storing the collected items like fruits and leaves. He also threw away whatever he had kept inside the folds of the blankets.

By the time he reached the location of the light, the darkness had set in. That was a small house with a thatched roof. There were many small houses of a similar type in the vicinity. But his aim was that house which led him towards that direction. No light was seen in other houses.

Holding on to the stick he smothered his beard and said in a mellow voice. 'I am too hungry. Please give me something to eat.'

No response was heard from inside.

Going still close to the house he again requested. 'I am hungry. Please give me something to eat.'

Still, there was no response. The people inside would not have heard him. That doubt made him walk around the house and found one door was open. Looking either side, he peeped inside through that door like a thief, silently. That was the kitchen. Again, he tried to draw the attention of the people inside by repeating the same. There was still no response. Looking both sides, with reluctance, he entered the kitchen. Found a few vessels inside. When opened the covered vessels, he found chapatis and dal inside. Looking around, like a thief, he took a few chapatis and dal on a small plate and ate with greed. Again, he kept looking around to ascertain no one was around. The food was tasty. After many days he was getting a chance to have any food and with greed he gobbled inside whatever he had picked up, looking downward. When he raised the head, he found one cute girl of about ten years dressed in typical Pakistani dress, silently standing by the door and watching him curiously. With fear, he opened the mouth and whatever was remaining in the mouth fell unknowingly.

After keeping the vessel down, while he tried to run away, that cute little child very softly said. 'Don't run away. Have the whole.'

Gaining confidence by seeing the attitude of that girl, he again squatted and completed the chapatis he had taken in the plate.

When he kept the plate back, she asked with a smile. 'Uncle, who are you?'

He looked at her. As the mouth was full of chapati, he tried to swallow fast for replying.

'Are you a thief?'

As far as the girl was concerned he had acted like a thief and her query was apt. He shook his head in negation.

'Then?'

'I am a passer-by.' He somehow completed the words.

'Where are you going?'

Finding no answer to satisfy her, he tried to get up showing urgency. 'I have to go. It is getting late.' He got up.

'No. You can't go.' She expressed sympathy. 'I think, you are unwell. When the father comes, he will give medicine.'

'Your father is a doctor?'

'Yes. Ayurveda doctor. Now he has gone to the neighborhood. To see a patient. One person came and took him just now. Here in this village, if anyone falls sick, he goes and gives the medicine.'

He smiled; a forced smile. 'I am also like that.'

A glow of happiness suddenly appeared on that little face. 'You are also an Ayurveda doctor uncle?'

He nodded in affirmation. 'What is your name?'

'Fathima.'

'Aren't you going to school?'

'Yes. In the third standard. I used to go with my father when he goes to treat patients. But, not during night time. He will ask me to sit at home alone.'

'How about your mother?'

Suddenly her face turned to be gloomy. 'She died. Allah took her away.' Her voice cracked.

'That means you are alone.'

'No uncle. Father is with me.' She closed her mouth and giggled realizing his folly.

Heard someone knocking on the door.
All four ears were focused to that direction.
'Fathima.' A loud call was heard.
The little girl smiled and said looking at Prabhakar. 'Father has come.'
Baffled, he got up with fear. 'I am going.'
'Don't go uncle. My father will like you. Especially as you are also a doctor like him. Sit down.'
'No. I will go.' He expressed fear.
'No uncle. My father is a good man. He will not tell you anything.'

She ran and opened the door. A tall and stout man, with a long beard and red cap, of about sixty years, came inside the room after pushing the door open properly. The very sight of that person spread a wild fear in Prabhakar. The scare of being caught hold and handing over to the police or army there with the help of other villagers crept in his brain. As he was very weak, making him surrender was easy, he thought.

That person came near him and asked politely. 'Who are you?' He turned to the girl. 'Were you talking to this person?'

'Yes, father. Poor man. He came here hungry. Ate chapatis and dal. He is also an Ayurveda doctor.'

'Have you come to treat any patient of this locality?'

Prabhakar struggled for proper words. 'I am on my way.'

Thinking for a while he said with compassion. 'Anyway, you go from here only tomorrow. In this late-night don't go anywhere. You may spend the night here with us.'

He was happy to hear that offer. Since how many days and nights he had not slept? That was a kind bliss.

Fathima moved to the kitchen. Others moved into the room.

-27-

Asking Prabhakar to sit on a cot, that person sat on the cot opposite.

'Fathima does all house-hold works?' Prabhakar just asked for asking sake to break the prevailing silence.

'Yes. She is eleven years old. This is the time she starts learning the kitchen chores. I was doing all myself before going out. As she was willing for this, I left the entire chore on her' He smiled. 'Once she goes to another house, she will be shamed if cooking and other works are not conversant with.' Heaving a long sigh, he continued.' After two years I have to think of getting her married.'

'I came to know that your wife is no more. Can't you think of marrying again?' Very politely he inquired.

He laughed. 'I often think of that. But, somehow, I did not like that. We Muslims can marry even four times, but you will not be able to love anyone sincerely. If you have only one wife, you will love her sincerely and you will be loved also. I realized that when I had only one wife.' He kept looking at the burning kerosene lamp.

'That means, you had more wives.'

Looking at Prabhakar he said. 'Yes. I married twice. When the second young wife arrived, my affection towards the first was reduced. That created a great lot of problems in her.'

'Then the first wife has left you?'

Thinking for a long time he said. 'That is a long story. 'He turned his face towards Prabhakar.' What is your name you said'?

Without hesitation and delay, he said confidently a lie. 'Ahamed.'

'My name is Javed.'

Fathima came with a plate with few chapatis and small vessels with dal and kept on the small table in front of Javed. He pulled that table towards him and said with emotion. 'The correct thing to tell is that she decided to leave me.'

How is that possible?'

He laughed. 'When she was fed up with me, she asked me to go away from her life.'

'That looks very strange.'

'Yes, you are right.' He shoved a piece of chapati with dal and chewed. 'It sounds strange. Our life is full of strange things.'

'That is perfectly correct.' Prabhakar vouched.

Till fifteenth August nineteen forty-seven, I was in India.'

That news dripped a lot of interest and courage in him. 'Where?'

'In a small village near Amritsar.'

The thought of father's ancestral home and relatives flashed in his mind. That was also in a small village in Amritsar.

'Twenty-four years back. I had two children in my first wife. I married once again. From a poor family. And we were very rich. Very big house, a lot many servants for any job. We were a landlord in that village. Then the independence came. Fifteenth August nineteen forty-seven. We heard the Hindus from here should go to the other side and the Muslims from there to this site. Many accepted that. I too joined the exodus. Everyone dreamt that once the Muslims come here, they would be very happy and life would be very comfortable without any sort of social or economic problems. But, my elder wife was not prepared for that. She decided to stay back with her two children. Then, with the newly wedded girl I came here.'

'But, Fathima is very small.'

'You are right. For fourteen years, she did not get conceived. Then, finally, I got this child.' He looked up and prayed. 'Could be due to the curse of the elder wife.'

Prabhakar shot out one question. 'Now, do you regret coming to this side?'

He did not like that. He looked at him with anger.

Prabhakar regretted asking that. 'I did not mean otherwise.' He tried to take bail.

Very seriously Javed looked at him. 'Are you trying to put a stamp on me that I am not loyal to this country?'

'Not at all.' Prabhakar decided to further probe. 'I just asked without any bad intention. Like this, I have asked many Muslims here. Few have expressed their sincere opinion that had they been in India, they would have been much happier than they are presented here. Many have come here leaving all properties and relatives there behind. After coming here, they have been toiling for their daily needs and had been repenting for the idiotic decision. Not able to gather wealth or get a comfortable life as they had been enjoying while in India. That doesn't mean that they are not patriotic. Every Muslim in Pakistan is patriotic to the core; and not otherwise.'

With hesitation Javed said. 'If I open my mind, they will cut my head off. I like India. I regret coming here. But, what is the use of telling now.' He looked up and said. 'My fate!'

Laughing uncontrollably Prabhakar said. 'Majority of people who crossed over and domiciled here regret, as you say.' He looked at him cautiously and thought of divulging the facts in front of him. Sometimes, he could be such a person who has switched his loyalty over to this country and if divulged he might turn to be an enemy and lead him to a trap. Could be an enemy of India and Indians. Then he decided to take a different way to present his case.

'I am also like you.'

Javed raised his head and raised his brows. 'I did not understand.'

'I was of four years. Father and mother decided to come here along with me. Later, on many occasions I have heard them saying, that was the biggest mistake they made in their life.'

'Leaning forward he asked. 'Where are they living now?'

'They have left me and gone to the hands of Allah.'

'Any other relatives?'

'No one. During my childhood father died. Mother was working in an Ayurveda medical shop to earn our living. I too was working there. I leaned the medicines and treatment from there.' Acting morose he continued. 'Mother died recently. So far, we could not make anything. We were living in a rented house. I started hating life itself.'

Javed felt sorry after hearing the pathetic situation of that young man. After thinking he said. 'You need not have to go anywhere now. Now on, you stay here with me and help me in my job of treating the people. You may live here without any problems for your daily needs.'

Prabhakar did not know how to admire his humanitarianism. His broad-mindedness was beyond words. He kept looking at him with open eyes. 'How wonderful a person he is?' He whispered.

'Why do you look at me like this?' He asked laughing. 'If you don't like, just leave it. The only way I found to alleviate your problems is the offer I made.

War Hero

Another thing, I am getting old. I find it difficult to travel long distances to treat people. Usually, I visit the villages near the border and treat the people. As the war is over, they would have come back from the places they had gone during the hostilities. I have to go to that place. If someone is willing to come along with me as kelp, that would be very nice. 'He paused. 'I just offered you that. If you do not like it, leave it. I have not spoken anything about that to you and you have not heard anything from me. Just leave it.'

From that conversation, he could understand that the war was over. 'Would have the villagers who were evacuated, come back after the war?'

He laughed. 'What are you talking about? Don't you know how many days passed after the war? The war was over on sixteenth December. The villagers would have come long back. There, I should conduct a camp and treat the people. There are people to make arrangements for our stay. Once we reach, Fathima will be very happy. A lot many girls of the same age group are there to play with and give her company.'

Prabhakar could guess that Javed was having a good relationship with the villagers near the border. 'I too will come with you to that place.'

Expressing happiness Javed laughed showing all his teeth. 'That will be nice of you. I am very happy to hear that.'

Looking at the yellow teeth Prabhakar said. 'I have a desire.'

'What is that? Let me hear.'

'Before dying, mother had told me one thing. I should go to Amritsar and meet her brother.'

Showing surprise, he asked. 'For what?'

'Once he is told of my condition, he might give a share of the property, which is due to my mother. If so, I will be able to lead a comfortable life there doing agriculture.'

'If such a desire is being nurtured by him, my ambition of getting assistance from him has to be ruled out'. Javed thought. Holding the long beard, he sat speechlessly.

'I don't know whether he will give me anything or not. If not successful, I will return.'

Those words gave little consolation. He smiled unknowingly. 'If it is so, let it be.' He murmured. 'The border is far from here. Around fifty kilometers. Buses ply from here to the border.' Thinking he said. 'After two days, both of us will go there.' His face suddenly changed to sullen. 'But, crossing the border is difficult. There will be many guards. We will be going to a village near the Wagah border. Crossing the border from there is slightly difficult. You may have to move either to the left or right and sometimes might have to crawl to cross the border.' He looked up into his face. 'Where your uncle is staying?'

'Amritsar.'

'Do you know the address? '

Prabhakar thought and said 'After going to the village if I mention the name of the uncle, mother had told that they will guide me to his house.'

Shaking his head, Javed called Fathima and asked her to spread a sheet outside on the verandah for Prabhakar to sleep. He got up. 'Now, let's sleep.'

Prabhakar took his blankets and moved out to the verandah.

Looking at his dress, Javed asked. 'Don't you have any other dress?'

Prabhakar stood looking at him thinking what his reply should be.

'Don't worry.' Javed said realizing his embarrassment. 'Don't worry about that. In the morning, after a bath, you can wear my dress.'

The cloth Fathima had spread on the verandah was very thick. That was a luxury for a person who had been spending nights till then, with the scare of attack from wild animals and reptiles. The war was over. The peace had been returned. But, in his life and that of Sujatha, the happiness had not returned yet. In both houses of their parents, happiness was yet to return. Similarly, in many other houses too. The messages of sons or fathers missing in the war would have been received by many houses killing their happiness. Their tears would have got dried of constant crying. The agonies created by the war! How many families spent sleepless nights? His thoughts went out of control.

-28-

On the next morning, after bath Prabhakar had worn the same soiled dress. Intending to help Fathima in the kitchen he went there and found her kneading the wheat flour. Asking her to sit aside, he squatted on the floor and kneaded the wheat flour. He kept talking to her while doing the job. Hearing the sound Javed went near the kitchen door and saw Prabhakar doing the job, in his dirty dress.

'Fathima, I told you to give one pair of my dress to him. See he is still wearing that dirty dress.'

He said with concern.

Prabhakar turned his head towards him and said. 'I am helping her. After this job, I will change. Otherwise, that will get dirtied.'

Javed smiled thinking of his simplicity.

They sat for breakfast. Fathima served them.

'Fathima also can sit. We will have together.' Prabhakar looked at her and said affectionately.

'I will eat later.' She refused the invitation politely.

When the breakfast was about to be over, a knock on the door was heard.

Turning the head towards the door Javed asked. 'Who is that?'

'Baba, I am Irfan.' The reply came from outside.

Looking towards the door, Javed said. 'Irfan, the door is open. Come inside.'

One mustached person, of about six feet in Pakistan army uniform, entered the room.

Pointing to the cot Javed requested. 'Please sit on that.'

War Hero

Looking at the breakfast items in their plates, he sat on the cot. He suspiciously looked at Prabhakar and said. 'Who is this person? I haven't seen him earlier here.'

Javed smiled. 'Oh, I forgot to introduce him.' He turned his head towards Prabhakar and said. 'He is Ahmed. He came in search of a job and I employed him. He will work with me. As an assistant' He looked at Irfan. 'He is also an hakim, like me.'

Irfan looked at Prabhakar. 'Where is your house?'

Prabhakar never expected any probing questions like that. His heart rate suddenly increased. He did not know what to answer. With fear, he looked at that person.

Looking at the fear and distress on his face Javed said. 'He is from a far-off place. He lost his father and mother. An orphan. When I heard his story, I felt pity and employed. As I am getting aged, I need some assistance.'

That army soldier was not fully satisfied and looking at the dress he was wearing he asked. 'From where did you get this dress.? This is the inner worn by Indian pilots.' The soldier looked at him with suspicion.

The lips of Prabhakar started quivering. Suddenly he felt everything was coming to an end. The efforts he had been taking to safely return to his unit, crossing over all impediments, were on the verge of crumbling into pieces. Finally falling into the hands of an army man shattered his mental courage. He felt like crying aloud out of despair.

Javed also had the doubt raised by Irfan. Looking at the dress worn by Prabhakar, he thought for some time and decided to help him whichever way he could. Bringing a mock smile on his face, he asked. 'What are you talking about? How would he get the inner of Indian military man?'

Irfan's face was full of suspicion. 'As per my knowledge, these sorts of inners are worn by Indian pilots.'

Javed laughed. 'I think you are wrong. These types of inners we will get in our market also. Do you want it? I can get for you.'

Irfan, with a determined expression, said. 'Let him say that.'

Javed could not deny personally the suspicion raised by Irfan. However, he felt it was his duty to help him and said. 'I gave him this dress last night. His dress was dirty and need to be washed.'

Irfan looked at Javed very crudely. 'From where you got that?'

That interrogative question was not expected and for a moment Javed looked hither and thither, confused. 'You know that I visit the border villages. Someone there gave me that. Otherwise from where I will get? I heard these dresses are available in the local market also.'

Not able to believe what Javed was telling, he said looking down. 'I can't believe you. He is an Indian pilot. The pilot who bailed out in our territory.'

With mock anger, Javed decided to withdraw from further supporting Prabhakar. 'If you can't believe, what can I do.? You may do whatever you feel like.' He turned his face away to exhibit his displeasure.

Refusing to accept defeat, Irfan sat motionless thinking. 'Ok. Alright. Let me confirm that he is a Muslim.' With a confident face, he got up and turned to Javed. 'I will take him to the adjoining room and check the veracity of your claim. If you permit'

All arguments and protective efforts were going to get crumbled like a pack of cards. Javed looked at Prabhakar and saw him sitting with a pale face and worried look. That very sight cleared all doubts he had and he firmly believed him to be an Indian pilot as told by Irfan. It was confirmed that he would not be able to help him out in

War Hero

any way further. He felt sorry for telling lies to assist him and repented for having taken such stand. The fear of exposing his lies haunted him and he was scared.

He looked at Irfan and nodded as if to grant permission.

Prabhakar go up and walked behind the army soldier to the adjoining room. Looking at Prabhakar who was moving slowly with a worried face, Javed cursed his ill luck for supporting him. He knew well that when Ahmed was being arrested and taken as a prisoner, he was not going to be left free of charges of betrayal for giving shelter to an enemy. No court of the country would ever pardon him and stringent punishment was sure to follow. Raising both palms upward, he called Allah. If so, what Fathima will do alone? He thought. He wanted to cry aloud for inviting the troubles unnecessarily by giving shelter to an unknown man without knowing the essential credentials. By bestowing all his future in the hands of almighty, he sat motionless closing both eyes, preparing himself to accept everything as it comes.

Irfan moved inside the room and asked Prabhakar to enter. When Prabhakar stood outside with hesitation, the doubts of Irfan increased many folds. He yelled. 'Come inside.' An Army manlike command!

Slowly, like a child with face half-covered, Prabhakar moved to the room and stood in front of him.

Pointing to the inner he shouted. 'Um. Remove that.'

Begging little sympathy, Prabhakar looked at him, as if he did not understand his order.

As the body structure of Prabhakar was better than that of his, Irfan had little apprehension of being forcefully pushing him down and escaping from that room. After moving slightly behind, he again ordered. 'Remove that.'

'What?'

'I want to confirm that you are a Muslim.'

'Ok. You may check.' Prabhakar exhibited confidence. He pulled down the inner bottom exposing his genitals.

Curiously Irfan looked and satisfied. 'Ok. You are a Muslim.'

When those two were seen coming out of the room without any commotion, Javed breathed comfortably. He turned to Irfan. 'When I told, you refused to believe. Now you are satisfied, isn't it?'

Irfan smiled. 'As a soldier, I have to suspect any new faces.'

Relieved from a great turmoil, Javed smiled and asked him. 'Now, you tell me, what is the purpose of your visit.'

Irfan sat on the cot and said. 'Last time when I came here, you had given medicine for my wife. She is yet not fully cured. I came to tell you that and take medicine for further treatment.'

Javed suddenly became serious. 'Then, you created all drama.'

'That was part of my duty.' He smiled.

'But, you refused to believe me.'

As penance, he bowed down to touch his feet. 'That's all over. Forget that.'

Javed gave him medicine and instructed how to administer. After giving money for the medicine, Irfan left.

When the atmosphere came back to normal, Javed said looking at Prabhakar. 'At least now, you change the dress.'

Prabhakar took a pair of kurta pajama from Fathima and went to the side room. Removed the inner and wore the neatly ironed white kurta-pajama and combed the hair with a comb he could lay his hand on. When he

War Hero

came out, Javed could not pull out his eyes off him. Wondered of having seen such a handsome personality in the nearby areas, he sat motionless praising him inside his mind. Had Fathima been slightly more grown-up, he could have thought of him to be his son-in-law, he dreamed. That dream made him smile and immediately corrected whispering, she is too small to think of that. When Prabhakar came and sat by his side, he inquired with more concern and affection.' In fact, who are you?'

He could not help laughing. 'I am Ahmed. Why such a question now?'

Javed scratched the back of his head. 'No. You are not.' Looked into his eyes. 'You are, as said by Irfan, an Indian pilot.'

Prabhakar sat motionless thinking. He decided to tell the truth without hiding any facts. He felt it did not fair on his part to hide the facts further. Javed had given maximum help when needed and he was confident of getting such help further, so long as he stayed with him. After letting him know all facts, he thought, he could seek his assistance for an escape to the motherland.

'You are right. I am an Indian pilot. My name is Prabhakar.'

Javed was seen shuddering with shock. He looked around and said. 'Don't say loud.'

Prabhakar sat without a change in his expression.

'Then when Irfan checked?'

'During my childhood, I had some problems. Pain while passing urine. To solve that the doctor had performed a minor operation. The foreskin was removed. Seeing that Irfan was satisfied. He confirmed to me to be a Muslim. A Hindu who performed the circumcision.' He laughed closing the mouth to muffle the sound.

Hearing that, Javed sat motionless with a wonder-stricken face. He looked up. 'Allah helped both of us; you and me.' He smiled. 'In India, which is your native place?

'A small village near Amritsar.' He said the name.

Expressing immeasurable happiness, he said. 'Allah, I am also from that place. Do you know Abdulla Haji? He is the owner of a big provision shop there. At present, I don't know if he is continuing with the same shop or even he is alive. He is from my first wife's family. My two children are with them.' Thinking, he smiled. 'They both might have grown up. I should have lived with them there. The madness of religion and caste got into the brain and spoiled my entire life and future. Here or there, we should be able to live peacefully and happily; isn't it? Had I been living there, I should have been like a sultan. With all comforts and respect from the entire society. After coming here, what have I achieved? Nothing. All happened due to my heavy headedness and dirty ego. Otherwise, what was the necessity of leaving them behind and coming over here? All my fate.' He heaved a long sigh. 'Before death, I want to go back to India. I want to die in my motherland. The country where I was born and bought up.' Again, he looked up with raised palm upward. 'Like me, there are many here repenting for their wrong decision. They also think on the same lines like me; but what can be done?' He looked at him. 'I am only talking about me. 'You must be getting bored up with my brakeless talking. I haven't been permitting you to say anything, isn't it? I am anxious to hear from you. Who are all there in Amritsar?'

My grandfather had gone to Kochi for doing business. There itself they got settled down. I was born and brought up in that place. In my house, my father, mother, and one younger sister. I am married.'

'You are in the army?'

'No. In Air Force.'

Hitting the forehead, he said. 'Oh, my mistake. Pilots are only in the Air Force. I forgot that.' Moving close to him, he inquired. 'How did you happen to come here?'

'That is a big story. My airplane was in flames and I bailed out. I fell in a deep forest. I had to undergo a lot of difficulties and finally, after a month I happened to reach this place.'

Showing surprise, he asked. 'In the forest, what was your food?'

He laughed. 'The fruits and leaves from the forest. And also, fresh fish caught from the small rivulets.'

After hearing that, Javed felt bad. 'Let me give you my heartfelt sympathy. Also, my sincere salutations for your grand work.' He got up and saluted him. 'You have suffered a lot from your country. I admire you.'

Javed looked around and confirmed that no one heard their conversation. 'At any time, you should never expose this news to anyone here.'

'No' He smiled with utmost happiness for meeting such a good-hearted man.

-29-

Javed was ready to undertake the long journey. He prepared two bags full of medicines. He did not forget to give one more pair of dress to Prabhakar before the commencement of the long journey. When he knew that Prabhakar had no money with him, he consoled him by saying 'I will take you up to Wagah border. Once you cross that, Pakistan currency has no use there in India.'

After locking the house, when Javed tried to take both bags, Prabhakar went near him. Picking both bags he said. 'I will take bags.' When Javed refused to hand over the bags to him saying, 'I will carry. I have been doing this always'. When both started pulling the bags towards them, Fathima who had been watching the scene with a smile said.

'I will carry one. No need for confusion about that.' She laughed showing her teeth and picked up one.

The other bag was held by Prabhakar.

They had to walk a little distance to the bus stop. On their way, many people who came across gave their obeisance to Javed and few even asked about his welfare. From that, Prabhakar could understand that he was a prominent figure in that locality. After all a doctor; will be respected by everyone, he thought.

'Who is this new face? I have not seen him earlier.' One policeman who was met on the road asked Javed looking at Prabhakar.

'He is my relative. Two days before he came from my place to assist me.'

'Where is his house?'

That question was not expected by Javed. 'Lahore.'

'There, where?'

'In the city itself.'

'Now where you are going?'

'I told you that. He is coming with me to assist in my job.'

'Ok.'

Prabhakar wondered why that policeman was asking all such questions. 'Why is he asking all these things?' He probed.

'I know that policeman. I am treating his mother. Would have asked for the sake of asking something.' Javed smiled. 'Otherwise, also, this army personnel and policemen suspect anyone whom they have not met earlier. It is their job. After all, the war is only just over. It is quite natural.'

After walking for a distance Prabhakar felt that Fathima was too tired by carrying the bag. He forcefully took that bag from her saying, 'I am fit to carry both these bags.' He looked at Javed and asked. 'Do you take her along wherever you go?'

'No. Whenever I go out to distant places, I take her with me. To nearby places, though she often asks for, I do not take her along. When I go to longer distances, sometimes I used to be back only after a few days. Leaving her alone at home on those days is not safe. She will accompany me on such occasions.'

'How about the accommodation at the places you visit?'

'Now we are going to a village near Wagah border. There I have a known person. I usually stay with them. Though their house is small, it has many small rooms. One room will be given to us. He doesn't take rent or anything from me. To be frank enough, I usually do not get much income from this profession, to live in rented accommodation. A very noble and humble profession. I do not take money from the poor. I give them medicines free. So, the people there consider me equivalent to God.' He smiled with contentment.

'People with such good hearts will be considered as God.' Prabhakar thought. 'It is very difficult to find people with such a kind heart. People do all sorts of indecent and illegal activities for money. A doctor practicing without charging and giving free medicines will be considered by the poor like that. There is no wonder. When the majority of people do not mind even to cut one's throat for money, a doctor who willingly gives everything free to the needy ones will be surely considered as such. This is a lesson for others. The poor trying to help other poor with whatever he could, when the rich, out of greed, do all malicious ways to gather wealth.'

On the roadside, they waited for the bus. After long waiting, they saw one bus coming and the faces were lit with rays of hope. They showed their hands for the bus to stop. The bus which was full of passengers did not stop and the faces went gloomy.

'Why the bus did not stop?' Fathima asked looking up to her father.

Javed looked at her. 'There was no space even for a needle. That is the reason.' He smiled and caught her chin showing love.

After half an hour, they saw another bus coming fast. They raised hands to stop that. That was also full. The kind bus driver stopped near them. Javed looked at the people inside the bus and said. 'There is no place at all inside.'

The conductor said looking at Javed. 'This will not go to the border. You may have to take another bus.' He knew Javed personally. 'You climb up. All buses will be full like this.'

Javed looked at Prabhakar as if seeking his permission. 'Will you like to go up and travel?'

Prabhakar nodded with a chuckle.

They climbed up with the help of the rear side ladder. There were also many people sitting cramped. Somehow, with the help of co-passengers, they could find a place to sit.

The bus was going at a good speed. The passengers on top were clinging to each other for safety from falling. After some distance, few top passengers got down and they found a place to sit comfortably.

'When people get down from inside, we will get seats inside.' Fathima looked at Prabhakar and said as if to console.

Hearing the young one's solace, Prabhakar felt sympathy and held her close to his body and pressed against his. 'Then you will find enough place to sit comfortably.' He smiled looking at her.

The road was very bumpy, with potholes all along and the bus jumped and jerked making the journey quite uncomfortable.

'If one travels on this road at this speed, the backache will remain as a companion throughout life.' Prabhakar said.

'You are right' Javed supported him with a smile and nod.

Whenever the bus stopped for the passengers to alight, Fathimalooked at the passengers getting down and counted to examine the possibilities of getting seats inside. To her dismay, at every bus stop, the number of passengers alighted and boarded in remained almost equal. She kept making her face to express her unhappiness over that and looked at Prabhakar, expressing helplessness. Looking at her Prabhakar kept smiling conveying sympathy. Suspecting that he was trying to tease her, she showed a long face cursing the bad luck.

It took a one-hour hazardous journey for them to get seats inside. After taking a comfortable seat near the window, she looked at him and smiled to show happiness.

Bus stopped. All passengers got down. They had to take another bus to reach their destination. Three of them quickly got into a waiting bus which was almost empty. They all got comfortable seats in the front itself and Fathima was the happiest.

Within minutes the vehicle was filled. The majority of the passengers were uniformed military personnel.

Inside the bus, Javed met many known persons and they conveyed regards and exchanged pleasantries. One person curiously asked. 'For how many days you will be available?'

'For three days. After that, we will go to the other village. Total for about ten days we will be spending near the border villages.'

That person looked at his daughter. 'How about her classes?'

He laughed. 'When we return, from the next day she will attend the classes. She is a small girl. That's more than enough. After her marriage, she has to live in someone's house. I am not interested to get her employed. I don't have such desires.'

On the crowded bus, when Prabhakar saw one standing old woman passenger struggling for proper balance, he got up and offered the seat to her. That female praised him up to the sky, saying such human behavior was seldom seen among the local crowd there. Hearing her words, few people looked at him and agreed with her.

War Hero

When the bus was stopped at a particular stop, Javed asked them to get down.

They got down in a hurry. The bus moved away, spraying heavy black smoke, with a roar.

'Now we have to walk little distance' Javed looked at Fathima. 'Are you tired?'

'No'

When a lassi shop was sighted, Javed reduced the speed and sought everyone's attention. 'Now, after a lassi, we will commence our further journey. With that, we can cool down our bodies.'

As he was not having money, Prabhakar was not in a position to opine. He stood mute.

They had lassi. The cold lassi cooled their body and felt they got a fresh lease of life. The weariness which was predominant on their faces got vanished. They gained more energy for further walking.

They continued to walk.

The expected house was in sight.

Seeing approaching Javed and Fathima, the occupants of that house came out and walked towards them.

'Since morning we had been expecting you.' One person said. Taking the bags from Prabhakar he asked Javed. 'Why so late? We thought that you might have changed the program for tomorrow.'

'We started late. And we could not get a direct bus.'

Looking at the unknown person he said. 'Today you are having a new person for assistance.'

Looking at Prabhakar Javed said. 'Oh, my mistake. I didn't introduce you. This is Ahamed. My friend and relative.' Turning his head towards that person he said. 'This is my friend Kasim.' Pointing to the woman and

259

child by his side he continued. 'That is his wife and daughter.'

Kasim welcomed Prabhakar with a broad smile. 'I have four children. Others have gone to school. This one did not go, as Fathima was expected.'

They entered the house and sat on the benches and chairs lying on the verandah.

Fathima was taken inside by Kasim's daughter. Happily looking at the kids, Kasim said. 'Now on, they both will be in a different world. Will not come for food and would not sleep. She has been waiting for Fathima's arrival enthusiastically and as you were getting late, I was being questioned of the delay showing her gloomy face with impatience.' He laughed. 'They will be throughout engaged in playing; day and night without even drinking water.' He said in a mellow voice. 'Childhood is the most wonderful day of a human being. Memorable days! He looked at Javed and said showing surprise. 'You have not told about this relative so far.'

Javed smiled. 'I might have told you. You would have forgotten.'

Kasim sat thinking. 'Not able to recollect. Leave that alone. Is he staying in your area?'

Thinking for a while Javed said. 'He is staying in our area only. Do you remember one Abdul Rehman who had come once with me?'

'No'.

'This person is the son of that Abdul Rehman. Poor man, both parents died. He is alone. He happened to come to me for some help. Before death, his mother had advised him to visit India and tell about his financial difficulties to his uncle in Amritsar for some help. He has the intention to try that way.'

'That isn't a problem. If you have a passport, getting a visa is not a problem.'

With mock anger Javed said. 'Am I lunatic to advise him that? When you people are here, I thought he will get your help. Ahamed had mentioned that to me. But, I dissuaded him saying that, for a few days going to Amritsar, I will get your help to cross the border.'

Kasim sat thinking as if in a great dilemma. 'What you said is right. I can help. But, these days the amount demanded by them is huge.'

Hearing that Prabhakar got a shock. He had no money with him and wondered how he will be able to meet that demand.

Javed was not perturbed by that. 'Don't worry about that. The amount they demand will be paid'.

Prabhakar looked at him, wondering what he was talking about. He looked perturbed and worried. He saw Javed looking at him and closing his eyes conveying some message, which he could not conceive.

They sat for food. Chapati and dal. To add taste, they were also served with Punjabi mango pickle. After dinner, they moved to the verandah. Kasim excused himself and went out saying he would come back quickly.

'When will you go for seeing the patients?' Prabhakar asked.

'Tomorrow morning onwards. I had asked Kasim to convey the message to the entire village informing them of my arrival and requesting to come tomorrow morning. There will be forty to fifty patients and I will be very busy. Sometimes I will be freed very late in the night'.

'Where will you sit and see the patients?'

'Sitting here in the same verandah. Kasim will assist me. That is my relationship with him.'

'With so many patients, you will be able to carry a good amount of money when you return.'

Javed smiled. Some people will give, some may not. I never care about that. Many times, I have given them medicine free.'

'You are a great man.'

Prabhakar praised him for his providential mentality to needy patients.

'He laughed. 'I am doing whatever is possible by me. I am not interested to make money. My only desire is that I should be able to find a person who will look after my Fathima. She should live comfortably without any problems. Nothing other than that.'

Prabhakar kept thinking. He asked. 'Your friend had said of paying money to someone for helping to cross the border. To whom it is?'

Javed showed ignorance. 'I don't know. Possibly that would be to the person on duty at the border post.'

Expressing helplessness, Prabhakar said most humbly. 'For that, I have no money.'

With a smile, Javed looked at him. 'I know that. You had told me that earlier.'

'Then, from where you will give?'

'Don't have to worry about that. I will pay for him.'

'After Going to India, I will pay for that. But, how will I be able to?'

'If I don't need that amount?'

'Oh, no. That should not be'.

Javed could not control his laughter.' How is it possible to give, when you don't have? You just don't have to bother about that. You are defense personnel looking after our country. By 'our country', I mean what I said. That is the truth. After coming from there, When I come to know of the freedom and the standard of living there in our country India, I repent. There are many here, like me.'

Heaving a sigh, he said. 'What is the use of crying over the spilled milk? All over, except the dissatisfaction of many.'

'How much we have to give him?'

Javed could not control his laughter. 'You are only thinking about that still? Could be five hundred or six. I don't know.'

'If they demand more?'

'Don't worry. I will give it.' He reassured him.

In the evening, Kasim came back.

'I have spoken about the whole requirement.' Kasim said with contentment. 'Tonight, my person is on duty. His duty is from ten to twelve in the night. If required, he is ready to help today itself. Then, if the date of return is fixed, he will adjust the duty for that particular day.'

'Next month tenth.' Javed said very confidently. He knew very well that such a requirement would not be there.

After dinner, on the same night, after bidding farewell to Javed and Fathima and thanking repeatedly, Prabhakar went out of that house with Kasim. Prabhakar kept looking back, till Javed and Fathima went out of his sight in the darkness. Extreme cold and darkness. As he was wearing the inner inside, he could adjust to the dropping temperature somehow. The mental tension added to keep him warm and he walked quickly behind Kasim, with the rising heartbeat. Sometimes he felt the jaws were quivering making the teeth touch each other producing sound.

They both walked silently. Though the fear was trying to control his movements, the thrill of joining the unit and his family dragged him forward, overpowering that. The fear was due to the suspicion of getting caught by the enemy forces while crossing the border and taking him, by them away, as a prisoner. They could keep him for as long as they desire; no one could question. All efforts for escape and the troubles undertaken for avoiding getting caught would entail futile. After crossing the border, even if caught by our forces, they might interrogate but once confirmed that he was an Indian pilot, the approach would be with respect and wait for the unit authorities for identification and rescue.

As they approached the border, Prabhakar was asked to wait and Kasim went ahead fast towards a person who was on duty at the border. Though moonlight was there, nothing was visible properly. Kasim was seen approaching that person and talking and handing over something. That would be the amount he had asked for, Prabhakar presumed. Again, and again he thanked Javed, in mind, for his magnanimity shown towards a stranger, knowing fully well that he would perhaps never meet him again.

Kasim was seen coming back. He came near and asked Prabhakar to go forward and cross the border. Thanking him Prabhakar walked fast. While he looked back, he saw, in the darkness, Kasim still standing there itself looking at him. Till Prabhakar vanished in the darkness, Kasim kept standing there itself. Prabhakar increased the pace and walked with boldness, at times looking back to see if he was still standing there. The person on border duty came near Prabhakar and asked to proceed further and cross the border peacefully. He also informed Prabhakar that he had already spoken to the person on duty on the Indian side and no one would ask anything.

The assurance given by that guard did a wonderful job on his confidence and with happiness his eyes were full. He felt nothing could be seen momentarily. Thanking him many times he quickly crossed the border. When the first step was placed on the Indian soil, he wept with happiness. He felt like crying aloud shouting that he had come back to the soil where he never expected to come back alive. He squatted on the ground and looked up and prayed all Gods he knew, with tears flowing down his cheeks. Calling Lord Ayyappa he lied down and kissed the ground many times. The soil received his tears with compassion. Taking a fistful of sand, he smeared over his face and body. He wanted to cry aloud, but for fear of others hearing him, he controlled by biting the lips.

- 30 -

Prabhakar knelt on his knees and enjoyed the very smell of Indian soil. So far, he was like a fish out of the water struggling for little oxygen. Suddenly he felt relief from the struggle. A feeling of fish from the land falling back into the water. A feeling quite unexplainable.

Wiping the face with the palm, he slowly got up and started walking. When a light was found at a distance he became more enthusiastic and the speed of walking suddenly increased. With the help of the villagers, he imagined reaching the unit at the earliest and meet Sujatha if she was not sent back to Kerala. 'Poor Sujatha, she would have shed all her tears thinking I was no more.' His thoughts went negative side.

With happiness, he felt like laughing aloud. 'I am free. I am back in my own country.' He shouted, though, he knew, no one was there to hear him. Increased enthusiasm made him walk faster aiming the distant light. As the distance to the light started diminishing, his walking speed increased exponentially. He saw someone approaching him from the farthest distance.

Seeing two persons walking towards him, he ran to meet them with a broad smile, expecting a heroic welcome. But, what had happened was beyond his expectations. They started manhandling him without mercy. A huge figure stood in front of him and gave a strong knock on his face. The pain was unbearable and he struggled to avoid further blows. The unexpected behavior from the Indian side made him nervous. 'One more Pakistani has crossed over and come to our soil.' Prabhakar heard one person shouting aloud.

'I am an Indian pilot.' Prabhakar kept telling them, but no one bothered to listen to him. They kept torturing him from left and right. More people gathered there hearing the shouting and commotion.

Prabhakar became helpless and tired of hearing abusive words and torturing. His throat became dry. His frequent request for pity was not heard by anyone. No one cared to observe his pitiable gaze begging sympathy. Instead, their anger multiplied like wildfire. He was on the verge of collapsing. He begged for little water, but no one bothered to offer. The unexpected inhuman behavior with torture pushed him to the point of collapse.

The commotion attracted more people to the scene. Whoever came, gave his quota of torture, not even considering that he too was a human being.

One person was heard saying. 'What is the purpose of hammering him like this? Sometimes, whatever he says might be right. First, why don't you check whether he is a Hindu or Muslim?

'That is the correct way.' Another person was heard supporting him.

One person took him perforce slightly away and made him stand with his back to the crowd. Another person pulled down his bottom dress and lighted a match stick and held towards his genital. 'He is a Muslim.' He declared.

Suddenly the people around turned furious and again started hammering him with all their might. Repeatedly he kept saying of the minor operation he had to undergo due to some ailment during his childhood, but no one bothered to heed to the facts.

With bruises and bloodstains, he fell on the ground and kept saying 'I am an Indian Air Force fighter pilot.'

'Every intruder says the same. Two days back one person came like this. He said he was a colonel and we treated him well. But, he exploded a bomb and killed eight innocent people among us.' One person said with anger. 'We will not leave anyone. We will not.'

'Why don't you hand over me to the police.' He requested them passing his mercy-begging gaze towards the crowd which they could not see in the darkness.

'We will not hand over you to anyone. Your punishment will be awarded by us. We will kill you inch by inch.' One person shouted. ''Do not give him even a drop of water. If someone gives him, that person will be considered by all of us as a traitor.' That voice was quite authoritative.

'No. I am not a Pakistani. I am an Indian Air Force pilot.' The words kept coming out of his mouth. Finally, that turned out to end in a whisper. But, no one bothered to show an iota of mercy or to find out more about him to get into the facts. Finally, the waning whisper withered away completely.

When he gained consciousness, he realized that he was dumped in a huge empty room. He tried to get up slowly. But, could not succeed. The limbs were not taking his commands. They refused to follow his mind. Dragging slowly, he managed to reach near a window. Slowly with all efforts, he caught hold of the window bars and raised the body slightly. Through the open window, he looked outside and realized the day had broken out.

How to get out of that place and escape? His mind was busy trying to find possible ways to escape. In the enemy territory, he had not faced such a precarious situation. The unexpected situation he was facing in his own country had ruined his enthusiasm and felt he was as good as dead. He felt all his faculties were inactive and not functional. All his courage suddenly faded away leaving him like a dead man with zero aspirations. He cursed himself shouting why God gave him such a miserable life. Suddenly his eyes got filled. Many times he kept thinking of ways of escape from that captivity, but all ways were found to be closed with a bleak future. He felt like crying aloud. But, for what? Who was there to hear him? Only his hope was pinpointed to the unknown force - his beloved Lord Ayyappa. The very thought of probable help from that unseen great power made his lips get elongated and his face suddenly became cheerful. He cleaned his face with the palm and brought in his mind the almighty's hill temple and the deity. A firm belief of escape with the help of that power made him feel confident. He thought of the impending possibility to meet his beloved wife and that very thought made him smile with satisfaction.

An eight-year looking girl in a dirty and torn frock with a dripping nose was sighted walking outside in front of the house. With a smile, he invited her attention toward him. She turned her head and eyes towards the window and looked at him but did not bother to respond. Disappointed, he again invited her attention by making shrilled sound and when she turned towards him, he gesticulated to approach him. Looking around, she slowly walked towards him with a lot of hesitation and fear of being observed by someone. When she stood near the window and asked for the reason of calling her, he said.

'Can you give me a little water?'

Expressing fear, that little lad whispered. 'No. Not possible. My father's order is not to give even a drop of water to you.'

Prabhakar could understand that the person who ordered everyone, not to give even a drop of water, was her father. His instruction was to kill him by starvation.

Begging sympathy, he looked at her. 'I am very thirsty. Give me a little water. I have not eaten anything and am hungry.' Those words were sympathetic and stretched his hand to fondle her. 'If you quench my thirst. God will reward you.'

'I don't want that. My father will beat me.'

'You bring without his knowledge. Then, I will tell you a very interesting story.' He smiled. But that offer was not found attractive to her. Without saying anything, she ran away from there, looking back.

With thirst and hunger, his morale got shattered with despair. "Why such an experiment on me, Lord Ayyappa?' He murmured and lied on the floor cursing his ill luck.

He heard the voice of that little girl from outside. Raising his head slowly, he looked outside through the window and saw the little girl standing like an angel with a broad smile showing all front discolored teeth. Her face was seen cleaned and the innocent smile was found very attractive. From her happiness, he could judge that she had something positive to tell him. Slowly he raised his torso and squatted on the floor.

Looking around she raised a glass of water and said in low voice. 'My father has gone out. Take this. I brought it from the kitchen without anyone noticing me.' There was fear on her little face but at the same time, there were traces of contentment in those eyes.

Expressing great satisfaction of getting a chance to quench his thirst, his hand moved through the window bars and grabbed the glass with greed, and drank the whole glass in one go. With a broad smile, he cared to caress her soft cheeks with love expressing gratitude. Withdrawing the hand, he kissed his fingers and looked into her eyes which he found glittering with satisfaction. 'You are a sweet angel. God will do all good to you.'

Without knowing the meaning of what he whispered she enthusiastically looked at him and raised the other hand and gave two chapattis which she was hiding from his sight. 'You eat this.' Her sweet words started ringing in his ears.

Taking the chapattis in his hand he smiled and said. 'Now you go. Otherwise, someone might see.'

'They all are not here. They have gone to the field.' She looked around. 'I am too scared of my father. He beats me often.'

He had no words to thank that minor girl for her kind-hearted behavior. 'Aren't you studying?'

Showing much enthusiasm, she uttered. 'Yes.'

'Then, why didn't you go to school? It is not good for a smart girl like you to miss the school.'

'Today I was asked my father not to go. Today there is a medical camp in this village.'

Thinking for a while he inquired. 'Where is the medical camp?'

Looking on either side she said casually. 'Somewhere in this village.'

Moving close to the window more, he asked with a smile. 'When you go there, can you tell the doctor about me?'

She shook her head in agreement. 'What should I tell?'

'You tell that doctor that one uncle is lying in this house half dead. You must not forget to tell you. Otherwise, I will die.'

Suddenly her face turned gloomy. 'No. You should not die.' Rubbing her eyes, she promised.' I will surely tell.'

'Tell them that I am an Air Force pilot.' He pinched her cheek with love and kissed those fingers.'

When she nodded in agreement, he felt satisfied and dreamt of freedom from that illegal confinement. Unknowingly he smiled. Seeing his sudden happiness, she was taken aback and laughed closing her mouth.

'You are a sweet girl.' He praised her. "What is your name?' He caressed her hair and asked.

'Saniya. And your name uncle?' Those words were very soft and lovely.

'Prabhakar. Air Force pilot. Flight Lieutenant Prabhakar.' He knew she could not grasp that, but unknowingly uttered and smiled at her.

-31-

When the normalcy was re-established after the war, the families who were evacuated from the border villages started coming back to their homes. Knowing the losses and damages suffered by such families, many voluntary organizations and kind-hearted people came forward with their helping hands. Many organizations came forward with medicine and food to all people of such villages. Everyone volunteered to share the sufferings of those villagers with money and food in kind.

Different hospitals with the help of defense establishments conducted medicals camps in such villages and ascertained their health conditions and supplied free medicines and treatments. Such camps continued for two or three days in each village. Similarly, a medical camp was planned for that village also. As the general public was informed of the camp beforehand through the public-address system, a huge crowd had assembled there in a public place from the early morning.

The public place was full of tents for the doctors to sit and examine the public and for giving treatment to the patients and for the resting purpose of patients. Few ambulances were also seen.

From nine o'clock songs were heard on the public-address system. For the sake of the public not knowing about that camp, frequent announcements requesting the public to avail the free medical facilities were also heard. The environment was of a festive mood. There were no sufficient seating arrangements for the people who had gathered there in huge numbers. Many were seen sitting under the trees at different places within the vicinity of the camp and whiling away time.

After some time, one ambulance with doctors and the medical team arrived. Two doctors were on the team. They moved to the tents meant for checking the people and took their seats. There were few medical assistants in the Air Force uniform. Without being instructed, the crowd gathered there formed two queues in front of each doctor's tent.

The announcement was heard on the speakers asking the public to have patience and wait for the local MLA's arrival and his formal inauguration. All people who had come there were requested to gather in front of the mike and listen to the inaugural speech of the local MLA, who was expected to arrive shortly. Only after that formal function, the medical checkup will commence.

Hearing the request, all people moved towards that tent and took their seats on the ground. Certain unhappy words were heard questioning the requirement of MLA in such a medical camp which was not organized by any political party.

'Wherever few people gather, these politicians show their presence. That is their bread and butter. Then only, tomorrow when they come to us asking for the vote, we will remember them.' Another person commented.

Hearing that comment one person raised his voice. 'Because of the efforts of our MLA this medical camp is being held here in this village. Otherwise, this would have been conducted in the neighboring village. Do you know since how many days our MLA had been running around to get it organized here?'

A person who heard him turned towards him and said sarcastically. 'These politicians claim every credit for any good thing happening in our place.' He laughed.

'Probably they would have known once the event takes place only. It is their habit by birth. None on this earth could change them. They will remain like this.' He looked around. 'This camp is being organized by a few civil hospitals and defense for the social benefit. It has nothing to do with the so-called efforts of any politicians.' From the facial expression of all gathered around there, he could understand that none was prepared to support him on what he said. So, he decided to keep mum.

Accompanied by a bunch of politicians, the MLA arrived. He straight went in front of the mike with folded hands and saw only one chair there. He asked the person standing by his side. 'Where are the doctors? Why no additional chairs are placed for them?' His face was reddish with anger.

Within minutes, additional chairs were brought and placed and the doctors came and sat by his side. He looked contented. Slowly he got up and stood in front of the mike and looked around with a broad smile.

'My dearest villagers.' He addressed everyone politely. 'We have just experienced a great war. The damage this war has caused is directly experienced by you all. Some people lost their houses and some others lost their very costly properties. Our government is committed to take account of the losses you people have suffered and to give assistance to all affected. The preliminary work towards that has been initiated and the benefits will start coming soon. I hope you people have already given your list of articles you have lost to the panchayath. If not, please do so urgently.'

He continued. 'You know, the most valuable thing over the properties is our health. If wealth is lost you lose something. But, if health is lost, you lose everything; money, peace of mind. Our effort is to find a solution to that. Our army and air force with the cooperation of civil hospitals are conducting medical camps in every border village. They will examine every person in these villages and give medicines and other treatments. I humbly request you to make use of this opportunity to your maximum. I can imagine that there will be some who have not known of this noble effort. It is the duty of one and all who have gathered here to apprise them of this and to insist upon them to come and at least carry out a usual checkup. There could be some who can't move out of their houses due to some incapacitation. Those patients will be examined by these doctors in their houses, on receipt of information.' He had a doubt, whether such efforts will be made by the doctors. He glanced and found them smiling from which he could realize that they aligned with what he said.'

He continued. 'Today we are lucky to have here with us doctor Sneha from BhatraHospital and Flight Lieutenant Doctor Pendarkar from Indian Air Force. They will examine you and give the required medicine and other treatment.'

He turned his head and eyes in all directions. 'I don't want to waste your valuable time anymore. I declare that this medical camp is opened.'

With the help of some volunteers, two lines were created; one in front of doctor Sneha and the other for doctor Pendarkar. The line in front of Sneha was full of youngsters. The reason behind that was the anxiety of youngsters to get the very touch by that beautiful and young doctor on their body and to derive pleasure. When the queue was seen, even Sneha could gauge the reasons for that particular behavior of people. She could confirm that when those youngsters came and took seats in front of her complaining of chest pain, cough, body pain, etc, requesting her to check them up physically. In order not to disappoint anyone, she took that into sportingly and carried

War Hero

out their body examination thoroughly. With the pacifying words when she placed the stethoscope on their chest and back and examined, their faces were seen glowing with satisfaction. As if their desires were fulfilled!

Doctors examined and prescribed medicines wherever required. Those medicines were handed over to them by the medical assistants.

All those who had come in the morning were examined and medicines administered. Some were advised to go to the nearby hospital and get the medical lab tests done and the prescriptions were handed over.

During the lunch break, Pendarkar and Sneha assembled in one of the tents for having their lunch. They opened their lunch box and shared whatever they had brought from their homes.

'What are the damages caused by war; isn't it?' Pendarkar asked Sneha.

'Definitely. How many homes get ruined? Someone's husband and someone's son. Ho. Can't even think of that.' She expressed her hatred. 'Most of the people join defense forces not for safeguarding the integrity and sovereignty of the nation. Each one of them needed a job and got inducted. After becoming a soldier or an officer, due to discipline, they become committed to doing their job of safeguarding the country. The implicit discipline forces them to obey the command and in turn volunteer even to accept martyrdom. The transition is great. 'She looked at him sitting without reacting to what she said. These are my feelings.'

Pendarkar suddenly turned pensive. 'From our station, we lost three officers.'

Sneha looked at him. 'Yes, we lost three. Wing Commander Mukerji, Flight Lieutenant Prabhakar, and then Flight Lieutenant Varma. Of these, the death of Mukerji and Varma has been established and Prabhakar is still missing. After a few days, he also would be declared dead. Poor man sometimes would have been under the captivity of the Pakistan army. If so, he may have to undergo heavy torture. Ho, I can't even imagine that.' She turned suddenly sad. 'That night I couldn't even sleep. I am so concerned for him, you can't even imagine. Poor man. He was a very good man. What to do? We have to console ourselves blaming everything to fate.'

Listening to her concern for Prabhakar, Pendarkar leaned towards her and said. 'I think you haven't forgotten him yet.'

Without uttering a word further, she kept mum with hatred for his such remark.

Pendarkar felt sorry for what he said, that probably would have hurt her feelings. 'I am sorry for what I said.'

She looked at him and said with an artificial smile. 'That's alright. That is a closed chapter.'

Time moved. People started trickling down. The doctors examined them and prescribed medicines wherever required. By four o'clock all work was completed. As per the announcement, the medical camp was up to four o'clock. When no more people were seen coming, they all decided to pack up. When one person asked Pendarkar that the medical camp would be on the following day also, he confirmed their arrival exactly at ten o'clock in the morning asking to give wide publicity for the benefit of those who were not knowing of the same.

Within ten minutes they were ready to pack up and all of them got into the vehicle. Pendarkar and Sneha got inside the front seat of the jeep. The medical assistant Francis who had come with Pendarkar got inside the back of the jeep. When the driver started the jeep, the girl from the house where Prabhakar was locked up, Soniya, went running towards that. She stood near Sneha and said.

War Hero

'Doctor aunty, one person from the Air Force is locked up in my house.' She struggled to convey those words showing her frontal teeth outside. Neither Sneha norPendarkar could understand what she wanted to convey.

'What?' Sneha asked her with anxiety. She looked at Pendarkar and asked.' What this girl is telling?'

Soniya did not like that. She got angry and shouted. 'One Air Force is locked up in my house.'

Sneha felt like laughing hearing her words which were not clear. She asked the driver to take the jeep forward.

When they moved slightly ahead, Pendarkar said. 'Actually, we should have tried to find out what she said. As someone said, a child's mind is always stainless. What they tell would be the truth. Why not we try to find out that?'

'What should we do for that? That is the job of the police.' Sneha was not inclined to find out the facts of what the little one had said.

'Sneha, please. That girl said one Air Force is locked up in her house. Why not we find out the facts of what she said? Having come over here, is it not our duty to find out that?'

Sneha looked at him. 'Is it required?' She raised her brows. 'We are doctors. Should we involve ourselves in this? Police have to find out.'

'Why not we just go there and find out?' It was a humble request. His words carried ample sympathetic feelings.

Without even showing an iota of sympathy, she asked the driver to turn back the jeep. When the jeep reached the campsite, they saw that little girl, Soniya, sitting on the road and crying. Sneha felt sympathy for the small one and got out of the jeep and asked. 'Why do you weep?'

'In the morning when I came to your doctor aunty, my father was with me.' Her speech was distorted with sorrow. 'Hence, I did not tell you about that uncle. When I went back home, he asked me if I could inform you about him. When I said no, I found him weeping.' She sobbed. 'That's why, without being noticed by anyone, I came running now to you.' She looked into the eyes of Sneha. That gaze was demanding sympathy.

Sneha felt sorry for what had happened from her side. 'Where is your house?'

Soniya pointed her fingers to distant places and said. 'There.'

'Will jeep go? Is there a way for the jeep?'

'Yes.' She put her fingers in her mouth and said with a smile, satisfied over Sneha's change of attitude.

Soniya was made to sit in the front along with the doctors and Sneha directed the driver to follow the directions given by her. Soniya was smart enough to guide the driver and they reached the front side of her house. They saw many people gathered there.

The attention of all those standing outside fell onto the incoming jeep with Sonia in the front. Suspecting something would have happened to Sonia, her father moved fast towards that and inquired. 'What happened to my daughter?'

Looking at the approaching person with melancholy filled face Sneha said very casually. 'She is perfectly alright. We came here to see that Air Force person who is locked up by you in your house. Where is he?'

That person looked at everyone around there. He could guess, who could have informed the doctor about that. He cast a dirty eye on Soniya and bit his teeth. Then, he looked at Sneha and said in a firm voice. 'Doctor should not interfere in this. We will deal with that person. He is a Pakistani.' He paused and continued. 'We saw him crossing the border and coming. All those who cross the border and come here always say the same words that they are from the Indian Army or Air Force.' He passed his gaze around and found everyone nodding to support what he said. 'A few days back, one person crossed the border and entered our territory. On questioning, he said he was a colonel and we treated him well with food and drinks. Before bidding farewell to all of us, he exploded a bomb here and eight of us got killed.' His eyes got filled. He cleaned his eyes and continued. 'These are done by Pakistan. They sent people like that and take revenge, even though the war is over. This is likely to continue'.

Sneha and Pendarkar got out of the jeep. From behind the jeep, Francis also came out. They expressed their desire to see the person who claimed to be from the Air Force.

'No doctor' That person talked tough. 'You have come here to conduct a medical camp. You people will not understand the heavy losses we suffered during this war.' He bit his teeth and said with anger. 'We also have a vendetta. Every possible way we will adopt to show our revengeful attitude. We will hand him over to anybody only after handling properly as we decide.' His words were firm and decisive.

Pendarkar said like a mature person. 'Having come up to here, let us just see him.'

The people around there did not permit.

After hearing the jeep sound and the serious talk outside, Prabhakar was anxious to find out what was going on there. He struggled to get up holding the window bars but failed and fell on the floor. Somehow, he managed to sit on the floor and tried to listen to the conversations outside. But, as the distance was more, he could not hear them. Still, with the rays of hope of some angels coming to rescue him, he tried to listen to them with sharpened ears. The enthusiasm overpowered his physical weakness and he struggled to get up and by holding the window bars he somehow managed to look outside. When he saw two persons outside there in air force uniform, his lips widened. He smiled with rays of hope of impending freedom. With sudden happiness, his eyes were widened. With difficulty, he wiped his face and eyes with the palm. He could see Sneha and Pendarkar. He also saw Francis. A firm belief got germinated in his tired mind that they had come to take him to the unit. He thanked the villagers for informing the Air Force authorities about him and momentarily forgot the torture and harm done to him by all of them out of sudden anger. He yelled. 'Sneha.' But, his voice was submerged in the general public voice and nobody could hear him.

Soniya moved close to Sneha and said holding her sari. 'Doctor aunty, he is calling you.'

Sneha refused to understand what the little one said. She just looked at Soniya and got the sari released out of her hold.

Again, Prabhakar shouted. 'Pendarkar, Sneha.'

Pendarkar heard that and inquired. 'Who is calling our name?'

Someone who knows the names of doctors who had come to the camp today.' One person said.

'That's correct. They were announcing the names of doctors in the mike.' Soniya's father said casually.

Pendarkar realized that the villagers were adamant of not entertaining them to interfere in their affair of dealing with the intruder. 'Do whatever you feel like.' He said with anger and climbed into the jeep. Seeing him, Sneha also followed. When Francis also got inside, the jeep started and moved forward.

Seeing that with disappointment, Prabhakar yelled with all his might. 'Francis.'

From the moving jeep, Francis heard that call and requested the driver to stop. He jumped down from the jeep and ran to the direction of the call. A person with a long beard and hair was seen through the window.

Seeing Francis running towards him, Prabhakar called him once more. His lips quivered. 'Francis, this is Flight Lieutenant Prabhakar.' With uncontrollable emotion, the words did not come out of his mouth as he desired. 'I am Prabhakar.' He yelled again; this time in the Malayalam language. The words were grief-filled.

Francis did not take much time to recognize him. He looked towards the jeep and shouted. 'This is our Prabhakar sir.'

Sooner those words fell into their ears, Pendarkar and Sneha got out of the jeep and ran to that place. They recognized him. Sneha turned her head towards everyone standing near the jeep and said loudly. 'This is our friend. Flight Lieutenant Prabhakar. Our Air Force pilot.'

Soniya's father hurried to that place and opened the room and brought Prabhakar out. There were traces of guilt on his face for confining him for so long without food or water. Though repeatedly, he had been telling that he is an air force pilot, he felt sorry for not believing him.

Pendarkar ran to him and hugged saying 'had we not recognized you, you would have been subjected to maximum torture by these people.' He ran his fingers through his hair and kissed him repeatedly.

Thinking of all the agonies undergone by Prabhakar, both inside Pakistan and in our territory, Sneha stood there aghast with filled eyes. She kept looking at him. When Prabhakar moved towards her, she moved forward. She jumped forward and hugged him with all her strength and kept moving her lips all over his body. 'Now I am very happy.' She moved her fingers through his hair and beard. 'Because of me, you could get freedom. I am very happy about that. That shows the harmony of our minds.' She kept murmuring something or other.

Observing Sneha's expression of utmost happiness and repeated kisses, Soniya moved close to them and asked covering her mouth. 'Is he your boy, doctor aunty?'

Hearing that, Sneha realized what she was doing with a sudden explosion of emotion and moved back from there. Looking at Soniya she smiled. A meaningful smile.

Pendarkar moved towards Sneha and talked something in her ears. Taking her consent, he asked Soniya's father of the possibility of getting a barber there.

That person called a person and instructed to get a barber quickly. Within minutes, a barber arrived there and shaved Prabhakar's beard and cut his hair. His wounds were bandaged after applying for medicine by Francis.

During this time, Soniya's father went to the nearby readymade shop and brought a pair of shirts and pants. Though initially, Prabhakar refused to wear them, when everyone including Sneha insisted, he yielded. When Pendarkar gave money for that to that person, he refused to accept.

With running eyes, Soniya's father stood in front of Prabhakar. 'Sir, we all have given maximum trouble to you. All those intruders always claim to be part of our Army or Air Force, when caught. In your case, we were under impression that you are also one among them. Hence, we refused to listen to you and did all that we could to harm you. Sorry for everything. Please do not keep anything in your mind. You should be kind enough to forgive all of us.' Those words were felt coming out of his heart. He fell on Prabhakar's feet. 'You should forgive for all harm done by me to you.'

War Hero

Prabhakar felt his feet got wet with few drops of his tears. 'Had I been in your place, I too would have done the same.' He made him get up by holding his shoulders. 'Forget everything. Everything is for the good. God is great.'

That person took Prabhakar inside the room and requested to change the dress.

Prabhakar felt he got a new lease of life. He went along with that person inside the room and washed his face and changed the dress. While coming out, he looked like an entirely different person. He went directly to Soniya and lifted her and kissed her many times. 'Hadn't she informed Sneha and Pendarkar, I would have still been inside there.'

Soniya's father quickly brought a glass of fruit juice and a few guavas and offered to Prabhakar. He needed something to regain the strength he had lost for days. He drank the juice and ate one guava and gave the rest to Soniya.

Sneha and Pendarkar moved towards him, looking at him thinking over the unexpected escape of their friend.

Witnessing all these from a distance, Francis wiped his eyes off tears and moved smartly close to Prabhakar and gave a smart salute. When he saw that, he remembered the toddy shop in Kerala where they sat together and had toddy. He smiled and returned.

-32-

Bharathi saw both Kishanlal and Rajesh sitting, looking at each other on the verandah, silent brooding over the thoughts about both Prabhakar and Sujatha. She went closer to them and said. 'Since no further information has been received from the Air Force authorities, why don't you think of bringing that girl back from there? Why should we leave Sujatha to live there and undergo all worries alone? If she is here we all can at least console her.'

Rajesh looked at her and said agreeing with her. 'I am also thinking of the same. Sometimes Prabhakar might take time to get back. Till then, should we leave her alone?'

After hearing their opinions, Kishanlal said shaking his head. 'That is also correct. So many days have passed. Since no information has been received so far, I think that is what we should do now.'

'That is what I have said.' Bharati said.

Rajesh looked at Kishanlal and smiled. 'Actually, ladies have more common sense comparing men.'

'Or are they lacking?' In that difficult moment also Kishanlal tried to keep others happy.

Bharathi felt such a comment was out of context and left to the kitchen in a huff. 'How many days have passed since we received the telegram mentioning that he is missing. Why they haven't done so far anything? What am I to do? Weep. What else?' She kept murmuring on her way to the kitchen.

War Hero

Looking towards the kitchen Kishanlal said loudly. 'Even after going there, the answer we are going to receive will be the same; still missing.'

'Could be.' Rajesh opined. 'You may be right. But, till he comes back, should she stay there alone?'

Again, they sat speechlessly. Breaking the silence, Kishanlal suggested. 'Why don't we do one thing? As she suggested, why not we both go there and find out the latest situation? Now, one month has elapsed without any information.'

With the firm intention of bringing back Sujatha, they both proceeded to the Air Force Station where Prabhakar worked. Till New Delhi, they traveled by airplane. From there by train. The next morning, they reached the place and hired a taxi for the further journey to the Air Force Station. The Sardar driver was knowing the way to the Air Force Station. Within half an hour the taxi reached the guard room. As the guard at the main gate refused their entry, the driver went and requested the Air Force policeman on duty for the entry. The policeman went to the car and asked.

'Whom you want to meet?'

Kishanlal said. 'I am the father of Flight Lieutenant Prabhakar and he is his father-in-law. We want to go to his house.'

Thinking, the policeman said. 'But, he is not there.'

'That we know. We got the information that he is missing. His wife is alone here.'

Without saying a word, that policeman went back to the guard room and spoke to the Security Office. He went back to the car with a peon from the guard room.

'This person will come with you After leaving you in that house, this person will come back in the same car.' He gave the required instructions to that peon and walked back towards the guard room. The gate was opened and the car moved inside the camp.

The car was stopped in front of Ahluwalia's house. They got down from the car. Hearing the sound of the car, Ahluwalia came outside. He was in uniform, ready to go to the unit. Looking at the persons who just arrived, he went near them and inquired. 'To which house you need to go?'

'What this Sardar is doing in the house where Sujatha is staying?' Kishanlal thought. He asked. 'Which is Prabhakar's house?'

'He stays here only.' Looking at Kishanlal carefully, he asked. 'Prabhakar's father?'

'Yes. This is Sujatha's father Rajesh.' He frowned. 'But, how could you recognize me?'

'I have seen you in his marriage album.' He ushered them inside.

Both ladies who were busy in the kitchen came out.

Sujatha ran towards them with trembling lips. Her eyes were filled with uncontrollable emotion.

looking at her, both stood motionless.

Rajesh moved closer to her and sobbed saying, 'Why god has pushed you to this condition?'

Sujatha acted boldly. Wiping her eyes with hands, she said. 'Why do you worry? Nothing will happen to Prabhakar. I am very confident. As he is the ardent devotee of Lord Ayyappa, nothing will ever happen. He will come back very safely. Now, the present position is that he is missing. He will be found out and would be brought back soon. In my ears, this is the assurance I often hear from some unknown power. And I believe in that power.'

In front of her self-confidence, both could not utter anything further.

War Hero

'We also firmly believe in that. But, you are staying alone in this condition....' Rajesh could not complete as his voice choked.

She tried to smile. 'I am not alone. There is Ahluwalia, Prabhakar's close friend, and Paramjit, his wife living in the same house. They are there for any help which I might require. Moreover, I am employed in the Station Health Center here. No problem to pass time.' She paused. 'By the grace of Lord Ayyappa, I am confident that he will come back safe without even a scratch on the body.'

They moved inside the house and sat on sofas in the sitting room. Sujatha quickly moved to the kitchen and prepared tea for everybody.

'When you saw me and my wife here, you might have thought that why we are here? Isn't so?' Ahluwalia asked casually.

Kishanlal shook his head in affirmation.

'In this station, the quarters' position is slightly tight. Very seldom officers get the house immediately on registration. He should have got one, but for the present condition. As every posting has been kept in abeyance, the officers whose transfer orders have been received have not moved out. Had they gone, the houses would have got vacated and he would have got one much earlier. Unless the houses fall vacant one can't get that allotted. Taking a house outside the camp is not safe and most officers do not prefer that. In such conditions, the officers resort to sharing houses. Here, it is the house allotted to me. Prabhakar is sharing with me. It is a huge house with so many rooms and two families could stay comfortably, provided the ladies could adjust with each other.' He explained the position clearly.

After spending some time with them, Ahluwalia took leave from them saying he would be back after showing his face in the unit. As said, he came back after a few minutes. When his scooter arrived, Rajesh went close to him and asked. 'Is there any news about Prabhakar?' The inquisitiveness was written down in his eyes.

When he read the emotion-filled face of Rajesh, his eyes were filled. He was at the same time happy that the commotion he had expected from the two gentlemen was absent. They remained well-composed showing the least anxiety, probably after seeing Sujatha's courage and confidence in Prabhakar's safe return. Sujatha was quite optimistic about his safe return as if he had gone out of the unit for certain Air Force duties. The firm belief in supernatural power was giving enough courage. Ahluwalia stood looking at him without knowing what to answer.

'Nothing has been received so far.' He managed to complete the sentence.

'We came here to take Sujatha back to Kerala.'

'But, will she come?' He was apprehensive.

Rajesh was not sure of that. 'You people must convince her.'

Ahluwalia smiled. 'I don't think she will listen to anyone. However, I will try to convince her.'

They went inside. By then, both ladies had prepared the breakfast and had laid on the table. After breakfast, they sat and talked on various topics.

Kishanlal looked at Sujatha and said. 'We came here to take you back home.'

She looked at everyone over there one by one and said. 'I am not coming. Without Prabhakar, I am not coming back to Kerala.' She sounded very firm.

'We have come with three plane tickets from New Delhi.' Rajesh said looking at her.

'No father. Please don't compel me.'

Ahluwalia decided to butt in. 'You should listen to both of them. If they return without you being

War Hero

accompanied, what will the mothers think? My opinion is that you must accompany them. When Prabhakar returns, you can come back.'

'Yes.' Kishanlal supported that.

Without uttering anything, Sujatha sat looking at the wilderness.

Paramjit went near her and kept both arms over her shoulders and stood looking into her eyes. 'What they are saying has some meaning. We have to obey the elders. Especially parents. That is my opinion'

Sujatha looked into her eyes. She could read the compassion she had been hiding in those eyes.

Paramjit added. 'That will be a wise decision.'

Sujatha said in low voice. 'If that is everyone's decision, I will.'

Both Kishanlal and Rajesh smiled hearing that.

Having gone up to that place, Rajesh expressed his desire to see the plane being flown by Prabhakar. Ahluwalia agreed to make the necessary arrangements for the same. He went to the unit and spoke to the Unit Commander and Station Security Officer and obtained their permission for taking and showing the fighter aircraft to civilians. He also arranged a car on 905(a form used for car requisition on payment) for taking them to the railway station in the evening. After lunch, in the same car, he took both Kishanlal and Rajesh to the tarmac to show the fighter aircraft. One aircraft was seen opened for technical work with technicians around and he took them there. He made each one of them enter the cockpit and explained all about the controls to their satisfaction.

The train from town was in the evening at seven o'clock for New Delhi. At six o'clock Kishanlal and Rajesh along with Sujatha got into the car and bade farewell to both Ahluwalia and Paramjit. Sujatha and Rajesh were sitting in the back-seat and. Kishanlal in the front. When they reached the guard room main gate, the driver parked the car on the side and hurried to the guard room with the book for booking out the vehicle, which is a mandatory requirement to take an Air Force vehicle out of the camp. Similarly, while coming back, the vehicle was to be booked in, writing down the time of entry.

Sujatha saw a jeep parked on the other side of the road for booking in and Sneha sitting in the front seat. Intending to meet her, being the best friend of Prabhakar, she got out of the car and moved towards the jeep and called her aloud. Hearing that, when Sneha looked in the direction of call, she saw Sujatha rushing towards her. She quickly came down the jeep and held her by hand and took to the back of the jeep.

Sujatha could not believe her eyes. She saw Prabhakar sitting inside. She yelled. 'Prabhakar, I am here.' Her voice got chocked with unbearable happiness.

Responding to that, like a mechanical man, Prabhakar jumped out of the jeep in a fraction of a second and briskly moved towards her. He felt all his body was shivering. Some unexplainable emotions made him surrender. Embracing her, he cried like a small child. His hands ran over her whole body without his control.

Unexpectedly, when Prabhakar was seen, both Kishanlal and Rajesh came out of the car and moved towards them with utmost unbearable happiness.

'Where you were so far?' Sujatha asked aloud crying. 'Didn't you know that I was alone here? Though I ate a lot of fire, I managed to control it. I was very sure, that you will certainly come back. I was confident that our Lord Ayyappa will protect you throughout.' She kept crying. The emotional bund she had been safely harboring on, had broken and the complete emotions were on its way out making her mad. She ultimately surrendered to her emotions.

'I was here itself. Just one call away from here. In Pakistan.' He hugged her again and cried aloud without taking note of the surroundings. Wiping the eyes, he stepped back and looked into her eyes. Slowly moved away towards Kishnalal and Rajesh. 'Because of me, you had to worry a lot.' He whispered.

'That's alright. You have come back, anyway. That's enough.' Kishanlal said wiping his eyes. Looking around he said. 'Now, we are not going back. We will go back to Ahluwalia's house.'

'You are right.' Rajesh supported. 'In this happy and auspicious occasion, let us not undertake any journey.'

All people gathered there watching the happy occasion and shed their tears of happiness.

Epilogue

No one likes war, but when inevitable, fearlessly is fought with all might. The sufferings and losses of lives and property are part of the evil. The officers and men at the forefront are a dedicated lot to sacrifice their lives for the security and safety of the motherland. These dedicated lots enable people to live elsewhere to sleep peacefully without worries or fears of being attacked by the enemy.

About the Author

Writing has always been a hobby for M K Devidasan. However, it was not always something he thought he could make a living with. After retiring from the Indian Air Force as a Wing Commander serving 32 years, he realized he has something valuable to share with the world and turned to write full time. Since turning his passion into a profession, M K Devidasan has written prolifically and is constantly exploring new themes, genres, and ideas. It's incredibly hard work, but he is never happier than when he sits down at his desk putting the opening words to a new book or story on paper.

Printed in Great Britain
by Amazon